Marching Song

Marching Song

A Play

Orson Welles

With Roger Hill

Edited by Todd Tarbox

ROWMAN & LITTLEFIELD
Lanham • Boulder • New York • London

Published by Rowman & Littlefield
An imprint of The Rowman & Littlefield Publishing Group, Inc.
4501 Forbes Boulevard, Suite 200, Lanham, Maryland 20706
www.rowman.com

6 Tinworth Street, London, SE11 5AL, United Kingdom

British Library Cataloguing in Publication Information Available

Library of Congress Cataloging-in-Publication Data

Names: Welles, Orson, 1915–1985, author. | Hill, Roger, 1895–1990, author. |
  Tarbox, Todd, editor.
Title: Marching song : a play / Orson Welles with Roger Hill ; edited by Todd
  Tarbox.
Description: Lanham : Rowman & Littlefield, [2019] | Includes bibliographical
  references and index.
Identifiers: LCCN 2019003916 (print) | LCCN 2019011309 (ebook) | ISBN
  9781538125533 (electronic) | ISBN 9781538125526 | ISBN
  9781538125526 (cloth : alk. paper)
Subjects: LCSH: Brown, John, 1800–1859—Drama. | Abolitionists—United
  States—Drama.
Classification: LCC PS3545.E522 (ebook) | LCC PS3545.E522 M37 2019 (print) |
  DDC 812/.52—dc23
LC record available at https://lccn.loc.gov/2019003916

In memory of Ruth Hortense Gettys Hill
(April 19, 1895–February 5, 1982)

Children . . . and their children . . . and their children . . . Like the seed of Father Abraham, it does almost seem that the descendants of Mother Hortense are to be numbered as are the sands of the desert. As for her adopted children, they are truly beyond counting. In that community, I lay claim to an honorary membership.

For myself, I don't believe I can lay claim to more than an honorary membership in that community. A semi-orphan with something close to a surplus of foster parents before I even went to Todd, I was, in my childhood, determined to rid myself of childhood, a condition I conceived to be a pestilential handicap. I counted Hortense—not as any kind of mother, but from the first as the very dearest kind of friend. What was an infantile presumption soon became, with the passing of a few brief years, a grown-up fact. And so, it is that I join your voices today—not really as a member of that enormous tribe which was (and is) her family—but from a smaller and dwindling choir. Ours is the simple song of friendship. A corny old ballad sums it up: "You are my sunshine." That's what I share with you today, and always: She was our sunshine. . . . For sixty odd years my friend, your mother, was the radiant blessing of my life.

She has gone away and left a black hole in our universe. And yet to mourn is to remember. Our grief brings memories. That shining, vivid, marvelously living presence is back with us again and our hearts are stabbed with happiness. For just to think of her can never be anything but an occasion for joy.

Of everyone I've known, she was the most truly passionate. Yes, passionate in every good meaning of a word I choose with care. Other great and good souls may be described as "warm" or warm-hearted. That's too tepid sounding for Hortense. Warm is a word for comfort and consolation . . . a blanket and nice cup of soup. The word for her was heat. Fire. The very element itself . . . The fire in the hearth.

Given her own earthy, intensely personal preoccupations, it's a safe guess that for most of her rich and lengthy career on this planet, she had little time for the sticks and carrots of religion. But if there is a heaven after all, then it's a sure thing that she's in it. . . . I like to think of her barefooted (she had such tiny ankles) wading along some celestial strand, searching for seashells . . . And waiting for her children . . .

Orson Welles's eulogy
April 17, 1982

~

Contents

Foreword

It is impossible to overstate the importance to Orson Welles's development of his time at the Todd School for Boys in Woodstock, Illinois, just outside Chicago, under its inspiring young headmaster, Roger Hill; in many senses, it was the making of him. He arrived at Todd in 1926, aged eleven, and stayed until he was sixteen; it was one of only two experiences of formal education he ever received, and even that was pretty informal. In fact, Welles had been sent there under a misapprehension: his troubled older brother, Richard, had been dispatched there some years earlier, when Todd was still under the leadership of the man who had made it what it was, Noble Hill. In that magnificently named man's day, the school had a fierce reputation for discipline and academic rigor, so rigorous that the ever-delinquent Richard was summarily expelled. However, by the time Orson was admitted, and unbeknownst to his father, Dick Welles, and Maurice Bernstein, his late mother's former lover, Todd had become a different place. Under the radical leadership of Noble's uncommonly open-minded son Roger, it had transformed itself in short order from something resembling a reformatory into a progressive school of the most imaginative kind.

It provided, in a sense, the ideal environment for the eleven-year-old prodigy, though it signally failed to instill in him what his alcoholic father and Bernstein, who was the anxious, controlling family doctor, had hoped for: instead of containing and curbing the all-but-ungovernable boy, the school—or, to be precise, Roger Hill—indulged him, allowing him to pick and choose his classes and encouraging him to explore his considerable artistic gifts. The school, as reconfigured by Roger Hill—"Skipper" to the boys—rejected the notion of instruction, believing instead that learning was best done by doing; in the case of the already theater-obsessed Welles, that meant giving him free access to Todd's remarkable facilities, the recording studio, the camera equipment, and above all the state-of-the-art playhouse. In addition, when his gifts as performer and director became ever more apparent, he was given a company of actors—his fellow pupils, who provided him with an inexhaustible source of manpower, or rather boypower, to mold to his will. An avid consumer of theater magazines, he was fully *au fait* with the latest developments in Europe, above all in Germany, source of the most radical experiments, from Max Reinhardt to Brecht to Expressionism. The concept of *regie-theater*—directors' theater—originated there, and Welles's young actors were duly subjected to a great deal of Teutonic drilling to achieve the desired results. The climax of his efforts at Todd was perhaps *Winter of Discontent,* his condensed version of Shakespeare's *Richard III.* In alarming makeup, more *Nightmare on Elm Street* than Plantagenet Crookback, the fifteen-year-old gave a startling performance, supported by a large company of his fellow students, who under his complex and intensely physical direction generated immense energy.

His highhanded ways did not make him especially popular with his schoolmates. He had already long forfeited the goodwill of the staff by baiting them unrelentingly, catching them out whenever he could, and, in the case of the popular head of sports, Coach Toney Roskie, simply refusing to participate. He could have gotten away with none of this behavior had he not had the unstinting support of Skipper Hill, who, from the time of Welles's arrival, made it clear to the school, teachers and pupils alike, that he was a special case—a bit of a genius, in fact. The relationship between Hill and Welles was uncommonly intense, and it remained so until the day of Welles's death, some five years before Hill's own demise. Skipper, only thirty when Welles came to Todd, was enchanted by the boy, who almost immediately became part of his family, warmly welcomed into it by his wife, Hortense, if less warmly by his daughter, Joanne. Skipper—it was the secret of his success as a headmaster—was a boy at heart ("the adolescent's adolescent," his son-in-law Hascy Tarbox, also a pupil at Todd, called him), and his breezy appetite for life in all its manifestations was a wonderful corrective to the hothouse environment in which Welles had been brought up—traveling around the world and mingling with theatrical lowlife with his dipsomaniac father; severely exhorted to serve the community by his avant-garde piano-playing mother, Beatrice; moving in operatic circles thanks to Dr. Bernstein's connections. Welles was never going to be allowed to be a boy, but Skipper gave him something that he had not known up to that point: practical enthusiasm, the encouragement of his gifts, and the opportunity to develop them, as well as experiencing Skipper's home life and thus discovering the importance of healthy emotional relationships.

Skipper spurred him on in everything he did and, unlike Dr. Bernstein, actively fanned the boy's determination to make the stage his living. He also advised Welles that the only way to wean his father from the bottle was to refuse to see him until he stopped drinking; with the result that the ever-affable Dick Welles died of cirrhosis of the liver, alone, in the Chicago Bismarck Hotel, not having seen his beloved youngest son for six months. This catastrophe, which cast a dark shadow over Welles's life, becoming an ever-greater source of guilt and grief, had the immediate effect of pushing him and Roger Hill closer together: Skipper became a central figure in Welles's emotional life, part father, part elder brother. Welles left Todd in 1931 and, under the pretense of going on a painting holiday in Ireland, found his way to Dublin and eventually onto the stage of the Gate Theatre, where he created a sensational impact playing a leading role, at the age of sixteen, in that theater's distinguished production of *Jew Süss*. When the novelty value of Dublin wore off, he went to London, where he found no work in the theater. His next stop was New York, where his luck finding employment as an actor was no better than in London. Next, he returned to Woodstock, where Skipper offered him a job as drama coach at Todd for the second semester. When the school year came to a close, to channel his restless energies, Skipper floated an idea he had for a play, the play to be found in these pages, *Marching Song*, about the legendary abolitionist John Brown. It was Skipper's idea to begin with, and he wrote an opening scene for the play, but he quickly handed the work over to his ex-pupil, who was already demonstrating great confidence in his handling of the material, even offering the occasional shrewd comment on Skipper's own contributions.

The play by the seventeen-year-old boy has struck many who have read it as demonstrably the work of the twenty-one-year-old who, only four years later, took the Broadway theater by storm and the twenty-five-year-old who, after another four years, transformed Hollywood with *Citizen Kane*. Like *Kane*, it starts with an investigation by journalists of a dead man's reputation; like many of Welles's films (and several of his unfilmed screenplays), it interrogates the notion of greatness: Does greatness exist? Is it healthy? Is it good? And, also like *Kane*, it constitutes an investigation into the nature of truth itself. If the play's dialogue is sometimes a little over-excited (something a little judicious trimming could easily remedy), it makes up for it with a tremendous sense of theatrical excitement. The play as written is, in fact, a matrix for a production. Its heart is most definitely in the right place—with the abolitionists, naturally—but it is not a tract: the play is more interested in the character of the protagonist than in the issues he raises. The treatment of the material is epic, revealing little of its author's own inner life, in stark contrast to *Bright Lucifer*, another play written by Welles a couple of years later, with its lurid account of the central figure, the self-styled "bitch-boy," Eldred, and his diabolical effect on the lives of those who love him. The play is an alarming kind of self-portrait of the young Welles, reflected in a distorting mirror. *Marching Song* is about many things, but it is not about Welles.

What is astonishing is the seriousness with which Roger Hill took the play as a commercial proposition; he epitomized the can-do attitude before it was ever given a name. He and Welles went to New York, where they took a suite in the Algonquin—a costly affair, then as now—from which they sallied forth to meet potential producers. None was forthcoming, but Skipper, who had to go back to his duties at Todd, encouraged Welles to stay on, albeit in considerably reduced circumstances, and plug away. Eventually, a number of people read the play but rejected it. There was a plan to print it on the Todd Press; this also came to nothing. So Skipper came up with a new idea with which to beguile, intrigue, and occupy his unemployed young genius: an edition of some of Shakespeare's plays, edited by Skipper and supplemented with copious marginal illustrations by Welles, who also contributed a rip-roaring introduction to the Elizabethan theater; the book—*Everybody's Shakespeare*—was still in print thirty years later. Before the book was even printed, Welles had met the novelist and playwright Thornton Wilder, who, having heard of the prodigious boy's Irish reputation from his sister in Dublin, secured the contacts for Welles that swiftly led to his landing the part of Mercutio opposite the Juliet of Katharine Cornell, the greatest actress of her day, which in turn led to him being seen by John Houseman, who asked him to direct the Negro Theatre Project's *Macbeth* in Harlem, which made him a theatrical superstar at twenty-one.

Thus, Welles's early career proceeded by leaps and bounds, good fortune intervening at every point. Whenever it did, he was always ready to make the most of it, thanks in no small part to his having had the good luck to find himself at an early and formative age in vibrant proximity to Roger Hill. Hill's faith in him, and practical demonstration of that faith, played an incomputably large part in creating the phenomenon that was Orson Welles, as Todd Tarbox brilliantly demonstrates in this riveting sequel to his no less illuminating *Orson Welles and Roger Hill: A Friendship in Three Acts*. These studies together provide essential clues to one of the most enigmatic but vivid personalities of the American century.

—Simon Callow

~

Preface

It's difficult to imagine any aspect of Orson's life and his prodigious outpouring of work in the theater, in radio, in film, and as a social commentator that has not been fully explored and captured in print and on film. At last count, there are more than fifty Welles biographies and critical studies of his work.

What I find most striking and unsettling about many of the Welles volumes is that after acknowledging his talents, not a few subtly or palpably portray Orson's professional life—despite his colossal contributions as a director and actor in theater and film, magician, artist, journalist, social commentator, and author—as unfilled, damning him as a squanderer of his talents to his and the world's detriment. He is cast in many accounts as a "failure" because of what he didn't accomplish, rather than viewing his life as a triumph for all that he did achieve during his seventy years.

The one aspect of his life that is often overlooked by critics and has yet to be plumbed in detail is his facility with words—his essays, newspaper columns, screen- and stage plays—that came to flower as an adolescent schoolboy at the Todd School for Boys, more than a decade before he won an Oscar for co-authoring the screenplay for *Citizen Kane*.

All of the volumes on Welles, including my own, *Orson Welles and Roger Hill: A Friendship in Three Acts*, bring to mind the tale of the Blind Men and the Elephant—each man examines one distinct physical feature of the animal's anatomy and expounds definitively on the shape of the pachyderm. The individual accounts are partially correct, but each fails at providing a complete description of the multi-dimensional animal. So, too, the accounts of Welles's life and work, however expansive or truncated, capture only a portion of this complicated, compelling, and creative fountainhead.

It would be a valuable contribution to American letters and to gleaning greater insight into Welles as a creative force and a dedicated humanist if his trenchant and limpid newspaper and magazine articles, radio and print essays, movie scripts, speeches, and letters were bound between the covers of a book. *Marching Song* and the accompanying illustrations of Welles's writing is a beginning.

Is *Marching Song* simply an impassioned history lesson, or is the play's leitmotif—addressing the need for radical racial regress in mid-eighteenth-century America—a plea that is relevant today?

~

Acknowledgments

The impetus to publish the play *Marching Song* and a collection of Orson Welles's youthful writing emerged from a September 30, 1985, telephone message my grandfather, Roger Hill, left on Orson's answering machine promising to gather and deliver a rich assortment of Welles's childhood literary outpourings he had saved, including a copy of *Marching Song*, the play they had written in 1932, not long after Welles graduated from the Todd School for Boys.

> I turned up a copy of *Marching Song*. It remains a compelling, if overly long, play. If that God-awful *Hearts of Age*—memories of your stumbling repeatedly on an absent step on the Wallingford fire escape and your bloody shin—is worth saving, *Marching Song*, written two years earlier, should rate a Pulitzer. At least it's worth publication.

For years, I had known of this Welles/Hill theatrical collaboration, but I had never read the manuscript. Hill's recommendation prompted me to read the play and agree with his assessment, vowing to one day take it upon myself to find a publisher who shared Hill's and my opinion.

That one day arrived last year when I sent my manuscript including the play and my Shavian introduction to Stephen Ryan, Rowman & Littlefield's senior acquisitions editor for arts and literature, who shared my enthusiasm for this project. My greatest gratitude is to Stephen for his faith in and steadfast support of the book.

In truth, where does responsibility for this book begin? One candidate surely is Orson's father, Richard Head Welles, for enrolling Orson at Todd, for had he not, the lives of his second son and Roger Hill would have been far diminished and there would be no cause to write these acknowledgments.

Abounding thankfulness is extended to not only my maternal grandfather but equally to my maternal grandmother, Hortense Gettys Hill, whose nurturing influence on my life, Orson's life, and the lives of everyone she touched was considerable.

Thanks beyond measure to my father, Hascy Tarbox, who directed *Marching Song*'s premiere performance at the Opera House in Woodstock and provided me with more than five decades of invaluable direction and affection, as did my mother, Joanne, who played Annie Brown, daughter of John Brown, in the Woodstock production. Kudos to my sister, Melinda Tarbox Reitman, who also appeared in the play as Mrs. Huffmaster's daughter and who provided insight into the play and a lifetime of joy to her younger brother.

Welles scholar, film critic, and historian Jonathan Rosenbaum's candid and considered suggestions after reading an early draft of *Marching Song* were deeply appreciated. Patrick McGilligan, author of *Young Orson: The Years of Luck and Genius on the Path to Citizen Kane,* and I share a particular interest in Welles's formative years. Patrick's support of and suggestions to strengthen *Marching Song* were most welcome.

Considerable credit to director, writer, actor, producer, and film critic Peter Bogdanovich for his support of and devotion to Orson and his kindnesses to me. Kudos to Ray Kelly, owner and editor of Wellesnet—a compendium of Wellesiana—for his prized advice and friendship.

I am indebted to American Civil War historian James McPherson, winner of the 1989 Pulitzer Prize for *Battle Cry of Freedom: The Civil War Era,* for kindly paying tribute to *Marching Song.*

For his infinite kindnesses, encouragement, and insights, my most profound appreciation goes to Promethean polymath Simon Callow, the English actor, writer, director, and cherished friend who in many ways approaches, if not equals, the theatrical and literary talents of Orson Welles, the subject to whom Simon has devoted more than three decades and three biographies—with a fourth and final volume in progress—examining in exacting and exciting detail the life of, in his words, "one of the most remarkable men of his time. He cannot be extinguished." Nor can my admiration for Simon.

Cheers to my son, Hascy II, whose quick, inquiring mind and caring soul—the ultimate reward of parenthood—proved a valued sounding board.

I tender ultimate credit to his mother and my bride of fifty years, Shirley, for her editorial and divine guidance.

~

The Gestation of Genius

Orson Welles, Roger Hill, and the Road to Marching Song

Todd Tarbox

Richard Head Welles and Beatrice Ives were married on February 9, 1903, and settled in Kenosha, Wisconsin, where Richard was a partner, treasurer, and general secretary of Badger Brass Company. The Welleses became parents of their first son, Richard Junior, on October 7, 1905. Ten years later, on May 6, 1915, their second son, George Orson, was born.

Richard was born in 1872. He was a successful businessman and inventor, who held twelve patents. His first, an acetylene generator, was used in bicycle headlights. When not engaged in the marts of trade and associating with business colleagues—or tippling spirits with his bibulous, high-spirited companions, who Orson characterized as "aristocratic philistines"—Richard was something of a Lothario, before and during his marriage to Orson's mother, who was eleven years her husband's junior.

Beatrice was devoted to the arts as a performer—a concert pianist, lecturer, and patron. Often when performing on the stage, between musical selections, Beatrice would intersperse lively and limpid commentary on the life and times of the composers whose music she was performing. In addition to pursuing a music career, she involved herself in civic and political affairs locally and nationally, becoming the first woman elected to public office in Kenosha, winning a seat on the city's Board of Education. By 1911, Beatrice had become an ardent suffragist and a prime mover in forming the Kenosha Chapter of the National Political Equality League.

Two years after Orson's birth, the CM Hall Lamp Company, in Detroit, Michigan, bought Badger Brass, netting forty-six-year-old Richard $100,000,

Three-year-old Orson with his dog, Caesar.

which permitted him to opt for an early and comfortable retirement. A year after the sale of Badger Brass, the Welles family moved to Chicago, where Beatrice immersed herself in the burgeoning arts scene, joining and later directing the Lakeside Musical Society. She transformed her home into a fashionable salon, which attracted numerous international musical and theatric luminaries, not a few of whom marveled at the wit and erudition of Orson.

Early in their marriage, the Welleses were a congenial "power" couple in Kenosha and Chicago, maintaining an active social life that included extensive global travel. However, Beatrice's interest in the arts and politics became all-consuming passions that were not shared by her husband. As their marriage began to fray, Richard spent increasingly more time away from home traveling the world, enjoying a sybaritic existence often accompanied by female escorts.

It wouldn't be unreasonable to describe Orson's first decade as complicated and conflicted. Critic Kenneth Tynan captured Richard and Beatrice's troubled relationship with candor and clarity, observing, "Where mother had her salon, father had his saloon." Reflecting on the increasingly disparate lives of his parents in Chicago, Orson observed late in his life, "I saw my father wither under one of her looks into a crisp, brown, and winter's leaf."[1]

Even before Orson's birth, the Welles marriage was beginning to devolve. Complicating the family dynamics was the presence of a young orthopedist, Dr. Maurice Abraham Bernstein, who arrived in Kenosha from Chicago in 1911 and opened a practice. Shortly after putting out his shingle, Bernstein was summoned by the Welleses to mend Richard Junior's broken arm.

Dr. Bernstein was twenty-eight, the same age as Beatrice, and he shared her enthusiasm for the arts. An amateur cellist, Maurice was particularly partial to classical music and opera, as was Beatrice, which led to their developing an aesthetic and emotional bond. In a matter of months, Maurice became enamored with Beatrice and developed an equal infatuation with her bright and effervescent infant son, Orson, whom he called "Pookles." In return, infant Orson referred to the doctor as "Dadda."

When Pookles was eighteen months old, Bernstein reported hearing the toddler declaim, "The desire to take medicine is one of the greatest features which distinguishes men from animals." Astounded at the child's precocity, Maurice pronounced Orson to be a "genius," a description not infrequently applied to Welles in years to come.

Shortly after the Welles family relocated to Chicago, Dr. Bernstein closed his practice in Kenosha and resettled in the Windy City, principally to remain close to Beatrice and Orson, adding to the domestic discord of Richard and Beatrice and increasingly straining the relationship between the two men.

The Welleses separated in 1919. Thereafter, Orson divided his time between the two households. His bifurcated home life continued for five years until 1924, when Beatrice fell victim to acute yellow atrophy of the liver (jaundice)—a disease that few in the 1920s survived—and died on May 10, four days after Orson's ninth birthday.

Estranged from Beatrice and finding himself financially comfortable, Richard's restless nature found direction through indirection, living a peripatetic existence, traveling the globe with frequent stops at his vacation home in Jamaica. When not in flight, he maintained an opulent residence in Chicago.

In 1925, Richard discovered one his favorite Illinois haunts, the Hotel Sheffield, in Grand Detour, Illinois, one hundred miles west of Chicago on the west side of the Rock River, was for sale and he bought it. To entice Chicagoans to his hostelry, his advertisements evoked nostalgia and the offer to return to a rustic setting: "If you love the country, if you would hear again the familiar song of the meadowlark, the bobolink, the brown thrush, and the whip-poor-will, if you sit down once more with the same old out-door appetite, to a meal such as you had on the farm—Come to the Hotel Sheffield in Grand Detour. Dick Welles, Proprietor." Three years later, on May 14, 1928, a week after Orson celebrated his thirteenth birthday, the hotel burned to the ground.

Orson's Arrival at the Todd School for Boys

Unlike the close bond that developed between Maurice and Beatrice, the relationship between the doctor and Richard Senior was at best complicated

The front entrance to the Todd School for Boys. Two students are headed toward Wallingford Hall.

and guarded and grew increasingly more so after Beatrice's death. The lone connection between the two was the welfare of Richard's second son. Both doted on Orson, each vying for the boy's attention and affection, exposing Orson to their disparate worlds. Both men adored the child, but neither believed the other fit to raise the protégé. As a result, and possibly feeling overwhelmed with the ultimate responsibility of parenting Orson, Richard opted to send his son to a private boarding school, the Todd Seminary for Boys, in Woodstock, Illinois, sixty miles northwest of Chicago, where he discovered that Orson would be able to develop his many creative gifts and be removed from the influence of Maurice Bernstein. Late in his life, Welles confided to a biographer, "I was sent to Todd in order to settle their hopeless battle."[2]

Although Orson's father took great pride in his younger son's quick mind and agile tongue, essentially Richard Welles was a disaffecting and detached father. Indicative of his distant parental nature, he was in Jamaica when Orson first arrived at Todd in the care of his rival, Dr. Bernstein, on September 15, 1926. This was two years before Noble Hill retired and placed the school in the hands of his son, Roger Hill.

ROGER HILL: ORSON WELLES'S FIRST COLLABORATOR

Among the dozens of Orson Welles's collaborators were Micheál Mac Liammóir, Hilton Edwards, John Houseman, Gregg Toland, Joseph Cotton, John Houston, Gary Graver, and Oja Kodar. Indisputably, his first and one of his most influential collaborators was Roger Hill.

A description of Welles that comes closest to defining him unreservedly from his Todd days and throughout his life is the one he ascribed to himself in the title of his unfinished autobiographical film, *One Man Band*. His "genius" came from the wellspring of his expansive mind and imagination. However, as he was quick to acknowledge, his creative life often involved collaborators, from his formative years producing plays at the Todd School for Boys through his last days collaborating with a diverse cast of characters attempting to start new projects and complete decades-long unfinished work, most notably *The Other Side of the Wind*.

No one knew Orson Welles better or longer than Skipper. Their partnership began at Todd when Orson and Roger co-directed several dozen stage productions including Shakespeare's *Julius Caesar*, George Bernard Shaw's *Androcles and the Lion*, and two Hill musical comedies, *It Won't Be Long Now* and *Finesse the Queen*, and ended shortly before Orson died when he assisted Roger in editing an anti-war film produced at the Todd School, *Rip Van Winkle Renascent*.

May 18, 1930: In front of Grace Hall on the Todd School for Boys campus. A freshman in high school, Orson stands in front of the tree. Roger Hill is fifth to the right of him.

Roger Hill was born in Woodstock, Illinois, in 1895, twenty years to the month Orson's senior, and lived there until the mid-1950s when he and his wife, Hortense Gettys Hill, moved to Miami, Florida.

He was Noble and Grace Rogers Hill's second child, their first being a daughter, Carol. His mother, referred to on campus as "the Mother of Boys," died on the school's commencement day, June 11, 1914. His father, Noble, died in May of 1953, days before his ninety-fifth birthday.

After graduating from Todd, Skipper attended the University of Illinois, where he met his future wife, Hortense Gettys. They married and moved to Chicago, where he began a career in advertising working as a copywriter at Montgomery Ward. Noble invited his son to return to Woodstock, where he and my grandmother would join the Todd faculty. They happily accepted Noble's offer and made Todd School their home until the school's closing in 1954.

Throughout his tenure as headmaster at Todd, Skipper provided one of the most progressive educational programs in the country. His educational philosophy embraced the concept that all youngsters were "created creators." Toward that end, Todd offered an extracurricular program that was generations ahead of its time. It included producing sound motion pictures and theatrical productions. Two buses, referred to as "Big Berthas," permitted students and faculty to travel throughout the United States, Canada, and Mexico. Crewed by the Todd faculty and students, the school's schooner, *Sea Hawk*, cruised the Great Lakes. A three-hundred-acre working farm, run in large measure by students, expanded their appreciation of agronomy and enhanced the school's cuisine. Todd maintained a winter outpost in the Florida Keys.

During the last decade of the school's existence, Skipper established the Todd Airport, which housed a Link Trainer and three Piper Cubs that afforded interested students flight instruction and flight time.

Hill's forebears were liberal and, in the nineteenth century, outspoken abolitionists. His maternal grandfather, John Almanza Rowley Rogers, was the co-founder of Berea College. Berea, in Berea, Kentucky, was the first school in the South to admit African Americans, a decade before the Civil War. Almanza's cousin Edwin Embree, grandson of Berea's other co-founder, John G. Fee, was the president of the Julius Rosenwald Fund from 1928 until the fund came to an end in 1948. Julius Rosenwald, head of Sears Roebuck Company, established the fund with the goal of promoting "the well-being of mankind," with a foremost focus on improving the lives of African Americans, particularly those living in the segregated South. The fund expended tens of millions of dollars building and staffing more than five thousand schools for black children in the southern states from the 1920s through the late 1940s, generously endowing black colleges, and offering hundreds of scholarships to black artists and academics to further their education.

Hortense shared her husband's progressive politics and desire for there to be an end to all forms of racial intolerance. Her father, an attorney, Arthur Lincoln Gettys, spent much of his career litigating against political corruption and defending clients who were at odds with the powerful in business and government.

Shortly after arriving at Todd, Orson began spending increasing amounts of time in the Hill apartment on the second floor of Wallingford Hall entertaining and being entertained by the headmaster and his wife. He soon began supporting their tastes in the arts and their views on politics and social issues.

Skipper was married for sixty-six years to Hortense, who died in 1982. They were the parents of three children, Joanne, Bette, and Roger II. My mother, Joanne, was their firstborn.

Also accompanying Orson to Woodstock were two oversized steamer trunks—one containing the "what to bring" items enumerated in the school catalog: a rug, a dark couch cover for the bed, four single sheets, four pillow-cases, twelve towels, six napkins and a napkin ring, a Sunday suit, two school suits, eight shirts with collars, one dozen handkerchiefs, overalls for use in woods, and a good hat. The second trunk was chockablock with Orson's most precious possessions: oriental decorations; books on performing magic; an extensive collection of paraphernalia for the young conjurer to employ when performing tricks that included the Vanishing Coin, the Wandering Rubber Band, the Bewitched Walking Stick, the Weeping Pencil, the Spoon Dances, the Walking Pen, and the Ghostly Gathering; capes, wands, stacks of trick

Orson, age unknown, performs a magic act on the Todd School stage.

playing cards, a makeup kit, and an assortment of his favorite costumes, none more treasured than a Sherlock Holmes Inverness cape and deerstalker cap.

Like all entering students, Orson was given the Stanford-Binet test measuring intelligence. It consisted of questions followed by multiple answers, requiring the student to underscore the correct response. His first test had this question: "Deserts are crossed by—horses, trains, automobiles, camels, donkeys." Orson underscored every item and wrote, "See other side." On the back of the test, he wrote, "All of these, but the writer was obviously too dumb to know it."[3] This and subsequent annual tests established his IQ at 185; 140 and above was considered the genius level.

Once at Todd, Orson quickly made his considerable creative presence known. During his tenure, he wrote prodigiously for the school's literary magazine, *The Red and White*; painted murals; captivated his classmates and teachers with his adroitness as a magician; and wrote, directed, and acted in dozens of plays that were performed on the Todd stage, at the Woodstock Opera House, and throughout the Midwest.

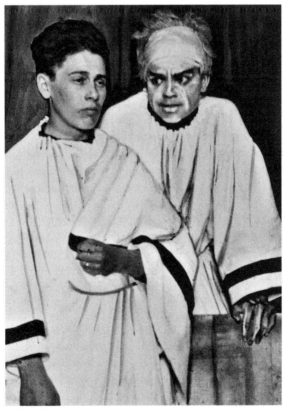

1929 Todd Troupers production of *The Tragedy of Julius Caesar*, performed at the annual Chicago Drama League contest, in which Orson played both Mark Antony and Cassius.

When Orson arrived, the school was in its seventy-eighth year—one of the oldest private boarding schools in the Middle Border, founded in 1848 by the Reverend Richard Kimball Todd shortly after receiving his theology degree from Princeton University. Todd journeyed to the frontier community of Woodstock with this wife, Martha Clover, to establish a Presbyterian church and school—intent on bringing God and enlightenment to this neophyte community on the Illinois prairie.

After forty years as the school's headmaster, Todd retired and sold the school to his successor, Noble Hill, who guided the seminary for the next forty years. Depicting the institution at the turn of the century, a reporter from the *Woodstock Sentinel* newspaper wrote:

> For more than 50 years this school has, without intermission, opened its doors each succeeding term, and from it has gone hundreds of sons, many of whom have reached places of influence in the world's great fields of activity. The sons of Todd seminary are scattered all over the continent, from New York to the Golden Gate, from the Canadian line to the Gulf. They are found in frozen Alaska, in London, in the "Dark Continent," in the very isles of the sea. . . .
> At the present time there are a few over forty pupils in the school, hailing from all parts of the country, who are carefully watched, instructed and disciplined by Prof. Hill, his estimable wife, three male and two female instructors. . . .
> Todd seminary is in all respects what its owner designed to make it—a model homeschool for boys, wherein is taught not only the rudiments of a common education but the finer essentials that go to make up model citizenship.[4]

A quarter of a century later, the school continued to be "a model homeschool" instilling the "finer essentials" of citizenship. The 1928 Todd Seminary for Boys catalog, sent to Richard Welles and the last to be written by Noble Hill, informed prospective students and their parents,

> Our ideal, "For every Todd boy a good citizen," is not a mere catchphrase, but a living principle in the daily life of the Todd boys. . . . Woodstock is a beautiful little town of 4,000 inhabitants, with a New England charm about its quiet, shady streets, and surrounded by a country of wonderful beauty and fertility. . . . True to its New England origin this school has ever stood for plain living and high thinking, and in harmony with Puritan traditions. It has had but two changes of administration in the eighty years of its history.
> Our teachers are all specialists. Their specialty is boys, and the varied interests which make up the modern boy's life. . . . The true work of the educator is developing character, and the true educator knows that character is developed on the playground and in the social circle even better than in the schoolroom. . . .

In the Todd woods, a 40-acre oak and hickory grove situated one mile north of the campus, boys "hold communion with nature in her visible forms" all year round and learn to understand the "various languages" in which she speaks to nature lovers. No other book contains so much ennobling truth as the great book of nature.[5]

In a final "word to parents," Noble avows with supreme confidence one of his hallmarks, "Like the great Teacher we can do nothing for those who do not believe in us while we are daily performing miracles for those who do."

Orson walking to class on the Todd campus with classmate and good friend Paul Guggenheim.

Twenty years later, in 1948, at a banquet celebrating Todd's one hundredth anniversary, Roger Hill said of his father, "To those Todd alumni who are over thirty years of age, Noble Hill is Todd. He was 'The King,' stern, mosaic, sometimes awesome, yet invariably just and deeply, deeply revered."

In his book, *One Man's Time and Chance: A Memoir of Eighty Years 1895–1975*, Roger Hill writes,

Todd was a laboratory, and I don't think there was any other school in the world that could have and would have let Orson express himself the way he did. He came to us at age 11 and immediately began to flourish on the Todd stage as a member of the Todd Troupers. His first performance at Todd was in a musical revue I wrote, *Finesse the Queen*. In other early performances, Orson played the Virgin Mary in the Nativity play, Judas Iscariot in *The Dust of the Road*, and a Christ-like figure, Mason, an English butler, in *The Servant of the House*. In *Wings over Europe*, a play that had the year before met with acclaim on Broadway, Orson was Francis Lightfoot, who discovers how to harness atomic energy. The British government's rapacious reaction sets Lightfoot on a course to destroy the world. Before his plan is set in motion, he is murdered, and the play ends portentously as the audience is told that planes carrying atomic bombs are flying above London.[6]

While at Todd, Orson wrote dozens of radio scripts and contributed essays, short stories, and poems, many illustrated with his clever pen, that were published in the school's newspaper, *The Todd Record*, and literary magazine, *The Red and White*, both published and printed by the students.

A sampling of his poems published in the latter—ranging from frothy to weighty—evince his youthful intelligence, wit, and adroitness with words.

Welles wrote in the spring 1927 volume poems that included "The Pilot—A Description," "At Noontime—A Description," "The Onaways and the Wendigos," and "At the Call of the Drum and Fife."

The Pilot—A Description

Staunch he stood, his great grim face, married by the wrath
    of the sea,
His burly hands gripped tight the wheel, his pose both wild
    and free.
The biting wind clawed for his face and kept his fingers
    there,
And the icicles came streaming down from his gray and
    sun-bleached hair.

At Noontime—A Description

The sun beat mercilessly upon,
The scorching heat cursed plain;
And the field that lay in sunny wealth
Was gold with sun and grain.
        ***

The toiler sought with lagging steps
The comfort of the great oak trees,
And there to taste with hungry lips,
The coolness of long-sought breeze.
        ***

The bloodstained sword and the earth stained plow
Now lazy and idle lay;
For all men's number and various task,
Are left in the great noonday.
Close by a knotted oak their laughter,
A silvery rippling stream,
Whose shining crags and glittering rocks,
Cut the water in between.
        ***

On one moss bank his head in air,
There dreamed a peasant boy;
Who from sun-bronzed feet to sun-bronzed hair,
Was a symbol of boyhood joy.

The Onaways and the Wendigos
The Onaways were hot and mad
And in their war togs they were clad;
Dancing up and down with might;
Dancing in the firelight.
Singing praises to Gods of war,
Of ancient legend and olden lore,
Of how they captured the fearless braves,
And made them serve them as slaves.
Waving scalps with thought of more,
With hopes of hearts they'd have to gore,
When suddenly from the forest trees,
Blown by the gentle waving breeze,
Came the cackling voice of an ancient hag,
Who silenced the braves by the wave of rag;
It is prophesied in the magic sands,
That a terrible curse is upon these lands,
And unless its braves shall turn to the wise,
The almighty spirt his children despise,
You of yourselves must not be talking
Or with Wendigo packs you'll soon be walking.
The warriors knelt down upon the ground,
And with attention most profound,
Promised these things they would do,
And kept their oath right well and true.
They won the war with the Wendigo braves,
And made them serve them as their slaves.

At the Call of the Drum and Fife
From scorching heat to freezing cold,
The men of whom these tales are told,
Come from every walk of life,
Come at the call of the drum and fife,
They come to fight the tyrant Huns,
Entranced by the song of blood and strife,
March to war with the drum and fife,
Thru fiery rain and gory mud,
The boys who bathed in the cleansing of blood,
Sacrificing more than life,
March to hell with the drum and fife.

The following year, *The Red and White* published Orson's "Pome—A Prevacation Parody on *America for Me*."

Pome—A Prevacation Parody on *America for Me*

'Tis fine to see the Old School, and wander all around,
Among the gnarly oak trees, and buildings of renown,
To admire the ancient Clover Hall and the office of our
  King.
But now I think I've had enough of all this sort of thing.
So, it's home again, and home again, Chicago town for me!
I want a train that's southward bound, to flit past field and
  tree,
To that blessed land of "Home" and "Folks" beyond
  Cook County line
Where movie shows are always good, and malted milks are
  fine.
Oh, Crystal Lake's a hick's town, there's hayseed in the
  air;
And Woodstock is a factory town, with Dagos everywhere
And it's sweet to dream in English Class, and great
  to march in gym;
But though this student may love Todd, home's now the
  Place for him.
I like our games, I like our shows, actor's nicely
  drilled;
I like our Beans, I like our Hash, with luscious thumbtacks
  filled;
But Oh, to take you out my lad, for just a single day,
And eat at Childs or Thompson's (that is, if you will pay).
I know that Todd is marvelous, yet something seems quite
  wrong,
The teachers like to make you work entirely too long.
But the glory of Chicago is "Not parking on the streets,"
We love our town for what she is, the town of "Home" and
  "Treats."
Oh, it's home again, and home again, Chicago land for me,
I want a train that's southward bound to flit past field and
  tree,
To that blessed town where Big Bill's frown has King
  George on the run,
Where the hours are full of leisure and the leisure's full of
  fun.

The spring 1929 volume included his "The Mump Song" and "I'd Like to
Be a Kite."

The Mump Song

There is nothing so fine as the
    Spring, Tra! La!
But the mumps are a different
    thing, Blah! Blah!
You grab at your neck
And it feels like heck!
Your throat has an awful sting,
    Ya! Ya!
To Mrs. Ereau you hastily go,
    La!
The truth you are anxious to
    know, Ha! Ha!
She sheds not a tear
As she looks at your ear,
And gives you the joyful "no,"
    Rah! Rah!

I'd Like to Be a Kite

I'd like to be a kite and sail the
    skies,
I'd like to see the school building
    from above,
I'd like to break off all my mortal
    ties,
I'd like to fly—gosh I'd love
To just keep sailing and not listen
    to the bell.
And what an end, to in an oak tree
    lie,
T'would suit me well—
To soar above the world—and then
    To die!

During his last year at the school, Orson wrote, edited, and illustrated the school's catalog, "Todd: A Community Devoted to Boys and Their Interests," in which he affirms:

Todd is not perfect. This we realized and this we rejoiced in, for if it were, the joy of making it finer would be gone. . . .
    Todd is a bustling beehive of activity from dawn until dark and, for some of us, on into the night. Skipper tells us there is no joy compared with having accomplished something worthwhile with your hands or your brain and we have found he's right.

Every boy can express himself in some line of useful or artistic endeavor, and the program at Todd is to give him this opportunity.

In the next few pages, we will try to give you some slight picture of this guild of young artists and artisans who are finding the thrill there is in doing the work of the world and who have learned that usefulness is the highest good and greatest joy.[7]

Orson's cover illustration for the 1931 Todd School Viewbook, which he also wrote, edited, and illustrated.

In 1928, at the age of thirteen, when on vacation from Todd, he divided his time living with his father in Chicago and Dr. Bernstein in Highland Park, Illinois. While staying with Bernstein, Orson met Louis Eckstein, owner of the *Highland Park News*, who found the young man exceedingly articulate, particularly knowledgeable in the arts, and so engaging that he offered Welles a summer job as the paper's tyro arts critic—reviewing philharmonic and opera performances at the nearby Ravinia Festival.

Introducing himself to the *Highland Park News* readers in his column, *Hitting the High Notes/Inside Dope on the Opera Stars*, Orson wrote: "'Cover the opera,' quoth the editor as he threw down the proof sheet." Orson's first assessment of the Ravinia opera offerings he'd seen was none too flattering. Concluding his lacerating account, he posited, "I will not admit that there have been any real performances as yet. Pray that both the opera and I will improve. I am Orson Welles."[8]

Welles's spirited, trenchant, and informed commentary was enthusiastically received, which prompted Eckstein to hire the teenager for the following two summers. Orson dubbed his second year's column *Stage Stanzas* and his third *Inklings*, which he illustrated with the word "Inklings" pouring from a bottle of ink.

"When he wasn't with us at Todd," Roger Hill recalls, "he traveled extensively with his father. Travel has ever been Orson's addiction as well as Orson's education. He had a fantastic capacity for absorption from books, people, and experiences."[9]

In the summer of 1930, prior to entering his final year at Todd, Orson and his father sailed to Japan and China, which proved to be their last extended trip together. He writes vividly about his trip in several *Inklings* columns.

Announcing the upcoming trip to the Orient in the July 4, 1930, edition of the *News*, Orson writes,

> More or less (in the manner of the COMING ATTRACTIONS AN-NOUNCER of the Talkies) Ladeez and Gentlemen . . . instead of lingering here in HP to prattle weekly—(voice from the gallery: "weakly is right!")—we are packing up and going far away . . . very, very far away indeed. Even unto the other side of the earth, i.e., China and environs—many thousands of miles beneath Central Avenue, to the underworld kingdoms of dog-stew and bird's nest soup. . . . We are broadening out, we will write about the East, and we'll spill you the whole business, absolutely everything. . . . All the clout, glamour, romance of the Orient will troop in Literary Caravan across the glowing lines of this, your favorite feature of your favorite journal. . . . I thank you!!!! (Loud sound of escaping steam as we take our bow).[10]

In his *News* dispatches, as well as his letters to the Hills and Dr. Bernstein and his literary outpourings at Todd, Welles writes with a maturity, urbanity, and command of the English language. One of his more insightful ruminations on this trip with his father was his final post from Japan, datelined September 5 with the headline "Midnight, Yellow Sea," that reads in part:

> The heart of the Japanese pirate country: the first day in Nara was an adventurous one, to say the least. Nara is picturesque and lovely, one of the most beautiful spots in Japan and particularly so in the rain. It started to sprinkle just as we left the station in our rickshaw and increased in violence as we rode. There was a thin green mist hanging over everything as we went scurrying over little-lacquered bridges across the willow-bordered streams under huge pines as old as time itself, crunching across temple yards, past age-old pagodas, and on up to the hill to our hotel. The furnishings in our room were typically Nipponese and most fascinating but not sufficiently so to keep us among them, so leaving our Dad to snooze under mosquito netting we stepped out the back entrance and took a walk. It had stopped raining. You know how lovely it can be right after a summer rain—everything clean and green and glistening? It was like that, just as fragrant as a flower, as warm and wet as the tropics in heaven. The willows wept liquid sunshine into the silver streams, lovely little-sacred deer stood in the deep, damp grass, a pilgrim shuffled along the road, his bell tinkling faintly from beneath his great straw coat, and behind the pagodas above everything, there hung a rainbow . . . ! In the park, we found an open space in the center of which was a gaily-curtained platform.
>
> We guessed correctly that it was a temporary stage erected by a company of strolling players. We parted the drapes and peered in. The actors were clustered about a tiny stove eating their supper. They invited us to join them and of course, we accepted. We shall not forget that meal. How we thanked our lucky stars we had learned to eat with chopsticks! We were stuffed with rice, raw fish and sake. And while our Japanese was more extensive than their English, we carried on a successful conversation of three hours' duration entirely with our hands. We taught them a song from a school musical and they instructed us in the art of Oriental theatrical fencing and make-up. It was a truly fascinating experience. We were shocked by their living conditions, their poverty. They told us that they had enough rice for one more day if no one came the next night. . . . They felt hurt when we offered them some money and laughed at our sympathizing. They would laugh at death. . . . We said goodbye and the last thing we heard as we walked down the road was the sound of their merry voices singing the American song we had taught them.[11]

Five months later, on December 28, 1930, Richard died alone in the Bismarck Hotel in Chicago. The death certificate signed by Dr. Bernstein read, "Cause of death: chronic myocarditis, a disease of the heart, and chronic nephritis, a disease of the kidneys, followed by cardiac failure." Days later, Orson selected Maurice Bernstein as his legal guardian.

Weeks after losing his father and at the start of his last semester at Todd, Orson delivered a lecture for the PTA on the stage of the Dean Street School in Woodstock recounting his oriental adventures. Surrounded by mementos from his trip and dressed in an exotic oriental outfit, Welles proceeded to bedazzle his audience with an impromptu narrative illustrated by sketches penned as he was speaking.

A reporter from the *Woodstock Sentinel* covering his tour de force wrote, "We traveled with him in mind, as he led us along the wide beautiful streets and also through the narrow, poorer districts of both of these countries." Summing up Orson's performance, the reporter commented effusively, "Orson is a young man fifteen-years of age and already a genius, with poise, expression, and ability beyond his years."[12]

In May 1931, Orson and his classmates graduated after their sophomore year. The culmination of Orson's acting career at Todd was his recasting of Shakespeare's *Richard III*, which he titled *Winter of Discontent*, that was performed at graduation. Reviewing the play, the *Woodstock Sentinel* enthused that *Winter of Discontent* was "the most outstanding affair of its kind ever attempted by the [Todd] Troupers," adding that the acting was "far beyond that

The caption for this photograph that appeared in *Todd: A Community Devoted to Boys and Their Interests* reads, "The Seniors in their formal dinner clothes—picnic dinner." Orson is fourth from the left.

usually found in school plays. . . . Orson Welles outdid himself. . . . Orson today leaves Todd. If he misses his school in the days to come, he may be sure that the school will also miss him."[13]

Graduating with honors from Todd, Orson wasn't at a loss for options. Harvard University was eager to welcome him to the school's prestigious "Studio 47" program. Cornell College in Iowa offered him a scholarship to take advantage of the school's nationally recognized drama department.

Autodidactic Orson saw little advantage or appeal to being "entombed" in an institution of higher learning. His path led him in another direction: the professional stage. Days after graduating from Todd, Welles attempted to find work as an actor by placing two advertisements in *Variety* magazine touting his talents and availability, alas, to no avail.

To explore another of his talents, painting, Orson enrolled in a summer class at the Art Institute of Chicago taught by the noted Russian émigré stage designer Boris Anisfeld. Anisfeld was quick to marvel at Welles's talent with a brush as well as his facility for stage design. Anisfeld was so impressed that he arranged for Orson to receive a full scholarship to study at the Art Institute beginning in the fall.

Tempting as the offer was, Welles was far more interested in exploring life and the arts outside the classroom. Restive and still smarting from the deafening silence his two notices in *Variety* generated, Welles longed to escape his overbearing guardian, who continually badgered Orson to delay his theatric dreams and enter college.

Eschewing higher education, at least for the time being, Orson opted to spend time touring Europe with paint brushes, canvases, sketch pads, and a journal to capture his impressions, and upon his return home, he would cobble together a book highlighting his adventures. He told his guardian if he discovered a college that intrigued him, he would consider enrolling. With serious reservations, Bernstein agreed and withdrew five hundred dollars from the trust fund Richard had established for his son and allowed the sixteen-year-old to embark on his creative sojourn.

～

Ireland: "Obsessed with Life"

In August 1931, rejoicing in his good fortune, Orson wrote the Hills aboard the Cunard White Star Line's steamship, the SS *Baltic*, shortly before arriving at Galway, Ireland: "The idea of Ireland—passionate, oppressed, mystic—was in every way the antithesis of the old tired civilized post-war world.

'Get out your Don Byrne and your Synge and your Gallic ballads—you can't trace my wanderings on the map!'"

"The critics tell us of Orson's obsession with death," Roger Hill wrote of Orson. "I tell you that he has always been obsessed with life, with its sensitivities, with its promises, and always an amazing gift for romantic readiness as witness his falling in love with Ireland the day he stepped ashore."[14]

The Hills and Dr. Bernstein shared Orson's letters with one another and saved them in the event he later would write a book about his Erin adventures.

Though Orson's Irish travelogue was never completed, my grandparents kept copies of Welles's letters and journal, extended snippets of which demonstrate his virtuoso mind and pen.

In late August, Orson wrote to Dr. Bernstein from the Leenane Hotel in Killarney Bay, Connemara, chiding himself for the paucity of letters to Ravinia and Woodstock. What he lacked in frequency he more than made up for in quality.

September 1931
Leenane Hotel,
Killarney Bay,
Connemara

Dearest Family,

I arrived in Ireland by way of Galway, the largest town on the West Coast and one of the more fascinating in the world. Surprises I have had in my travels—countries like Japan and China have exceeded my expectations, but in sixteen short, very full years of living—nothing comparable with Galway—or the west of Ireland—has looked so unexpectedly, so breathtakingly on my horizon. I wish I could describe that first moment. Our very landing was dramatic—the tender pulled up to the side of the ship full of luggage and relations—everyone aboard it seemed was Irish—men and women got on their knees, weeping with joy, there was much craning of necks and pitiful waving and then little cries of recognition as first one passenger and then another picked out their "Paddy," or "Michael." A fine tall man with flowing silver hair and a face like Wotan, brandished his silver-headed cane fiercely over our heads crying in a voice like thunder— "Sure and it's God's own country." I looked out over the rolling indigo sea to the misty mountains, blue and gold at the horizon—they were singing "The Wearin' of the Green," and on the tender, people, separated for years, were locking and unlocking in the intricacies of an Irish jig. "Home is the sailor, home from the sea, and the hunter, home from the hills." I unarmored, as Wotan, leaping madly down the gangplank, sang out for the hundredth time— "Sure, and it's God's own country." It was then that something in the lilt of the song and the color of the hills got under my skin, and quite impulsively, I ran down to my stateroom, packed to the last sock, was off to Ireland before the purser could do much about it. I must say I don't regret it—if I had gone on to Cobh, I should have missed Connacht and the Gaeltacht entirely—and the West Coast of Ireland is unknown and unbeliev-able. In all Europe and the Western Hemisphere, there is nothing to approach it—in this Americanized three-quarters of the globe, it is unique—the last frontier or romance.

Galway is a promise and that world between Spiddal and Benegal is its fulfillment. Nearly at my journey's end, I look on it all feeling very much like another Columbus who set out to find the Indies and came instead upon the Americas—the first man withal.

There have been—like the Danes before Columbus—other Marco Polos to penetrate the wild splendors of this glamorous backwoods—but on the whole, it is as known to the humoral world as Iceland was in those dark days when mapmakers dismissed it with the laconic "Here be dragons."

Civilization, like a gigantic spider, has thrown its web—or the beginning of it—aside and between the mountains, that commercial travelers,—our modern answer for the missionary and the trader—may bring to the men of the West, shoes, and toothbrushes and newspapers—and a realization of the existence of an outside world.

Climbing a mountain at dusk, I have lain in the heather and watched the sun fall into the mouth of a distant valley somewhere beyond the Twelve Pins, in the farthest reaches of the hills. I have found myself out of sight, and miles from the humblest habitation—only the single meandering line of one of those roads shining in the dark purple of the valleys. "A ribbon of moonlight over the purple-moor," is never more appropriate a description for the roads are literally ribbons, roads that tie Connemara to the outside world, a world of moving pictures, and chocolate malted-milks. It is difficult to believe that I'm twenty-four hours from London and civilization.

In those thatched cottages, soon to be sacked, I have lived—and, as the honored guest, attended feasts, weddings, wakes, and match-makings. I have lived in the midst of this Homeric simplicity as intimately as anywhere on earth—and after a month of journeying in this wonderful land of fine, tall friendly people, I find myself at the postern gates of Valhalla, not an authority on the lands thru whence I've come—but certainly a very dear friend.

I have circled half of Ireland in the simplest and safest of vehicles, the donkey-cart! This takes us back to Galway and my first days on the island.

On the third or fourth day I checked my baggage and chucking tons of oil-paint into the lately acquired army-store haversack, I marched down the road towards Clifton, the capital of Connemara. Here I was inspired—a donkey—drawing a donkey-cart, came down the road. The commonest sight in Ireland, but the heaven-sent answer to the most uncommon problem that land ever offered. Shaking like the traditional leaf in the October wind, I overpaid the bar-boy and stumbled hysterically out on the road, demanding the price of the rig from its owner—the rig was not for sale and further, I learned, somewhat at the expense of my high spirits—no rig nor no donkey was for sale. I questioned this and learned that the donkey-fair was just over and everything in the donkey and donkey-cart line had been bought up for use in the haying and gathering of new turf to follow forth for the next two months.—I might ask Mr. O'Malley—Mr. O'Malley had a rig he might be wanting to sell—I asked Mr. O'Malley—and I asked Mr. Flaherty, and Mr. Bian, and Mr. Machoown, and Mr. Greally, I asked everybody in Galway and finally found myself at the door of one of Mr. McDonough's numerous plants—in which donkey-carts were newly made.

A gentleman was standing at the door of the donkey-cart shop smoking a clay pipe. When I told him my story a great light shone in his brown eyes and I learned he was the brother-in-law of the great Pádraic Ó Conaire—one of Ireland's most notable literary lights, who somewhat like Diogenes, had lived his life in donkey-carts. I was taken at once to Mr. McDonough, himself, a great fine man in a bowler hat and overalls, who owns and is worshipped by the entire West of Ireland. The light came into his eyes as I have since seen it come into the eyes of every true Irishman.

From that moment onwards, we three were friends. I lived in their houses, danced with their daughters, and swam with their sons.

The cart—a magnificent creation of blue and orange, was given me at cost. For two days Mr. McDonough ceased work and drove me around the countryside in his Rolls-Royce in search of a suitable donkey, and in the fullness of time, she too was found. A three-year-old Spanish lady with original ideas and a beauty of face and figure, which won her the name of "Shimoga," Gaelic for a certain species of fairy.

The blacksmith considered himself honored to do the shoeing and refused pay and all who considered themselves honored to turn out in thousands for the purpose of instructing "Shimoga" and myself (both novices) in the mysteries of cart driving and pulling. And before I could escape all this attention the races were upon us. In all Ireland, the Connemara races are the most important of all the year's events. Everybody with sporting blood in their veins—that is—everybody—comes to Galway—and for three days there is carousing funmaking, fighting, gambling, drunkenness, and gaiety of every conceivable description, rivaling and out rivaling anything of the kind to happen in Europe or America at any time, inclusive of New Years!

A month's adventuring through the West of Ireland, the wildest, most fascinating and one of the most beautiful spots on the earth's surface, will never go on record. I shall have to tell you about it. My week with the band of gypsies, my mountain-climbs, my night in a quagmire, and finally, at the end of it all, the auctioning off of "Shimoga," at the Clifden Fair—should all make tolerably interesting after-dinner tales. As for the rest of it—I doubt if I could even begin to write it down. We traveled a good percent in Ireland together, Shimoga and I—from Galway to Donegal and the giant causeway, and nearly back. At night we camped at the roadside—Shimoga feeding on the mountain grass and I cooking over a turf-fire, and when the stars were out, Shimoga went to join the "Sidhe," the fairies—and I curled myself up under the cart and fell asleep. There were nights, too, spent in cottages at wakes, weddings, and match-makings.

I've come to love the folk of the West—and the mountains and the scenery of the West—but I can never tell you how much!

Having sold Shimoga for a fair price, I came out of the land of James Stephens, and into that of Synge, but enough said—I shall be here at the Aran island, Inisheer, for a few weeks painting—and the next boat will tell you about this new dreamland I've penetrated.

The mainland of West and North Ireland is behind me—I shall never forget it!

Hastily, and lovingly,
Orson

Writing to Dr. Bernstein several weeks later, from Inisheer, Orson captured the essence and antiquity of the "three tiny piles of limestone off the West Coast" of Ireland that constitute the Aran Islands.

September 1931

Dearest Dadda,

That I shall not make Scotland causes me little anguish. I have heard things concerning Scotland, and Ireland has certainly spoiled me for it. I have spent over eight weeks in unequaled adventures and I have nothing but a half-dozen hideous abortions on canvas to show for it. This is a painful admission, particularly so when I add that I am at the end of a second week on this island—an island of not three miles in circumference, and not exceeding four hundred inhabitants, to which supposedly undiverting exile I have isolated myself for the sole purpose of work!

The wind, the rain, the flies, to say nothing of the thousand and one diversions to which the adventurer in Ireland is tempted, were instrumental in the ruination and eventual physical demolishment of precisely ten terrible landscapes. Ireland is really a water-color country—and I have learned to my sorrow that whatever craftsmanship I can lay claim to, lies only in the channels of still-life, composition, design, and portraits—. Heretofore, I have never essayed landscape and an almost unearthly quality of this countryside and the mountains in the West and North completely stumped me.

The Aran Islands are three tiny piles of limestone off the West Coast. James Synge of whose plays take place on them—has lent the islands fame but not popularity. The weekly, (weather permitting—and it never does!) mail-boat bears, once in a blue moon, an occasional tourist for an hour or two on the big island.

Eighty years ago, the English government performed the remarkable engineering feat of erecting a coast-guard station that has gone out of use, and which I use as a studio. There is a priest who braves the waves when the Sundays are fine to say Mass, but despite these vague hints of civilization, Inisheer remains as it has been for many centuries, the most primitive spot in Europe. In those dim ages following the downfall of Rome, when all of the Western hemisphere, saving Ireland, was plunged in darkness, Erin was a world-famous seat of learning, and Enda, Columcille, Kevin, Corbett, and a great many others gained for it the title of "The Island of Saints." But that day has long since seen its twilight—remembered only in ruins and old men's tales. Earlier glories, too, have filled the earth with Erin's fame—as temples and palaces built three thousand years ago still standing—attest. And through the ages these people whose fathers produced and flourished in Tutankhamun's time—and kept alive the flame of Christian culture in the days of Genghis Khan—these people have achieved in modern centuries the climax in the history of their noble race, after many thousands of years in the making of it, their paradise has come into creation. A race as old as humanity has grappled with life since the dawn of time and discovered in the twentieth century how best to manage it. It is almost beyond belief that two days journeying from the world's greatest metropolis brings one to a land where intelligent and aristocratic people live in archaic simplicity, surpassing anything in Homer.

I am doing nothing but portraits now, and at the end of three weeks, I shall carry away with me perhaps a half dozen of them—simple sketches of men and women I have known here. Some of them will be bad pictures and some fair—most of them will be good likenesses, but as portrayals of that undefinable Erin spirit, they will all be dismal failures. There is a quality in the Erin eye a thousand times more elusive than the blue in the Connemara hills, a something in the clean, naïve smile that plays on the Erin mouth, a twinkle that dances in an Erin's eye—an intelligent candor and something more—to paint that—is to paint God.

"Good-night, tons and tons of love,"
Orson

Waxing additional virtues of Inisheer in a letter to the Hills, Orson enthused:

Dear Hills,

Here life has attained simplicity and is lived with an artistry surpassing anything—I am sure in the South Seas . . . somewhere there may be a forgotten land where eyes are as clear and hearts as open, but nowhere is candor so remarkably combined with intelligence, an intelligence which results from nearly five thousand years' cultural background. Being then fully cognizant of these several underlined wonders—you may gather that my wanderings have brought me a kind of lost Eden, rich in romance and of bounteous beauty. . . . I shall find it very hard to leave my little cottage by the sea for the world of tram-cars and leather shoes I used to know.

Love,
Orson

Shortly before departing Inisheer, Orson wrote to Dr. Bernstein extolling the ineffable glory of Ireland and the challenge of capturing the country's essence in words. However, he had little difficulty informing his guardian that his travels had come at a cost and he was "in desperate need of money!"

My Dearest Dadda:

Another Sunday will find me taking leave of Inisheer, and a sad leave-taking it will be. I can't tell you how I love this island and the people on it. Faced with the problem of recording experiences and impressions, I find myself in the same predicament as on the mainland. So much has happened. I am really drinking too deeply of Ireland to write well about it. The best travel books, one might almost say the only ones, are written by those who go with comparative haste from atmosphere to atmosphere. If I had hurried through the West—and seen but a few sunsets, a single wake, a single dance, a single wedding, instead of dallying along in a donkey cart, seeing countless of each, and calling Connacht by its first name—so to speak, then I might write interestingly of those few experiences, each impression would be clear and bright in my memory, and in consequence any record of them would make a continuous and rapidly moving narrative. As it is, I have such a fund of adventure and romance to draw from that I cannot attack any one particular of my story with quite the freshness and interest that an informative letter or a readable journal demands. I have lingered in these parts so long I have almost ceased to become a traveler. Neither of us could write an amusing article on Kenosha from the tourist standpoint. We could, however, do ourselves justice in a play, a story, an analysis, a poem, or a novel concerning itself with one or more phases of life and manners of that estimable metropolis.—To write a travel-book, compose a travel letter, or give a travel talk, one must be comparatively ignorant of the countries with which he deals. Of course, I don't profess an all-embracing acquaintanceship, but—I am sure you understand me.

This is written—as everything I write is—at 4:00 in the morning, after a very full evening. A few hours at Patch Litman's Cottage yarning and "talking fairies," and then a shindy at John Connely's. A shindy is a great thing, and scarcely an evening goes by but what one of us doesn't rout the old fiddlers out and stage one. You would hardly recognize "Paddy" as everyone here calls me, jigging away into the wee small hours!

Irish dancing is not delicate, but it is a hearty, joyful, genuine expression of the dance impulse. It is a great sight to see the kitchen of, let us say, Maggie Flaherty, (dealer in the mountain dew,)—sichh! —cleared of impediments and full of fine Erin men in indigo homespun and beautiful— (I use the word unhesitatingly) and smiling colleens in nice red skirts and sienna jackets, all whirling about in the intricacies of the "The Wind That Shakes the Barley," and stamping their leathern slippers on the flaggings as the orchestra plays on into the night. It was fine tonight, and when the dancing was over, there were ballads sung, and stories told, and a long walk across the moonlit strand brings me here.

As I must be up betimes tomorrow, I must come quickly to the point. The point is an old one—and one which you are much accustomed to hearing—I am desperately in need of money! The deficiency in my checkbook, of which I wrote you, has upset my budget considerably, and unless financial aid awaits me in Dublin, I shall never be able to leave this country alive but will die a swift but painful death by starvation. I have no ticket from New York to Chicago, remember, and Dublin is a long way from the nearest seaport.

Bidding adieu to the Aran Islands early in October, Orson's wanderings brought him to Limerick, where he bought a bicycle he dubbed "Ulysses" and rode twenty-two miles to the village of Shannon, where he went aboard a barge on the nearby Shannon River. Arriving at the town of Athlone, he debarked and spent the next day exploring the town before catching a bus to Dublin.

Riding along the town's battery, located on the west side of the town—built in the early seventeenth century to defend against the possibility of a French invasion—Orson came upon a young amorous couple and their chaperone that he limned and sketched in his journal:

The hill of which I have spoken is called the Battery and is crossed by a stone-breasted gully impregnable from vulgar gaze. There I came upon three little boys, their bellies flat upon the grass, peeping furtively over the brink. I tiptoed up behind them to see what the object of their attention was and was amused to discover two young persons of the opposite sex reclining in the trench and making violent and enthusiastic love. But what delighted both performers and audience most was the presence of a matronly lady—fat in a respectable kind of way—and obviously, the chaperone of the party—snoring lustily alongside the delighted lovers! Rather than disturb so happy a scene, I descended the hill on the side farthest from Romeo and his dark-eyed Juliet. This brought me quite near the slumbering chaperone. Imagine my astonishment upon passing, to discover that lady manufacturing the sounds of sleep with her twinkling eyes wide open! Dumbstruck, I gazed down at them and, as I turned away, one of those very Irish organs closed in an elaborate wink!!!!

I am riding into Dublin thinking glad thoughts of Ireland.

Monies from his trust fund awaited him in the capital city. So, too, within weeks, was his first opportunity to appear on a professional stage.

Recounting his first weeks in Dublin, Orson writes Roger Hill:

Dear Skipper,

A donkey cart, a bicycle, a port-barge, and a gypsy caravan have taken me round and round Ireland and finally dumped me—as Dr. must by this time have told you, in the Gate Theatre—Dublin. Here I shall probably remain until Christmas and more probably spring—playing, painting scenery and signs, and writing publicity for the press.

Here is the opportunity I have been praying for. The Gate is just organized. We are a kind of Irish Theatre Guild—that is to say an art theatre on a commercial basis. Mr. Hilton Edwards and the equally formal, Micheál Mac Liammóir, have a producing staff and acting company of really excellent professional

In a 1931 letter to Roger Hill, Orson writes of his donkey ride in Dublin, Ireland

people—neither mellowed and jaded "old-timers" and hams, nor inexperienced beginners. They represent the best of that vast army—larger on these islands than across the Atlantic, where the talkies have reduced them to job hunting.

Hilton Edwards came over to Dublin and took double pneumonia. When he recovered he found himself at loose ends for the summer season, and meeting Mac Liammóir, conceived the idea of the Gate. A part of the present company was rallied together from across the channel, native Irish and British colonial sources—and the Gate Theatre opened with "Peer Gynt" in the late spring.

I really didn't think such a company existed, where people were serious-minded and highly intelligent and well educated and contributed those virtues with the more cardinal sense of humor, wholesomeness, and rationality.

There are fifteen professionals in the company besides the technical staff, the directors, dancers and musicians, and everybody works "for the joy of working and each in his separate sphere"—and so on. The phrase "nobody works for money" being particularly applicable—salaries are of chorus girl's dimensions and are all of the same amount regardless of one's position.

I went to the Gate on my second evening in Dublin simply for entertainment's sweet sake. It was there that I met Hilton, our dynamic, hot-tempered and golden-hearted Lord-of-Lords. There was much talk and finally an application for a job. He was gracious and candid. He would be delighted, he said, but the budget would not permit of another member. He could find me a small part in *Jew Süss* just going into rehearsal but I would have to work on amateurs' wages. If I cared to stick and if we got along together bigger parts might even persuade the committee to pay me an extra guinea. I accepted.

There are two big parts in *Jew Süss*. One is the George Arliss title role and the other is the half Emil Jannings, half Douglas Fairbanks contrast to the Jew, Karl Alexander, and the Duke. I read the play, decided I had no chance as Süss, and though I scarcely dared dream of getting it, learned Karl Alexander. My first audition was a bitter failure. I read a scene and being terribly nervous and anxious to impress, I performed a kind of J Worthington Ham bit with all the tricks and resonance I could conjure up. The real climax to the whole thing is that Charles Margood—actor—press agent and assistant scene painter has left and I am hired in his place to fill the various departments in which he functioned! Step back John Barrymore, Gordon Craig, and John Clayton, your day has passed. A new glory glows in the East. I am a professional!!!

Love,
Orson

When the curtain descended on the opening night of Welles's first performance in the four-hundred-seat Gate, the silence was broken with deafening applause for Orson's performance. Reminiscing more than five decades later he recalled, "It was thunderous and totally unexpected. I got more acclaim for that than for anything I've done since."

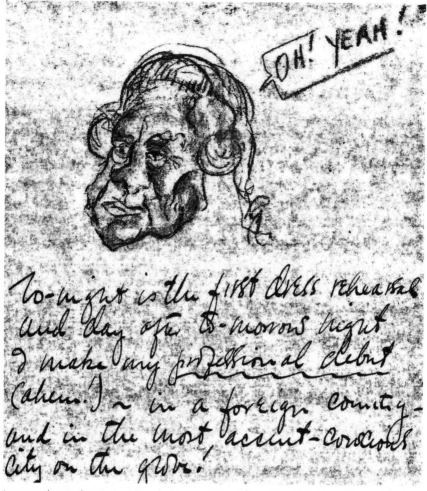

In an exuberant letter, Orson includes a sketch of himself as Karl Alexander in *Jew Süss*.

In the still hours after the performance, Orson wrote to Hortense Hill, "Tonight I took six curtain calls alone—with the galley and the pit shouting and stamping and calling out my name. This sounds like an appalling boast, and it is!"

Commenting on Welles's opening night performance, the *Irish Times* reviewer lauded praise on the sixteen-year-old actor: "A new actor, Mr. Orson Welles, made an excellent Karl Alexander. It will be necessary to see him in other parts before it can be said that he is the accomplished actor that he seemed last night in a part that might have been especially made for him."[15]

Micheál Mac Liammóir writes vividly in his book *All for Hecuba: An Irish Theatrical Biography* how the opening night thunder affected young Welles.

> When Orson came padding on to the stage with his lopsided grace, his laughter, his softly thunderous voice, there was a flutter of astonishment and alarm, a hush, and a volley of applause. That, of course, was at the end of each act, and when the play was over and Hilton and he took their curtains together, and Hilton said some words of praise and introduction, Orson swelled visibly. I have heard of people swelling visibly before, but Orson is one of those who really does it. The chest expands, the head, thrown back upon the round, boyish neck, seems to broaden, the features swell and burn, the lips, curling back from the teeth like dark, tropical plants, thicken into a smile. Then the hands extend, palms open to the crowd, the shoulders thrust upwards, the feet, at last, are satisfied: they remain a little sedately; that they should realize him like this merits a bow, so slow and sedate the head goes down and quickly up again, up higher than ever, for maybe this is all a dream, and if the eyes are on the boots, blood rushing to the ears, who knows that sight and sound may not double-cross and vanish like a flame blown out, and Orson will be back at school again, hungry, unsatisfied, not ready yet for the world? NO, the people are still there, still applauding, more and more and more and more and back goes the big head, and the laugh breaks out like fire in the jungle, white lightning slits open across the sweating chubby cheeks, the brows knit in perplexity like a coolie's, the hands shoot widely out to either side, one to the right at Hilton, the other to the left at Betty, for you don't mean to say all this racket is for Orson . . . ?
>
> So that was Orson's first night with us, and although of course it was said in Dublin that he never did anything half as good as the Duke again, it was, I think, untrue. Everything he touched took on a queer and gruesome magic, a misshapen and indescribable grace; and he himself, though no one could describe him as a clinging sentimentalist, has remained through all these years one of the most loyal men I have known, the kindest and most un-forgetting of friends; and somewhere through the turbulent vapors of his temperament there flows a broad river full of stars.[16]

On November 29, 1931, six weeks after the opening of *Jew Süss*, Welles was featured in the *Chicago Tribune*, the headline reading, "Chicago Boy makes Hit as Irish Actor/Aged 16, He Wins Praise in Leading Roles at Dublin Art Theatre." After chronicling his recent triumphant weeks on the Irish stage, the article concludes, "He is fixed up in the Gate Theatre programs until well into the new year, by which time the wanderlust will probably have gotten him again. He is a wanderer, and though only sixteen has been to China and Japan. He has also been to England, whence his forbears originally came."[17]

∼

Return to America

"At the end of the season at the Gate," Hill writes in *One Man's Time and Chance*, "and after raves from his Irish employers, and Hilton Edwards, Micheál Mac Liammóir, Irish press, and Irish audiences, he traveled to London and pounded pavement looking for work on the stage, and met with no success, though he met George Bernard Shaw, who, in his mid-seventies, Orson found quite cordial. He sailed to New York and looked for work in the theatre. In 1932, America was embroiled in the Depression. Many theatres in New York were dark and those that were not didn't offer Orson a part, leading, or otherwise."[18]

Photo of Orson at seventeen inscribed to "The Skipper."

Crestfallen, he boarded a train to Chicago to the welcoming embrace of the Hills. "Hortense and I met him at Union Station," Hill recalls, "and he bounded from the train sporting an over-sized wool coachman's cloak and a Gatsby Donegal Tweed Cap. As he stepped off the train, an overloaded suitcase sprang open and scattered its contents causing him to stumble into the ballast of Hortense's arms. As we helped him gather his sketchbooks, makeup kit, books, and rumpled clothes, he effervescently entertained us with his Irish adventures and dreams for the future."[19]

At Hill's encouragement, Orson began working as Todd's drama coach for the remainder of the second semester. The capstone of Orson's months as Todd's drama coach was directing with Skipper Shakespeare's comedy *Twelfth Night*. The production was entered in the Chicago Drama League competition that included dozens of Chicago area high schools, some of which had enrollments in the thousands. Todd, with a student body of one hundred, won the first-place silver loving cup and later performed at the Chicago World's Fair, which celebrated the city's centennial.

Hill suggested that at the close of the school year, they write a play about the riveting, polemical John Brown—the man, the myth, and his enduring legacy. It took little coaxing for Orson to agree.

"I suggested the upcoming summer would be an ideal time to begin this project," Hill recalls. "My own contribution to writing *Marching Song* was the first draft of the first act. In other words, just enough to motivate our tireless boy, and more importantly, send him off. It was summer, and in that hectic season, I ceased being a carefree schoolmaster and became a salesman, a recruiter of tuition-payers for a new year. To get him out of my hair, I sent him to Lake Mercer at Lac du Flambeau in Wisconsin to complete our play."[20]

The progression of the first draft of Orson's contribution to the play by the seventeen-year-old neophyte co-author is captured expressively and delightfully in Orson's correspondence with Hill during the summer of 1933.

Skipper introduces Orson's first Wisconsin letter in *One Man's Time and Chance*.

> I show you now the first of many letters from the co-author living in a wigwam on an Indian Reservation that summer of 1932. I give you a facsimile so you can appreciate the boy's ease of expression. You remember how Shakespeare's fellow actors described his facility when, after his death, they published that First Folio edition of his plays: *His mind and hand went together and what he thought, he uttered with such easiness that we have scarce received from him a blot on his papers.* Just so with Orson.[21]

Dear Skip,

I've been away for three days now and haven't done a lick of work. But there! When I tell you where I am and why you'll understand.

The story begins with Mr. Meigs [James B. Meigs, father of two Todd boys, James and William, and the business manager of *The American Weekly*, Hearst newspapers' Sunday magazine] and it will persuade you that there is indeed a destiny, which shapes our ends. I met Bill and Jim Meigs' father recently and we talked at some length. He, it appears, maintains a summer establishment on *Lac du* Flambeau in the Indian reservation. He said that between Mercer and Flambeau, there is no comparison. Would I stay on the train a few more miles and give Flambeau a trial? I certainly would.

At Lac du Flambeau, that delightful capital of the Ojibwe Reservation, boasting a main street like an illustration from somebody's novel of life in the early lumbering and Indian-fighting days, there waiting, big and little, rose-faced and multitudinous: the Meigs. They drove me over miles of picturesque Chippewa trails, through pine forests and past myriad little lakes to their luxurious "Lodge," and here I was given as demoralizing a breakfast as has ever been fed to a co-dramatist. Later there was swimming—the water here is crystal and can be drunk with relish—and successively: sailing, in a snappy sloop that would put, I think, the old glitter in your seaman's eye, game fishing, Jim caught a Muskie.

But need I go further? Need I say that when it developed that the reservation was as kind to my tortured nasal passages and be-spasmed bronchial tubes as anywhere South of the Fifty, it required only the opportunity to buy a wigwam and live in it in a pine grove, a million miles from a telephone, and entirely surrounded by water? Need I add that I have decided to stay?

I am serious about the pine grove and the wigwam and lest I be accused of extravagance, let me state the entire arrangement is eminently economical. The pine grove, you see, is part of the Meigs estate and the wigwam which I have caused to be built by squaws and a few antiques of the neuter gender for the total reward of twenty-five fifty, gold, is something the Meigs have been long wanting. So, by making the grand gesture of giving it to them for their own for as long as birch-bark and rush mat shall remain incorporate (which, I am informed, is a matter of generations), I feel easy at accepting their hospitality— meals, that is, delicious meals, and camping materials de-lux.

A wigwam or, more correctly, a wig-i-wham is emphatically a thing of the forest. It is fashioned of wild things; deerskin and bark, soft maple and basswood. Even the rope in the bulrush screening is of native manufacture. And being primitive and far removed from the high-pressure world of our civilization, its construction is a matter of time—exactly two days. So of course, I haven't worked. The building of this great inverted salad bowl of a house of mine has been too fascinating a diversion. But tomorrow, tomorrow I shall roll up the proverbial sleeve and lay to. Write me in care of J.B. Meigs (God Bless Him) Lac du Flambeau, Wisc.

I have been so many centuries from John Brown and Marching Song during the past weekend that I rejoice in returning to it, to find my mind freshened and enthusiastic. If things go as promising as they began in this Utopia, I shall probably linger for the Autumnal turning of the leaves. Or what do you think?

Love without end,
Orson

Weeks later, Orson writes to his co-dramatist of his delight cobbling the play together in his "pine pillared wigwam by the water" and that he is including in the letter a draft of the second act.

Dear Skip,

Flambeau is simply all that a Northern lake can be. I can scarcely think of a more perfect workshop than this pine-pillared wigwam by the water. A tuneful country this, here on the reservation, now that noisy outboards have been packed away. A little sad, perhaps the song the marsh-folk sing, and sadder yet the endless dirge of the wind in the fir trees. At night there are stealthy little sounds, and always the unbelievable, ceaseless throbbing drums.

Here, you will say, is a place to write.

But writing is like my outboard motor. Need I elaborate? Well, I have got started now, and the mail that carries this should include the completed second act of Kansas Days.

What cheer? I don't envy you your Concord, indeed I view the imminent Arsenal with greater complacency! And how kaleidoscopic are one's moods! After a soul-satisfying dinner, with the most charming of hosts, I completed a moment with Preacher White and peace treaties that hustled me into a whole series of transports over the play at large. Now, through the murky spectacles of early morning (one does keep barbaric hours in this bee-loud glade!), I search in vain for rosy pigmentation. Courage my soul! Hopes rise with the falling sun.

Orson

In Welles's next dispatch, he compliments and critiques Hill's first draft of Act I and expects the first draft of the play to be finished "within a week or a little more."

Dear Skip,

After your wonderful first act, referred to by you as a mere day's work, a pretty fair history lesson but, just a fulcrum on which to rest the lever of my thought, I am definitely and permanently shamed. I don't believe you wrote that in less than two hard weeks nor that you didn't think yourself, in your heart of hearts, that it's mighty damn good. Personally, I think it's great. Wonderful!! And with this opinion clearly understood, may I offer the inevitable criticism?

In the beginning, I don't think there's too much history at all. I rather think you've struck the note admirably and made incredibly dull expository material genuinely dramatic. But I do think there's too much Thoreau! He completely dominates the off-stage individuality of John Brown, whose shadow should be more real than any of the persons actually presented. . . .

But the marching on line is superb. "I have peered into the nightly chasm of his purpose—etc." is a line among many hundreds of thousands of lines, and unless I am badly mistaken in my ideas, it is one of those rare speeches, the kind that lives because it combines a literary quality with a very real dramatic theatric power.

But other of your speeches—some of them—I think at this moment are too good. There is something to be said of course for reproducing the period's predilection to the well-turned phrase, and I think myself that the whole scene smacks emphatically of the authentic. But this is, nonetheless, a different age, very different, and we don't want to be accused of bombast. I think neat lines are a fault of mine, too. We must both beware, for that way leads to floweriness. . . .

That's about all. . . . You speak of immediately rewriting. I look forward with pleasurable anticipation the possibility of anything greatly better. The scene should certainly be very thoroughly done over and snapped up, like all the rest of it. But the workable skeleton you said you had hoped it was, I would vote an enthusiastic Yes.

Tomorrow I shall begin the prison episode. It is delightful to contemplate the prospect of a completed draft within a week or a little more because if I plug madly on, it will be possible.

This third page is begun at ten thirty, a ten thirty that feels, even to this inveterate nighthawk, like the cold moment before dawn in a Dublin scene-dock. These rural regularities are cramping my style!

The Old Ghostly Galleon is full up to the brim and tossing madly about somewhere outside. I looked at it before I came in tonight and thought of how delightfully unexpected everything turns out for me. South Manitou, for instance, and even this, I reflected, I never dreamed when I purchased tickets to Mercer that I should end up among the red men, living now in the birch-bark wigwam. In the seventeen kaleidoscopic years of this present existence, I have not once successfully predicted any one-minute of my following future!

Search out the spare moment, sir, and make it count. The barest word from Woodstock sends me into perfect trilogies of delight.

Orson

The first draft of Marching Song was completed in early September. Upon Orson's return to Woodstock, he and Roger spent time working on emendations until both considered their creation worthy of being produced in New York.

⌒

Searching for a *Marching Song* Angel in New York

"In the fall, the play finished and duplicate copies prepared," Hill writes in *One Man's Time and Chance*,

> Horty and I took Orson in the school's land yacht, complete with a chauffeur-cook, to New York. There we moved into a suite in the Algonquin suitable for entertaining lucky Broadway producers who would be offered our opus. I would give Dwight Deere Wiman first chance. He had been my childhood roommate at Todd and America's most prolific producer during the Depression; now the only one using his own dough which consisted of all that ancestral plow money from Moline. When he and others said thanks-but-no-thanks, I peered into an empty purse, moved our boy into the cheapest of rooms to continue sales efforts via pavement pounding, and headed home.[22]

Throughout the next three months, while Orson remained in New York passing out copies of the play to theatric producers and agents, he kept a per-fervid correspondence with Skipper reporting on the emotional roller coaster he found himself riding.

Snippets capture his myriad moods ranging from confident expectation to dour doubt.

Dear Skipper,

This may discourage you even more than it did me. I never quite shared your optimism, nor quite believed that Madden and French would be fighting for the rights to *Marching Song*. Yes, it's true. Madden refused it! Their criticism, or rather Miss Trimblealab's, for which we paid, if you remember, five dollars, is enclosed.

I got it early this afternoon and it discouraged me terribly. I actually agreed with the verdict: not "suitable for the market!" If Madden turned it down, then what's the use? Nothing to do but write another play. Then I went to French. They hadn't read it, and finally to William Harris. They had. The play reader had had the script sent back to her by Harris without his reading it. She had read it over again. Her statement that it was "extremely interesting" was repeated, but with the additional "not the kind of thing for Mr. Harris." I went over to Riverside and stared moodily at the deep black water. . . .

Now, however, I've been to the movies and I've had some food, and I feel slightly better. The play may still be bad, and I've still a sinking suspicion it is, but we can always write more can't we? We must write another play—at once!

Hectically,
Orson

Hill wrote back suggesting the possibility they write a political operetta, to which Welles responds:

Dear Skipper,

You have spoken and with enthusiasm of writing an operetta-like *Of Thee I Sing*, a satire on some major phase of Americana. I disagree with you that the subject matter must be of necessity something big and complex such as American Politics. The only thing that keeps *Of Thee I Sing* from being absolutely soul satisfying is the largeness of its theme. One feels that all the possibilities of humor have not been exploited and the result is a sense of incompletion. Nothing could be as funny as American Politics except American Politics. By the same token, nothing could be as funny as Ford's *Ship of Peace* and so on. . . . Let's take a subject of great simplicity, some phase of life in this great country and make it screamingly funny to an amazed and happily surprised world.

Even as I write this an idea for a half-opera/half-revue pops on the horizon. A history of America in, let's say, ten scenes! Discovery. Revolution. Pioneering. Abolition. Civil War. Suffrage. Prohibition. Bootlegging. Advertising. The Newspaper Business—Whoa! There's an idea! The newspaper business as an operetta! A Front Page Gershwin only more so.

Love,
Orson

One of Orson's highest points during his weeks peddling *Marching Song* came late in October 1932 at a supreme moment of optimism when he shared a publisher's introduction to the play that he drafted for Skipper's consideration.

Dear Skip,

Your telegram and letter, which arrived at one and the same time have excited me so much I just can't write. . . .
    You must get started at once on the preface to *Marching Song*.
    The introduction, by the publishers, might read something like this:
    Mr. Roger Hill is known to most of you as a producer. Besides being a big name in the executive offices of the theatrical world, Mr. Hill is, as this publication attests, a playwright, also a poet, and a lyric writer, and a yachtsman, and strangest of all—an educator! He is principal of Todd, the world-famous "boy's community," perhaps the finest boarding school of its kind in the Western Hemisphere! Strange? It's only the beginning of a far stranger tale—
    A couple of years ago, at the commencement exercises held at Todd, a chubby little boy stood upon the stage just when things were beginning to drag and recited a piece. He delivered it exceedingly well and was given a medal for declamation. Later he was given a diploma. Now this chubby little boy, whose name, as you've probably guessed, is Orson Welles, being a notorious globetrotter, had

no sooner acquired the sheepskin than he set about acquiring steamship tickets and the next thing his friends knew he was in foreign lands painting pictures. The rest of the story is in newspaper headlines. He became a stage star literally overnight, a featured player at seventeen. There was no question about it, the local boy had made good. But Orson never forgot that piece he spoke on the last day. It was called John Brown's "Farewell to the Court." Neither did Roger Hill, who had heard it. The two wrote letters about it, and pretty soon they began studying in libraries and looking up old manuscripts. They traveled about the country quite a good deal, too, retracing John Brown's footsteps, talking to people who could still remember him, uncovering everything they could that would throw a light on the man. Finally, in the early part of this summer, in the year of our Lord Nineteen-and Thirty-Two, they started this play—etc. etc. etc.

Silly as Hell I know that. But I had to do something to work off steam. Just you wait till I get back to town, which I will the minute I've distributed the last of the scripts, sometime this week. What a preface! What illustrations! What stage instructions!

Much love, hysterically,
Orson

Weeks later in a less hopeful mood, Welles wrote to Hill expressing his growing frustration and suggested that Skipper abandon Todd and join him in forming a "producer-playwright-actor-manager team."

Dear Skipper,

I've sat day after day after day after day in offices. . . . Yesterday I spent the afternoon and early evening in the Schubert's [office] along with at least twenty others. Somebody told me there might be a chance for an understudy in their revival of *The Silent House*—the Chinese thriller. There wasn't. Somebody got it days before. They always do . . . Always. . . . Strangely, I've had a renaissance of optimism over *Marching Song* as a play. Wish I had your rosy outlook on its possibilities for production. . . . I don't think anybody will ever produce it. Ben Boyer hasn't read it yet. . . . Producers, my, what children they are. I doubt if any business anywhere is run so inefficiently as the theatre business is here in New York. Nobody has office hours. Nobody tells the truth. Nobody does what they say they're going to do. Nowhere is there the remotest vestige of a system. In a director that might be excused on artistic grounds or something, but in an executive office! This waiting for somebody to produce the play is likely to be a matter of years and years and years and years and years, and . . . We'll make a Producer-Playwright-Actor-Manager team that will go rolling down in history. . . . Big money, fame, and fortune!

Love,
Orson

Despite Orson's beseeching, Skipper remained at Todd and the world knows what became of Welles.

Dear Skip,

I am now firmly convinced that *Marching Song*, despite its merits, will never be produced, at least not this year, unless maybe by The Gate.

Sometime when we're famous . . .

I am aware that disappointments, it matters not how many, should in no way affect my confidence, but they do. Today, for example, it was not a shock, nor a sense of failure, just the realization of a fact, the cementing of a profound conviction. I refer to Ben Boyer's returning the manuscript. I wasn't even surprised. He said, "It's a swell show. It makes good reading. It would make a good book. I think maybe it's even a good play. But that doesn't matter. It won't make money. It isn't a commercial piece. At least that's what I think. Maybe I'm wrong." He thanked me for letting him read it, nicely, I thought, repeated himself, and said goodbye.

GET IN TOUCH WITH SAM RAPHAELSON! Advertise in the papers. *Variety* or something. I've seen his name a lot on big-time movies lately. He is our man! There must be some way of reaching him, of enthusing him. . . .

I got an idea earlier this evening (it's now half after three) for a comedy, a comedy-drama let us say, on the subject of aphasia. That's the medical word isn't it, for loss of memory? The idea, like so many others on ice, is merely embryonic. . . .

Now, for the first time, I'm determined that publishing *Marching Song* is the thing to do. Of course, I've got to be around for that.

Write me. Please.
Orson

December arrived and Welles had yet to interest a producer in mounting the play. At Hill's suggestion, Orson was about to pack his bags and return to Woodstock to write an introduction to *Marching Song* and fill the pages with his line drawings and publish the play as a book.

Shortly before boarding a train to Chicago, Welles was contacted by the noted theatrical producer George C. Tyler indicating interest in the play and that he would try to interest financial backers.

With the prospect of *Marching Song* being produced and published, Orson returned to Chicago. Shortly after his arrival, at a party he hosted, Orson, assuming all the characters, read *Marching Song* to the gathering and the next day wrote an impassioned letter to Skipper in Woodstock recounting the event:

Dear Skip,

The play-reading went over with an emphatic bang! Everybody kept awake and Lloyd Lewis, like your father at the Lyceum Course, was "an inspirational face."

Surprised to learn that *Marching Song* is revolutionary in its technique of dialogue.

I have decided not to go to college. Pretty soon there's going to be a powerful inflation or something and my money, if I still have it, won't be worth anything. I propose to enjoy it now. The sun is shining down in the Isle of Pines, the palms wave a beckon, and natives are dancing at the crossroads and the pineapple is poking out of the red earth.

Come to Chicago and let's talk this thing over. The year is tearing by depressingly swift and boats are sailing all over the world. I'm sick of Ravinia; sick and desolate. I want to finish our book in peace. I want to get going. I'm going mad.

So, do come in. As you love me, do this little thing. Drive in tomorrow or at most the next day.

Please.
Orson

Tyler was unsuccessful in attracting backers for *Marching Song*, which dampened the enthusiasm of the co-authors to publish the play as a book. *Marching Song* has yet to be produced professionally. However, in June 1950, my father, Hascy Tarbox, directed the play in Woodstock.

The June 2, 1950, edition of the *Woodstock Sentinel* announced, "The world premiere of 'Marching Song' a play written by Orson Welles and Roger Hill, will be presented in the Woodstock Opera House Wednesday

World premiere of *Marching Song*, June 7 and 8, 1950, performed by the Todd Troupers in the Woodstock Opera House.

and Thursday, June 7–8 at 8 p.m. by the Todd Troupers of Todd School. The late Lloyd Lewis, drama critic of the *Chicago Daily News*, and noted civil war historian calls *Marching Song* a 'great and stirring play.'"

The Hills sent a poster of the production to Orson in Paris, where he was starring in his play *The Blessed and the Damned* at the Théâtre Édouard VII, which prompted Welles to respond warmly and whimsically:

Théâtre Édouard VII
Paris, France
July 29, 1950

Dearest Hortense,

This is just a short note and will be followed by an informative and affectionate letter. I have been meaning to write you for many weeks. . . .

It was a big thrill getting the posters for *Marching Song*, and I wish that you or Skipper would write me a little more about the production and its reception on the occasion of its world premiere. Also, inform the producer that, as far as my royalties are concerned, he is at liberty to invest them for me. I suggest something safe like Government Bonds—or a chocolate malted at Allen's Drug Store.

All my love always . . .
Orson

⌒

Marching On to *Everybody's Shakespeare*

"After *Marching Song*, I needed a new project to absorb this boy's bubbling energy and to satisfy his constant creative urge," Hill observed.

The solution: write a Shakespeare book. Tell other teachers some of the tricks we used at Todd to make the Elizabethan popular in the classroom as well as on the stage. Orson was ecstatic. The idea of a single volume grew into the plan for a series. He started making sketches.

"They're wonderful, Orson! Kids will love them," I enthused. "We'll fill the margins of every page." "Do you really like them?" he asked. "You say we could do these plays? That'll mean scads of drawings. I could work faster off alone somewhere. I've never been to Africa. I hear it's wonderful. And I met an important Arab in Paris, Brahim, eldest son of Thami el Glaoui, the Pasha of Marrakech, a great lord of Morocco, who invited me to visit him there anytime. What do you think?" "Great with me, Orson," I responded. Off he went on a small freighter to Casablanca via the Azores. His first letter from Africa was written at sea. I had piled new duties on him. He was not only making the drawings but also writing the stage directions.[23]

At sea, aboard the *Exermont* en route to Africa, Welles reflected on the humbling task of interpreting Shakespeare and his "very Eugene O'Neill and salty" voyage.

Spring, 1933

Dear Roger,

You'll find grotesqueries in my stage directions, repetitions, and misfirings. You'll have to do a clean-up job. I'll be relieved when I can get this off in the mails. The mere presence of Shakespeare's script worries me. What right have I to give credulous and believing innocents an inflection for his mighty lines? Who am I to say that this one is "tender" and this one is said "angrily" and this "with a smile"? There are as many interpretations for characters in Caesar as there are in God's spacious firmament. What nerve I have to pick out one of them and cram it down any child's throat, coloring, perhaps permanently, his whole conception of the play? I wish to high heaven you were here to reassure me.

Mainly I just wish you were here. You'd love it! Everyone from the captain down is a real character. Here's a crossing that's rare fun chasing the plates and cups around the mess and trying to keep chair and self within the shifting scene of the table. I tried to put some of it into verse:

Days now numberless it seems to me
We've lolled and wallowed in a lusty sea.
Time is a thing that used to be.
The order and ascent of days is nothing now
A March-blown ocean mauls our plunging prow,
An acreage hysterical for us to plow
Crash in the galley. Crashes are constant now
Shiver the empty Exermont from stern to prow.
Time is a thing that used to be.
The order and ascent of days is nothing now.

Today for the first time it is fairly calm. There is only one other passenger beside myself. Radio won't work which is another blessing. It's all very Eugene O'Neill and salty. Quite the crossing of my experience.

Orson

The fruit of their collaboration was four of the Bard's plays edited and arranged for staging: *Julius Caesar, Twelfth Night, The Merchant of Venice,* and *The Tragedy of Macbeth,* first published by the Todd School Press, later by

Harper Brothers and McGraw-Hill. For more than three decades the books were best sellers, with more than three hundred thousand copies in print.

While completing *Everybody's Shakespeare*, Roger wrote a letter to Orson that illuminates why their collaborations were so productive and their life-long friendship so meaningful.

> In the simple acceptance of each other, per se lies the beauty of our relationship. Let's never spoil it with too many words. Or with too little realization. There are some things too solid, too genuine to be made articulate. Lord! Life is so full of explaining ourselves and justifying ourselves and masquerading ourselves before folks. Thank God we each have a friend for whom we need apply no make-up.

Thank God, too, for *Marching Song*.

～

The Opening Chords of *Marching Song*

It could be argued that *Marching Song* was the first flowering of Welles's liberal social consciousness—defending the defenseless, the oppressed, the forgotten—that remained in full bloom throughout his life.

Early in Hill's childhood, he learned of the abolitionist zealot John Brown and the firebrand's impact on Berea College. He had read John Almanza Rowley Rogers's autobiography, *Birth of Berea College: A Story of Providence*, that chronicles Brown's decisive role in closing the college and forcing the faculty to leave Kentucky with two weeks' notice. Hill also read the eponymous autobiography of Berea's other co-founder, John G. Fee, that provides additional insight into John Brown's Berea legacy.

While soliciting funds for the college in Worcester, Massachusetts, in the fall of 1859, Fee wrote:

> A request came to me from Henry Ward Beecher, pastor of the Plymouth Church, Brooklyn, New York, to come to that church and present the claims of Berea College. This was the time of the John Brown raid in Western Virginia. The country was in a state of intense excitement.
>
> In my address before the church, I said, "We want more John Browns; not in manner of action, but in spirit of consecration; not to go with carnal weapons, but with spiritual ones; men who with Bibles in their hands, and tears in their eyes, will beseech men to be reconciled to God. Give us such men," I said, "and we may yet save the South." My words were carefully reported and published in the *New York Tribune*. The *Louisville Courier*, then conducted by Geo. D. Prentiss, garbled my words and misrepresented my real attitude by saying, "John G. Fee is in Beecher's church, calls for more John Browns."[24]

Rogers writes in the third person of the rapid and draconian reaction to Fee's "garbled" and "misrepresented" words:

> The stir in Madison and adjoining counties was greatly increased by false rumors, some of which were published in newspapers as facts. It was said that Sharpe's rifles had been intercepted on the way to Berea. . . .[25]
>
> At a meeting at the Court House, sixty-two leading citizens of the county were appointed to a committee to remove the most prominent Bereans from the State; peacefully if possible, forcibly if necessary, and John G. Fee and John A.R. Rogers were mentioned by name.[26]

The Bereans reluctantly complied and within days departed the state, not to return until the conclusion of the War between the States.

Not surprisingly, since childhood, Roger Hill was fascinated with the fervent, contentious abolitionist John Brown and, like his ancestor, abhorred the zealot's methods but championed his cause. When teaching American history, Skipper spent significant time considering the causes and effects of America's Civil War. His mesmerizing lectures on the personalities engaged on both sides of the Mason–Dixon line held his students in thrall. One of the most indelible characters on the Civil War stage that Hill brought to life was John Brown. None of Hill's students became more fascinated by the sinning saint than twelve-year-old Orson.

JOHN BROWN: *MARCHING SONG'S* CENTRAL PROTAGONIST

John Brown (May 9, 1800–December 2, 1859) was a militant abolitionist who championed violence as a means to end slavery. He first gained national prominence in 1855, when he and five of his sons settled in the Kansas Territory shortly after the Kansas-Nebraska Act (that would determine whether Kansas would enter the union as a free or slave state), joining the cause of the Free-Soil colonists against their proslavery adversaries. After the "free state" community of Lawrence was devastated by Southern sympathizers, Brown—insisting it was God's will—along with four of his sons, retaliated by murdering five allegedly proslavery homesteaders living near the Potawatomi Creek, in present-day Franklin County, Kansas.

His murderous acts in the Kansas Territory instantly transformed him into an inspiring hero in the eyes of many in the North, and a brazen villain in the view of the majority in the South.

Emboldened by his Potawatomi "victory," Brown spent the next several years recruiting young men—white and black—to join his "army" dedicated to overthrowing slavery in the South. When not enlisting followers, he spent considerable time meeting with sympathetic Northern abolitionists willing to finance his "divine battle."

The apogee of his impassioned but imprudent campaign was his thirty-six-hour assault on the U.S. Arsenal at Harpers Ferry, Virginia, on October 16, 1859, to secure more than one hundred thousand armaments, arriving, in the words of Stephen Vincent Benét, in his poem, "John Brown's Body," "with foolish pikes/And a pack of desperate boys to shadow the sun." Brown's integrated "army" of eighteen, after kidnapping several local slave owners, including a descendant of George Washington, was captured by the U.S. Marines commanded by Colonel Robert E. Lee.

Was John Brown an Old Testament saint or an irredeemable sinner? This inquiry is at the core of the drama and is argued by many of the characters throughout the production; the most absorbing are two journalists, Rufus Wentworth and Choley Archer.

In Act I, the question is first posited by the two. Archer suggests that Brown "must be a great man" to which Wentworth replies, "He's a great fanatic—a lunatic if you ask me. Seems to think the Lord put him into the world 'specially to free the slaves."

Two years later, in the passageway before John Brown's cell in the Charles Town, Virginia, jail, forty days after Brown was captured and shortly before his hanging, Wentworth and Archer continue to ponder Brown's essence and impact. Archer contends, "John Brown has fought a bigger battle right in there, in that cell, than he did in all his Kansas wars put together."

Wentworth simply replies that Brown has "caused a good deal of talk," which stirs Archer to declare:

What's wrong with you up in Boston, are you asleep? Why he's shaken the world! I said this was a historical morning. It's more than that. My God, it's epic. This isn't the end. The execution of John Brown is only the beginning.

Moments later, Archer continues to rant:

Here in the South, we hate him for a miserable old fanatic, and because he fought against us and everything we hold to be right, and up in the North, folks have canonized him, even before his death.

Wentworth scoffs,

Nobody's canonized Old Brown unless it's Virginia. . . . Do you think John Brown would let himself be rescued? I should say not. He wants to be a martyr and the South is willing to play Pilate.

In the final scene, Brown stands at the gallows observing presciently:

You people of the South, you had better prepare yourselves! Prepare for a settlement of this question that's coming up! The sooner you're prepared the better! You may dispose of me very easily; I am nearly disposed of now; but this question is still to be settled—this Negro question I mean. The end of that—is not yet!

The play ends with direction from the authors:

The sound of marching feet grows louder and louder. But the note is gradually changing. The chains are gone and a martial ring has taken their place. The drum and bugle insinuate themselves. The tempo is quickened and the cadence is now that of a great army of free men—Marching, Marching, Marching, Marching. Indomitable. A thunderous, deafening, and triumphant rhythm. Now the bugle sound has melted into a vaster harmony, the full chords a song, a marching song beaten out by hundreds of thousands of feet. The old man still stands, a silent figure on the hill— and as the play ends the whole theatre is filled with the song— JOHN BROWN'S BODY LIES MOULDERING IN THE GRAVE, BUT HIS SOUL GOES—MARCHING ON!

After Hill read selections from John Redpath's sympathetic biography, *The Public Life of Captain John Brown* (written by Brown's friend, abolitionist, and journalist; published less than six weeks after Brown's death), Welles read the book and numerous other volumes concerning the controversial, confounding, and compelling zealot. Orson became so fascinated with the man that at the end-of-the-year oration contest at Todd he performed Brown's gallows speech, winning top honors and the roaring applause of the entire school. Days later, he again delivered Brown's ringing words at the school's graduation, receiving a standing ovation.

"'I have a Great Idea' has been Orson's theme song since the age of eleven," Hill recounts. "If for any reason this melody was temporarily silenced, I knew it was my duty to hum the air awhile until he was back on pitch. But the necessity for my own hum has been only at very rare intervals. The tune is his and I feel confident he will never forget it."

Marching Song was a "Great Idea" and a theme song Welles and Hill sang in perfect pitch. It's my hope that like Orson's first film, *Citizen Kane, Marching Song* will come to be appreciated as another prominent example of his boundless creativity.

~

Marching Song

ORSON WELLES AND ROGER HILL

A play of the stirring days just before the civil war, concerning chiefly John Brown, prophet—warrior—zealot—the most dramatic and incredible figure in American history.

The locale of the scene and the tenor of the times are presented before each act by stereopticon slides on a plain traverse curtain. These views, blending into each other with kaleidoscopic effect, depict newspaper headlines and views of the immediate surroundings, ending, in each case, with the exterior of the scene about to be opened. In two instances, there is some action played in front of the final projection. The orchestra carries popular tunes of the period.

SETTINGS
SCENE I   Concord, Massachusetts, 1857
SCENE II   The Empire House, Pine City, Kansas, a month later
SCENE III   The Empire House
SCENE IV   The Empire House
SCENE V   A year later, before Colonel Washington's home on the Washington Estate in Virginia, about five miles from Harpers Ferry
SCENE VI   Colonel Washington's study
SCENE VII   A few days later, the parlor, kitchen, and back-porch of Kennedy Farm, John Brown's headquarters near Harpers Ferry, on the Maryland side

SCENE VIII   Several weeks later, the Engine House in the United States
              Arsenal at Harpers Ferry
SCENE IX   Three days later, The Engine House
SCENE X   The passageway before John Brown's cell in the Charles
              Town, Virginia, jail
SCENE XI   Next morning, December 2, 1859, the Gallows

Every character and every situation in this play is historically accurate.

Characters in Order of Their Appearance

William Lloyd Garrison, American abolitionist, editor of The Liberator
    newspaper and a founding member of the American Anti-Slavery Society
Rufus Wentworth, hard-faced, elegantly dressed Boston journalist
Choley Archer, a young newspaperman with a round boyish face and earnest
    brown eyes
David Henry Thoreau, American writer, philosopher, and abolitionist
John Henri Kagi, a writer, cynic, and hero
Reverend Giddings
John Brown, Perfervid American abolitionist who attempted an armed insur-
    rection to end slavery in the United States
John Edwin Cook, theatrical, egotistical, chivalric young anti-slaver
John Brown Junior, an idiot, with a loose, wet mouth and saucer eyes
Jeremiah "Jerry" Anderson, a tall, chalky-faced young man, placid as an idol
    sleeping in an old shrine
Little Chick Tawky, an Indian and proprietor of the "Empire House"
"Killer Tim" Fugert, a big black-haired, red-faced bully "Border Ruffian"
Reverend Martin White, an oily little man with a complacent smirk
"Dutch" Lieder, Border Ruffian
Peely Hopkins, Border Ruffian
"Red" Emery O'Driscoll, a tall and scrawny, mean-faced Irishman Border
    Ruffian
Jo Austin, Border Ruffian
Aaron Dwight Stevens, a heroic figure, a huge bearded man with kindly
    bright eyes; member of John Brown's "Army"
Albert Hazlett, a happy-faced lieutenant in John Brown's Provisional Army
Billy Leeman, a slim, handsome boy with a dazzling smile; the youngest mem-
    ber of John Brown's Provisional Army

Charles Plummer Tidd, dark-visaged, ugly captain in Brown's Provisional Army

Frederick Brown, son of John Brown

Owen Brown, son of John Brown, and lieutenant in Brown's Provisional Army

Oliver Brown, youngest of Brown's three sons at Harpers Ferry

High Sheriff

Jeff, slave owned by Colonel Lewis William Washington

Colonel Lewis William Washington, great-grandnephew of President George Washington

Tom, butler slave of Lewis William Washington

Mrs. Huffmaster, sharp-eyed, sharp-featured little rodent of a woman

Annie Brown, daughter of John Brown, who has experienced a life full of unexpressed joys and sorrows

Jepp Huffmaster, son and oldest Huffmaster child

Second Huffmaster son

Huffmaster daughter, all three children are hard-faced and of a common stickiness; a perfect diadem of Huffmasters

Dangerfield Newby, an extraordinarily handsome man, bearded, beautifully proportioned, standing six-foot-two

Shields Green, a fugitive slave from Charleston, S. C., known as the "Emperor," member of John Brown's Provisional Army

Martha Evelyn Brown, wife of Oliver Brown, truly a beautiful girl with golden brown hair and serious baby-wide blue eyes; there is something puckish and youthfully impish about her

William Thompson, large-featured, ruddy-faced, rustic looking man with good-humored eyes, member of John Brown's "Army"

Barclay Coppoc, An audacious adventurous spirit; bold-eyed, big featured, and consumptive

Osborne Perry Anderson, born a free African American, member of John Brown's Provisional Army

Dauphin Thompson, brother of William Thompson; one of John Brown's lieutenants, and a North Elba neighbor of the Brown family

Watson Brown, a quiet, thoughtful young man; John Brown's fourth son

Edwin Coppoc, brother of Barclay

Steward Taylor, the only non-American Brown raider; born in Canada, a stocky, heavily-built, large-jeweled, dreamy-eyed spiritualist

John Allstadt, slave owner, taken hostage by Brown's provisional army, who freed his slaves

Lt. J.E.B. Stuart, an aide to Col. Robert E. Lee, who commanded 90 Marines to Harpers Ferry at the direction of President James Buchanan to recapture the Armory from John Brown and his Provisional Army; Stuart's negotiations with Brown for a peaceful surrender proved feckless

Captain John Avis, Justice of the Peace, Deputy Sheriff, and Jailor of Jefferson County, West Virginia

John Wilkes Booth, actor, and assassin of President Abraham Lincoln, who, six years before, joined the Richmond Grays, a volunteer militia that was present at John Brown's hanging

Scene I

Scene—A passageway in the Town Hall at Concord, Massachusetts, in the year 1857. The scene is mainly taken up with a large entrance, the great double doors of which are closed as the play begins. To the right, Choley Archer lounges against the wall smoking a cigarette, a young newspaperman with a round boyish face and earnest brown eyes.

In the next room, a meeting is in progress, the murmur of voices rises in an excited argument. When the hard-faced, elegantly dressed Boston journalist, Mr. Rufus Wentworth, opens the doors, a voice booms out—

The voice of WILLIAM LLOYD GARRISON
(Orotund and pompous)
—of the Negro! The South has dared to call slavery a "Divine Institution." Gentlemen, I repeat—slavery is a covenant with death and an agreement with hell!
(The murmur of voices grows much louder; then Wentworth closes the door and the sound is muffled.)
WENTWORTH: Well—there seems to be a—difference—in opinion—
ARCHER: What's it all about?
WENTWORTH: *(Stretches and yawns at great length.)*—Slavery. *(He strolls over to the other side of the door and strikes a lucifer on the wall. Taking the unlit cigar out of his mouth, he looks at Archer.)*—and this man—John Brown.
(Archer steps to the entranceway and opens one of the doors. Above the angry roar, a new voice is heard, ringing, resonant.)
The voice, (DAVID HENRY THOREAU)
Platitudes, Mr. William Lloyd Garrison! All platitudes!
(The excited rumble grows to a crescendo.)
WENTWORTH: *(To Archer)* They won't let you in, I'm telling you.
(A voice distinguishable in the confusion.) Platitudes did you say?
The voice of THOREAU

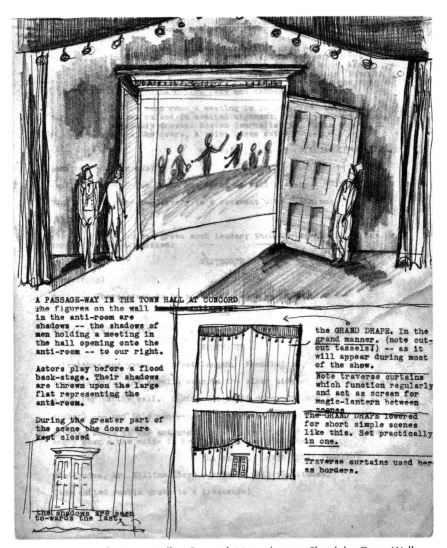

A passageway in the Town Hall at Concord, Massachusetts. Sketch by Orson Welles.

Certainly, I said platitudes! They're at a discount in Kansas, believe me! Sharps rifles are at a premium!

ARCHER: (*Closing the door—to Wentworth*) I can't understand it. (*Throwing away his cigarette.*) It's because I'm a Southerner, I suppose.

WENTWORTH: Well, as a Northerner to a Southerner—is there anything I can explain?

ARCHER: (*Perplexed*) This is Concord. We're right in the heart of the most violent anti-slavery sentiment. Every man in there, in that room, is an abolitionist. What in the name of heaven are they fighting over?

WENTWORTH: The old question. How to abolish slavery—with moral persuasion or force. John Brown has raised it again.

ARCHER: Force—what do you mean? Abolition is one thing, but these men are intelligent. They can't mean war.

WENTWORTH: Of course not. The thing is impossible; you know that as well as I do. Oh, there're a few that talk about some sort of armed attack. But they just talk. There's only one man in the world crazy enough to really do anything, and that's—John Brown.

ARCHER: John Brown. Who is this John Brown?

WENTWORTH: That's a hard question to answer. Nobody knows exactly. He's a Kansas fighter. A Free-Stater.

ARCHER: It's a name to conjure with. I've heard it a lot lately.

WENTWORTH: A kind of bogey in Kansas. Just whisper "John Brown" to an army of border ruffians and—Psst!—they're back in Missouri!

ARCHER: Great warrior, eh?

WENTWORTH: Had some pretty wonderful victories. The stories I've heard about him are just like fairy tales. (*Laughs*) I s'pose some of them are!

ARCHER: He must be a great man.

WENTWORTH: He's a great fanatic—a lunatic if you ask me. Seems to think the Lord put him into the world 'specially to free the slaves. Long white beard, glittering eyes, you know. Another Moses.

ARCHER: All the same when a man's a legend even before his death, he has something to offer.

WENTWORTH: Yes? Well, we'll see tonight, when he makes his speech.

ARCHER: (*Looking at his watch.*) Half an hour yet.

(*The murmuring in the next room continues and then John Henri Kagi comes in, the rarest of all combinations: a cynic and a hero. One remembers clear, wide eyes set well apart in an unusually handsome pallid face delicately molded. The lips are fine, too, full and firm and the mouth is ruled in the long, straight line of the logician and the scientist. Indifferent of dress, almost slovenly, careless of appearance, he handles himself badly, with a deliberate clumsiness. Kagi possesses a harsh manner and an intellectual callousness; seeking to hide a tender spirit, and unselfishness and an infinite capacity of love. He goes up to the door and is about to open it when Wentworth calls to him.*)

WENTWORTH: Sorry, mister, I'm afraid they won't let you in. (*Kagi turns to Wentworth, his eyes questioning—*) It's a private meeting.

KAGI: John Brown's lecture? I thought it was public.

WENTWORTH: It is, but the hall hasn't been opened yet. This is a meeting of the Concord Chapter of the Kansas Immigration Aid Society.

KAGI: Really?

WENTWORTH:—Or rather a meeting of the officers. They're to sit on the platform with Brown tonight when he speaks. (*A particularly loud burst of noise at this, from the next room.*) And there seems to be some disagreement about the endorsement of his policies. You a newspaperman?

KAGI: At times.—I've been a correspondent in Kansas.

ARCHER: (*Perking up*) Kansas! Honestly? Say, I'd like to talk to you. My name's Archer, I'm from Atlanta,—*The Clarion-News.* (*He extends his hand.*)

KAGI: (*Taking it*) Mine's Kagi, John Henri Kagi. Glad to know you.

ARCHER:—And Rufus Wentworth of *The Boston Transcript.* (*Kagi and Wentworth shake.*) Tell me, Mr. Kagi, what's the real truth about Kansas?

KAGI: (*Smiling*) Bleeding Kansas?

ARCHER: That's right. Atlanta's a long way off, you know, and so's Boston. We hear some strange tales.

KAGI: (*Gravely*) You'll hear the strangest tale tonight, gentlemen. Well, the story is simple enough. The Territory of Kansas is in a state of Civil War. The South wants it to enter the Union as a slave state and the North, naturally, wants it free.

WENTWORTH: But it's already decided—by the ballot box. The territory has voted in favor of slavery.

KAGI: There're two hostile governments operating in Kansas today. One under the constitution adopted at Topeka by the Free-soilers and the other under the Slave Constitution of Lecompton. This latter has the sanction of Washington, at the present time, but the election next November will settle it. Frankly, I can see no fair doubt as to the outcome.—There are twelve thousand settlers in the territory with an honest and legal vote today. Seven thousand of them have been sent by Northern emigration aid societies like this one, all pledged to vote anti. (*To Archer*) Two thousand have been sent by your societies in the south: The Blue Lodges,—they'll vote pro. The other three thousand have come of their own volition and are predominantly anti.—And why not? From a purely economic point of view, there's no excuse for slavery beyond the cotton belt.

ARCHER: Personally, I agree with you.

KAGI:—The last election—the election which gave so much comfort to your people—took place before the arrival of John Brown. At that time, five thousand Missourians armed with pistols and bowie knives and a generous supply of bad whiskey crossed over into Kansas and cast fraudulent pro-slavery votes. They threatened to shoot the Governor if he dared refuse certificates of election to their candidates. That's the gospel truth! 'Though I'll grant you, I'm in no position to give an impartial view of the situation. I'm an anti-slavery fighter myself. More of a fighter than a newspaperman.

WENTWORTH: That's very interesting. You a follower of this fellow—John Brown?

KAGI: No, not exactly. I've tried to join him. But John Brown is elusive, gentlemen. He's all over the west at once. You can never get at him, (*laughs*) but always somehow, he can get at you!

ARCHER: Surely, you've met him?

KAGI: Once or twice. Never can tell where he'll turn up. Half the time, he's traveling with the enemy, in disguise. I followed him up here to Concord and we had a talk this afternoon. I think I've a chance now to join his company.

WENTWORTH: You consider that a privilege?

KAGI: (*Earnestly*) Oh, I do sir. A rare privilege. I can think of no greater.

WENTWORTH: But a zealot—a madman! Perhaps your regard for this fellow is religious. Do you—do you believe in his divinity?

KAGI: In me, gentlemen, you behold the strange spectacle of a rationalist and an atheist—devoted to John Brown not because of his biblical delusions, but in spite of them!

WENTWORTH: (*Looking at him.*) I can't understand it.

KAGI: Have you ever met—"this fellow"—John Brown?

WENTWORTH: No—

KAGI: Well, then, of course, you can't. (*The murmuring increases, Kagi turns to the door.*) What's the argument? Who are these people?

ARCHER: (*Smiling*) The executive committee. An aggregation of the most brilliant minds in America. They're split right up the back on this new question—the question of endorsing John Brown's policies.

KAGI: But they're all abolitionists. They will endorse him of course.

WENTWORTH: Concord isn't Kansas, Mr. Kagi, and few abolitionists, even the most extreme, sanction John Brown's unique method of attacking slavery—by armed force. He has one staunch backer, Henry David Thoreau of Walden Pond, and of course, there're others—men like Garret Smith, willing to finance any of his projects. The pacifists, however, are very much in the majority.

KAGI: I remember something Thoreau once said about that. "Any man more right than his neighbors constitutes a majority of one already." (*He turns to the doors, opens one of them slightly and peeks in.*)

ARCHER: Tell me, Kagi, why is John Brown in Concord, why this lecture?

KAGI: (*Without turning*) To get money. He's penniless.

ARCHER: Money for what? The Kansas Campaign?

KAGI: Partly.

WENTWORTH: And what else?

KAGI: (*Turning to him. Gravely—*) Another campaign. A gigantic plan to free the slaves.

WENTWORTH: Free the slaves?!

ARCHER: What are you talking about Kagi?!

KAGI: I hardly know myself—though I hope to.

ARCHER: But—

KAGI: (*With finality*) I'm sorry, I can't go into it. (*He turns back to the door. The murmuring continues and the two newspapermen look at one another.*)

ARCHER: Just one question Kagi.

KAGI: (*Absently*) Yes.

ARCHER: Are you joining him? Are you joining Old Brown in this—this "new campaign?"

KAGI: I'm to meet him in Kansas—later in the year.

WENTWORTH: At least you can tell us what—

(*Suddenly Kagi opens the great doors wide, revealing a bare expanse of wall, obviously an ante-room opening into the meeting hall. Strong light plays on the wall from the other room and we can clearly make out the shadows of a group of men seated at a table. When the doors open the voice of Thoreau drowns out that of Wentworth—*)

The voice of THOREAU

(*The standing shadow gesticulating angrily—*)

Legality! I hate the word! You would have Christ dicker with the money-changers in the Temple when it requires only one strong hand to overturn the tables!

ARCHER: (*Coming up behind Kagi, staring through the doorway into the far-room which we cannot see.*) That's Henry Thoreau. I heard him speak in Baltimore.

The voice of THOREAU

(*Continuing*)

Mr. President, I make a motion—that you, this evening, introduce John Brown to our members and to the public, as one having the complete and unequivocal endorsement of our executive committee.

Another voice

Mr. President, I object. Are we to be led by the type of ruffianism we condemn in the Missourians? Heaven forbid. Our policy must first of all be legal and then forceful.

The voice of THOREAU

Legal! The sacking of Lawrence resulted from the call of a "legal" sheriff, legally elected, for "law abiding" citizens to come to his aid. At his call, the town was pillaged by a drunken mob!

The voice of REVEREND GIDDINGS

Mr. Thoreau, we believe in law enforcement and the rights of property, can we
honestly assume from John Brown's record that he will uphold those beliefs?

The voice of THOREAU

On the "sacred rights of property" I imagine, Reverend Giddings, you will
find John Brown heretical as myself. And even you or the United States
Government will find it hard to convince either of us that one man
owns another.

The voice of GIDDINGS

I abhor the law that says it is so, but while it is the law I uphold it.

The voice of THOREAU

Is it not possible that an individual may be right and a government wrong?
Are laws to be enforced simply because they were made? Or declared by
any number of men to be good, if they are not good?

The voice of WILLIAM LLOYD GARRISON

(*His shadow rising.*) Mr. President—

The voice of the PRESIDENT

Mr. Garrison?

The voice of WILLIAM LLOYD GARRISON

I am afraid Mr. Thoreau is blinded by the personality—the undoubted mag-
netic personality of this man, John Brown. But we must not allow emotion
to overrule reason. John Brown is a great man, a zealot—probably a fanatic,
working in a great cause though with sometimes doubtful methods. The suspicion of his hand in the Potawatomi killings is still strong. He will no doubt
meet a violent end himself—while we must carry on. We dare not die.

(*The shadow sits down*)

The voice of THOREAU

Mr. Garrison, I agree with you. John Brown will die—a glorious thought. You
and I, gentlemen of this assembly, will never die. We haven't life enough.
We'll simply run down like a clock. We'll be merely missing one day. No
temple veil will be rent—only a hole dug somewhere. We'll deliquesce
like fungi. Yes, John Brown will die. But I have looked into his soul. I have
peered into the mighty chasm of his purpose and glimpsed a spirit that
could no more fail than Arnold Winkelried. A million years have gone
behind. A million years stretch on before. And standing at this junction
of two eternities, standing almost alone, I say, in this world of creeping
things is John Brown—a body born to death—glorious death—but a soul
to go marching on.

The voice of GIDDINGS

I am unimpressed by Mr. Thoreau's idealism. I believe with President Buchanan that the acts of the Free Soilers are unlawful and revolutionary. When men resist the government, their acts are treason.

The voice of THOREAU

Is it treason—treason to any government worthy of allegiance when a man forcefully resists the buying and selling of human flesh?

The voice of GIDDINGS

(*His shadow rising angrily from the table*)

But it is the law!

Another voice

(*The shadow jumping to its feet after Giddings*) Law is the foundation of our land!

The voice of THOREAU

I care not for lawless Pharisees, but for right. It was law that pronounced Washington a rebel. It was law that excommunicated Copernicus.—It was law that crucified Christ! There is a higher law!

(*Confusion—The entire committee is standing. Now a new voice is heard.*)

The new voice

Gentlemen!—Gentlemen! (*The others are quiet.*)

(*Somewhere another door opens and the shadows of Thoreau and the rest are faded out as the wall in the ante-room is flooded with a new and even brighter light.*)

The new voice

—John Brown!

(*A new shadow appears; the shadow of an old man. It covers the whole wall, dominant, as the scene ends.*)

Scene II

Scene—Before the Empire House, Little Chick Tawky's place at Pine City near the Missouri Border. The combined saloon and general store is an ancient one-story frame structure boasting a faded sign and a roofed porch. This and a handful of deserted log-cabins nearby is Pine City. There is a great deal of Kansas sky in evidence, and endless miles of open prairies. While pictures of Kansas and the Southwest are appearing and changing, a frontier ballad is sung carried by a single voice, to the accompaniment of a mandolin. Now, as the scene already described blends into view, we can make out the figure quite distinctly. It is John Edwin Cook, the theatrical, egotistical, chivalric young anti-slavery fighter.

He is impetuous, passionate, as credulous of life as Kagi is incredulous, and with all his golden hair, fair cheeks, and boyish ways, a veteran fighter in his late twenties.

(Enter Kagi)

KAGI: *(To Cook as he comes up.)* Hey! I say!—You sir!

COOK: *(Turns and regards him for a moment before speaking. He stops singing, but continues to play.—Pleasantly—)* Hello.

KAGI: It sounds damn silly, I know, but is this Pine City?

COOK: Is this Pine City? *(He strums his mandolin for a bit before speaking again.)* Yes, I think so.

KAGI: *(Taking out a handkerchief and wiping his brow—laughingly.)* Thank God! *(Cook stops playing—looking about.)* I thought I knew my Kansas, but this strange territory. I don't see any pine.—Pine City—

COOK: Neither do I. And it isn't a city, it's a saloon.

KAGI: But these houses?

COOK: Deserted. People have all been killed or driven out.

KAGI: Why, how's that?

COOK: Raids. This is a funny spot you've come to, stranger, it's right square between the two camps.

KAGI: Pro-slavery and Free-stater?

COOK: Exactly. There's a lot a' prairie between here and the border, and there's more yet to Osawatomie. It's neutral ground right enough, but it isn't healthy.

KAGI: Anybody's country, I take it. A sort of battlefield?

COOK: That's right. *(He begins to play again. After a minute, speaking as he plays.)* Nobody lives here anymore, except Little Chick.

KAGI: Who's that?

COOK: *(Still playing)* Little Chick Tawky—he runs the Empire. He's an Indian.

KAGI: And you?

COOK: Arrived two hours ago—just scouting.

KAGI: *(Incredulously)* Scouting? You're no Border ruffian! *(Cook laughs heartily at this and goes on with his music.)* You're a man of education, not an ordinary Kansas Fighter.

COOK: *(Stops playing suddenly at this and fixes Kagi with a haughty eye.)* I should say not, sir! *(Resumes his playing. Then casually—)* And you're not an ordinary newspaper correspondent.

KAGI: *(Quickly)* How did you know that?

COOK: *(Smoothly)* What?—That you're not an ordinary newspaperman?

KAGI: *(With a wave of his hand.)* I'm going to be perfectly frank with you, Mr.—Mr.—

COOK: Cook—John Edwin Cook.

KAGI: Very well, Mr. Cook, I'll put my cards on the table. (*Cook goes on playing his mandolin without replying. Kagi continues bravely.*) I'm—I'm here to see a man—John Brown.

COOK: (*Stops playing again, and looks at him.*) Who?

KAGI: John Brown.

COOK: (*Whistling*) Old Brown! You've come to a strange place to find him. (*The two regard one another with veiled glances.*)

KAGI: Oh, I don't know. Isn't he due here about four o'clock?

COOK: (*Suspiciously*) Who sent you here?

KAGI: (*Slowly*) Captain Whipple—maybe you've heard of him. He was called Stevens before he escaped from Leavenworth.

COOK: (*After a pause*) Where's your horse?

KAGI: Tethered, down at the Creek.

COOK: I'll go get it, maybe it hasn't been noticed.

KAGI: Why, what do you mean?

COOK: There's no such thing as law in this country, Mr. Kagi. (*He starts off, strumming a tune, and Kagi calls after him—*)

KAGI: Hey! How about John Brown?

COOK: Go into the Empire and have a drink.

KAGI: Sorry. I'm a teetotaler.

COOK: (*Laughing*) I was right, you're not an ordinary newspaperman. (*He strikes up another tune on his mandolin and saunters off. Kagi, completely bewildered, stands looking after him as the orchestra picks up the strain of Cook's melody and—the scene ends.*)

Scene III

Scene—Inside the Empire House. The building, one large undecorated frame room, is dominated by a big "main entrance" near the center, raised three steps above the floor level and opening onto the porch, parts of which, railings and roof supports, baking in the hot Kansas sun, are glimpsed through the open doorway and the windows to either side of it. There are chairs and a table to the left and a side door. The bar graces the right. Old paint peels on the badly finished timber, some government proclamations and printed political announcements, pro-slavery and anti, are tacked about, but the saloon is otherwise barren.

A tall, chalky-faced young man with a long thin beard and blue-black hair hanging to his shoulders sits at the table, arranging cards, ordering strange patterns and raising a delicate white finger occasionally to change them. This is Jerry Anderson. Red-lipped, dark-eyed; placid-faced as an idol sleeping in an old shrine, unworldly looking.

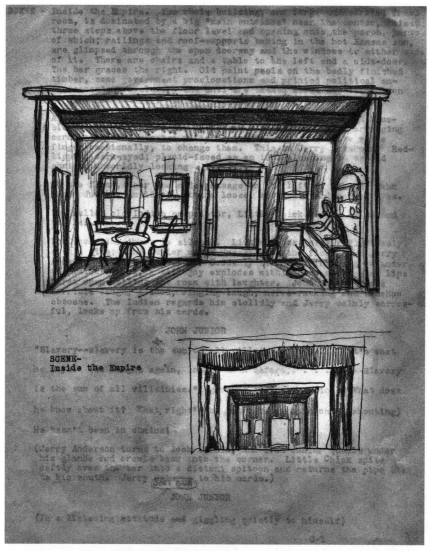

Inside the Empire. Sketch by Orson Welles.

On the floor, near the side-passage to the left of him, is John Brown Junior, an idiot, with a loose, wet mouth and saucer eyes.

The sullen old Indian proprietor, Little Chick Tawky, is behind the bar.

For some time, there is silence. Little Chick puffs reflectively at his pipe; John Junior moves uneasily on the floor, and Jerry Anderson ponders his cards. Suddenly strange wrinkles grow under the idiot's eyes, a wild joy explodes within him and his fat lips burst open filling the room with laughter. John Junior has a horrible laugh, a loud, ringing laugh, nerve-racking and somehow obscene. The Indian regards him stolidly and Jerry calmly, sorrowfully, looks up from his cards.

JOHN JUNIOR: "Slavery—slavery is the sum of all villainies." That's what he says. (*He laughs again, louder than before*). "Slavery is the sum of all villainies." (*Growing suddenly vicious.*) What does he know about it? What right's he got with an opinion? (*Shouting*) He hasn't been in chains! (*Jerry Anderson turns to look at him and John Junior quails under his glance and crawls back into the corner. Little Chick spits deftly over the bar into a distant spittoon and returns the pipe stem to his mouth. Jerry goes back to his cards.*)

JOHN JUNIOR: (*In a listening attitude, giggling quietly to himself.*) D'you hear that, Jerry? (*Jerry goes on shuffling his cards, paying no attention.*) Listen, Jerry. Listen to it . . . (*His eyes are fixed upward, he nods in time to a rhythm which he seems to hear, regular and clod-like*) You've never been in a chain-gang have you Jerry, so I guess you don't know what that is. It's marching—the sound of hundreds of chained feet—thousands—marching. (*There is a silence, John Junior goes on nodding his head like a metronome*) Marching, marching. (*Suddenly he stops, tense and motionless, listening. After a moment, breathlessly—*) One leg is chained and the other is free—that's what makes it sound so funny. (*He suddenly comes to life. Simpering foolishly, he scuttles around the floor after a piece of chain, picking it up he exhibits it to Jerry, who pays no attention.*) This is my chain, the chain they hammered onto me. I'm saving it to show to the old man. Look, it's worn all shiny from the road! The brown stuff is blood, where it dug in when they fastened it too tight. Jason couldn't stand it and he nearly died, so they dumped him in the wagon for the flies to eat, but me they kept marching—all the way to Osawatomie. They tied up my hands too, but that weren't so much—Can't move the fingers right yet—that's count a' the fine hemp they used, cuttin' clear to the bone. (*Slapping a card noisily down on the table, Jerry Anderson rises to his feet abruptly.*)

JOHN JUNIOR: (*Looking up at him and laughing.*) You hear it too, now, don't you?

ANDERSON: (*Sharply*) What?

JOHN JUNIOR: That marching. (*Jerry turns away with a little sound of disgust.*) It's a funny sound, isn't it? (*Laughs*) That's easy to explain—one leg is chained and the other is free. Like this—(*He drums on the floor, pounding alternately with a bare fist and the chain. Jerry stands it as long as he can, and then reaching down, he seizes the loose end of the chain. John Junior laughs wildly,—and for a moment, he keeps his hold on it using both hands, until Jerry, with an angry jerk, snatches it away from him. Instantly he is silent. Jerry Anderson looks at him and then, striding suddenly across the room, he slams the chain down on the bar-top.)*

TAWKY: *(Knocking the ashes out of his pipe and regarding John Junior with a grave, beady eye.)* It don't take much to drive 'um crazy in this country.

ANDERSON: *(Quietly)* He's had plenty. *(He turns to walk back to the table when something he sees outside causes him to start. Drawing a revolver from his breast pocket, he backs around to the other side of the entranceway and flattens himself against the wall. John Junior stares stupidly before him and Little Chick goes calmly on with the filling of his pipe. A minute or so passes and nothing happens. Then Kagi appears.)*

KAGI: *(Peering in at the door and speaking to Little Chick. He doesn't notice Jerry.)* This is the Empire House, isn't it?

LITTLE CHICK: *(Striking a light, his pipe in his mouth.)* Sign over the door.

KAGI: *(Dryly)* I thought that's what it said. And you're the proprietor, aren't you? Mr.—Mr. Little Chick Tawky?

LITTLE CHICK: *(Lighting his pipe.)* That's me.

KAGI: *(Descending the steps and approaching the bar.)* Well, my name's Kagi, I—

ANDERSON: *(Coming up close to him, covering him with his revolver.)* And your business?

KAGI: *(Turns quickly to Anderson and confronts him. After a slight pause—)* Hello. Have a drink?

ANDERSON: *(Insistence and menace in the rising inflection.)* And your business?

KAGI: *(With perfect composure, he walks calmly past him to the table.)* I don't think it's any of yours. *(Calmly)* I was sent here by Mr. Cook.

ANDERSON: You Pro-Slavery or Anti?

KAGI: *(And now he wheels suddenly around. He has drawn out a pistol while his back was turned, leveling it at Jerry)* Anti! *(For a moment, we expect shooting; then Jerry calmly pockets his revolver.)*

ANDERSON: *(Smiling in his faint way.)* I thought so. *(He sits down in a chair next to the bar, near the doorway.)*

TAWKY: *(Solemnly)* Best play safe in this country.

KAGI: *(Laughing quietly)* It's always best. *(He puts his pistol away and sits down at the table. There follows an unpleasant pause. Little Chick sucks at his pipe. Jerry sits quietly in his chair, and Kagi fidgets uncomfortably, looking about the room, occasionally, and playing idly with the cards. Suddenly John Junior begins to laugh, and Kagi who has not noticed him before starts up with an involuntary movement towards his gun.)*

KAGI: Oh, Hello—

JOHN JUNIOR: *(Laughs)* Funny, isn't it?

KAGI: What's funny?

JOHN JUNIOR: The sound of marching. *(Laughs)* It's the chains that does it! *(He laughs again, wildly; Kagi looks wonderingly at Little Chick.)*

TAWKY: Don't bother talkin' with him.

KAGI: What's wrong? Isn't he—right—mentally?

TAWKY: He's crazy mad. It's this country—

ANDERSON: John is the victim of a temporary derangement, due to shock and prolonged physical agony.

KAGI: Sickness of some kind?

ANDERSON: Mistreatment. Extreme cruelty.

KAGI: Cruelty? How's that?

ANDERSON: He was arrested and then taken to jail in Lecompton. They marched him for weeks in a chain gang.

KAGI: But why?

ANDERSON: *(Dryly)* On account of his political views. If you have any views, Mr. Kagi, you'd better give them up. It's dangerous.

TAKKY: It's dangerous anyhow. I seen a man shot in this saloon not two-weeks ago, a travelin' man, didn't have a view in his head. It was the pro-slavery men done it, they shot him 'cause he come from Michigan.

JOHN JUNIOR: *(Laughing wildly)* Murder! Murder! I've seen murder! Real murder!

ANDERSON: *(Angrily)* Be quiet John!

JOHN JUNIOR: *(Confidentially to Kagi)* Jerry's angry, 'cause he don't want me to tell. *(Whispering, his eyes glittering like glass.)* Did you ever hear talk of a killing at Potawatomi?

KAGI: Potawatomi? The Potawatomi Massacre? Why that was John Brown!—Do you know him? Do you know John Brown? *(John Junior goes off into another fit of laughter.)*

KAGI: *(To Jerry and Little Chick)* Does he? *(Jerry looks at the Indian)*

TAWKY: Know him, Stranger? He is John Brown!

(Kagi leaps up, glaring at John Junior who rises slowly, unsteadily to his feet. After a tense moment, John begins to snicker, and, at this, Kagi wheels about facing Little Chick and Jerry.)

KAGI: Liars! *(John Junior laughs hysterically and Kagi has to yell to make himself heard above the laughter.)* That's what you are! A couple of damned liars! *(He turns quickly and seizes John by the front of his collar, shaking him violently as he shouts into his face.)* I know John Brown I tell you! I've seen him! *(Suddenly John Junior stops laughing and the room is quiet.)*

ANDERSON: You're speaking of Old Brown—his father.

KAGI: (*Starts, after a moment, hesitatingly.*) Then this—?

ANDERSON: His eldest son, John Brown Junior. (*Kagi, too shocked to speak, stares horror-stricken at the idiot. Little by little he relinquishes the grasp on his collar and John Junior sinks slowly to the floor.*)

TAWKY: It don't take much. They go off their heads easy in this country.

KAGI: Does his father know?

ANDERSON: I'm taking him to him now.

JOHN JUNIOR: (*Dully*) Five men it was, at Dutch Henry's Crossing; shot down in the night, butchered—because they believed in slavery.

ANDERSON: (*To John Junior, sharply*) Because they'd committed murder in their hearts. They were marked for death.

JOHN JUNIOR: They died, right enough. Some was stabbed to death with knives. Old Man Doyle had his eyes shot out. John Brown did that—

ANDERSON: (*Testily*) He didn't. John Brown didn't touch a soul. It was only his men.

JOHN JUNIOR: I was right nearby, Captain of the Potawatomi Company. When I heard what happened, I resigned that same night.

ANDERSON: (*To Kagi*) And that same night he went stark raving mad.

JOHN JUNIOR: (*Intoning strangely*) Frederick was there. He saw the whole thing. I'll never forget the look of his face when he told me about it. All grey it was, in the dawn. He'll never leave Kansas—He told me so. Fredrick'll never leave 'til that crime is expiated. (*Laughs*) There's a lotta blood here to answer for. There's a lotta blood in just five men. (*Little Chick knocks the ashes out of his pipe with a sharp rap on the Bar-top. John Junior leaps up, terrified at the sound—shouting—*) Don't shoot! My God! (*He falls to the floor weeping hysterically.*)

TAWKY: (*Looking at his pipe.*) It don't take much.

ANDERSON: (*Quietly*) We're all fanatics in this country. We're all a little crazy—(*A pause*)

KAGI: (*His eyebrows raised*) I suppose so.

ANDERSON: (*Reflectively*) Even—John Brown.

KAGI: Old Brown?

ANDERSON: John Junior's a saner man.

KAGI: (*Anger creeping into his voice.*) Just what do you mean?

ANDERSON: (*Indicating John Junior*) God in his wisdom has hung only a thin veil between his world and ours—between lunacy and inspiration there isn't anything at all. (*John Junior sobs softly to himself.*)

KAGI: So, you're one of those who calls John Brown a fanatic. I never could.

ANDERSON: Don't misunderstand me. Old Brown is a greater man than you and I will ever know. He sees a great light and he speaks—with God. *(Quickly)* I don't know your religious opinions, Mr. Kagi, but—

KAGI: *(Shortly)* I have none.

ANDERSON: *(Continuing)* But there is a God, call it a spirit if you will, an idea, a principal, a Great Unrest, it amounts to the same thing. A God—walking these prairies. You may not know it, Mr. Kagi, but you're seeking John Brown so that you may find that God—

KAGI: Nonsense—

ANDERSON: Some of us find Him and some of us are called, tapped, ever so gently on the shoulder. His mighty footstep has sounded in men's brains and they have gone mad. His shadow has fallen upon the hearts of men and they have died. Nat Turner aspired to the hem of His garment and he reached upward and perished. Moses has named this God, and John Brown has—looked full into his face.

JOHN JUNIOR: *(Laughing to himself quietly.)* Chains . . . chains . . .

ANDERSON: Someday, like Jesus Christ—John Brown may—may come to—understand what he has seen. *(There is a slight pause and then the silence is broken with a roar of rude laughter and boisterous conversation. Jerry draws his revolver and steps warily to a window. Satisfied, he runs to the side door and is out just as "Killer Tim" Fugert appears in the center doorway. He comes right in—a big black-haired, red-faced bully, three other "border ruffians" at his heels. "Dutch Lieder," Jo Austin, Peely Hopkins, and a tall and scrawny, mean-faced Irishman called "Red Emery" O'Driscoll—all stomp noisily down the steps and crowd up to the bar.)*

FUGERT: *(Heartily)* Five o' the best, Little Chick. It's on me! *(Cheers and roars of assent from the others. Fugert notices the chain on the bar, picking it up)* What the Hell's this? *(The Reverend Martin White appears at the entrance, an oily, little man with a complacent smirk.)*

FUGERT: *(To White, throwing the chain back on the bar-top.)* Well, Rev'nd, will ya start off on an Ole Crow? We got some powerful celebratin' ta 'tend to!

REVEREND WHITE: *(Rubbing his hands together as he comes down the steps.—Neither he, nor any of the rest have noticed Kagi and John Junior)* Well, boys, I don't mind if I do. *(A roar of approving laughter and cheers.)*

LIEDER: 'Ats a'talk, Preacher!

HOPKINS: 'Ole Crow fur Preacher White!

(Little Chick has put a bottle and glasses on the bar-top and the men have been busy pouring their drinks.)

FUGERT: *(Handing White a glass.)* Here y'be Rev'rund.

REVEREND WHITE: *(Taking the glass)* I thank you, Tim. *(Loudly)* Gentlemen, a toast! *(The talking and laughter subside. The men raise their glasses.)* To "Killer Tim" Fugert, the handiest man with a knife in all Kansas, may he keep up the good work!

KAGI: *(Stepping up just as the drinks are finished.)* Once again, Little Chick. The next round is on me. If you boys will permit? *(The men eye him suspiciously.)*

FUGERT: *(After a pause)* Well, Stranger, where y' from?

KAGI: That's rather a delicate subject in this country, isn't it? *(An ominous silence, then—)*

O'DISCOLL: Y'd better answer up, Stranger. You oughta' seen what happened to the last fella Killer asked that question of. He didn't say the right thing.

LEIDER: "Killer's" a hard man. Even that feller's mother wouldn't recognized him, I betcha, after "Killer" got finished.

KAGI: *(Dryly)* Not much of an incentive to speak. Well, I'm a journalist, among other things, I write for papers. *(Another silence)*

FUGERT: There was a settler up Middle Creek jest read the wrong newspaper. They found him a couple weeks back, out on the prairie. The critters had 'et most of him, but there was enough left so's you could tell how he died, slow and unpleasant-like. Somebody—somebody's went and throwed acid on him. Acid all over his face.

KAGI: *(After a slight silence)* Let's have a drink and talk this thing over later.

FUGERT: Sorry, stranger, we're kinda' pitikaler about our company. You'll have to tell us what we wants to know. Are ya—*(Craftily)* Are ya sound on the goose?

KAGI: What's that?

FUGERT: You heard me—Are you "Sound on the goose?" *(The Border Ruffians are lined up against the bar with their backs to Little Chick. Kagi falters, opens his mouth to answer and then catches the Indian's beady little eye. Little Chick nods his head.)*

KAGI: Why, yes, yes. I'm—pro-slavery. *(The tension breaks up immediately. Everybody is smiles and goodwill)*

FUGERT: Well, why didn't you say so in the first place?! Once again, Little Chick, the stranger's treatin'. *(Little Chick begins to pour drinks. Fugert lolls against the bar, arrogantly, his head thrown back.)*

REVEREND WHITE: *(To Kagi)* You find us in a holiday mood, Mister, we're celebratin' a great event, a momentous occasion as y' might say.

KAGI: *(Taking the glass Austin hands him.)* And what occasion is this?

REVEREND WHITE: The acquittal of Mr. Fugert, here—

KAGI: *(Looking at Fugert)* Acquittal? What was the charge?

FUGERT: *(Calmly)* Murder.

KAGI: Really. *(Takes a drink)*

REVEREND WHITE: *(Coughing apologetically)* These are perilous times, stranger, perilous. Times when it behooves us all to mark well the difference between a devil crime and a military act.

KAGI: Oh, I agree with you, sir. *(Putting his glass down on the bar.)* Another all around, Little Chick. *(Puts money down.)* Never mind me. *(To White)* This time, I gather, the law was wise enough to differentiate.

REVEREND WHITE: Quite, sir, quite. The Leavenworth authorities were very apologetic, as well they might be. "Killer's" tactics may have been a trifler sensational, but nonetheless the blow struck at the anti-slavery idea was highly effective, one calculated to inspire terror, and, speaking as a minister, I may say, the fear of God, sir, in the hearts of the Free Soiler element.

KAGI: What exactly was the nature of this blow?

REVEREND WHITE: *(Laughing nervously)* Well, as I say, it was a bit sensational. Killer is inclined to be a little—hasty.

FUGERT: It all started with a bet I made with Red Emery, here. A little matter, six dollars and a new pair a boots *(Laughs)* again' a scalp—an abolitionist's scalp.

KAGI: What?

FUGERT: A scalp—you know—the hair part off a fella's head. Little Chick's an Indian, he kin tell ya about scalpin', can't ya Little Chick?

LITTLE CHICK: *(Lighting his pipe.)* I ain't no authority.

FUGERT: Wall, as I sez, I made a bet with Red Emery, that inside two hours I could bring him a scalp, a fresh one, guaranteed out off an abolitionist—

O'DRISCOLL: *(Laughing)* Well, stranger, he got his boots.

FUGERT: And I got four dollars still comin', Red Emery. *(To Kagi)* So I started off and it weren't long afore I met up with a minister a-ridin' in a buggy. Old Skinner, he was with white hair. "Where y'come from?" sez I. "Lawrence," sez he. So, I takes out me bowie knife and I gives it to him.

KAGI: And he died?

FUGERT: Well, Mister, I reckon he's dead by this time. *(John Junior laughs, loudly, and so suddenly that the big men are startled. As it continues, all look in his direction. Reverend White walks to the other side of the room and confronts him.)*

JOHN JUNIOR: *(Looking up at him.)* Hello, Preacher White—*(Sobering)* Can you hear it? The sound of that marching? *(Jo Austin comes behind White and looks at John Junior.)*

JO AUSTIN: Kind 'a simple, ain't he?

HOPKINS: Reckon so. (*John Junior laughs again.*)

PREACHER WHITE: Simple. He's crazy-mad. (*The others chuckle*) D'ye know who that is? (*No one replies.*) Well, it's a Brown boy. One of John Brown's sons! (*The laughter stops abruptly and the men are silent.*)

O'DRISCOLL: You mean?

REVEREND WHITE: That's just what I mean.

FUGERT: (*After a pause*) What's he doin' here? How'de get here Little Chick?

TAWKY: Dunno. Figger like he jest came.

O'DRISCOLL: He ain't up to no good, I betcha.

JOHN JUNIOR: You made enough bets Red Emery; this one'll be your last. (*They all stare at John Junior in silence, finally—*)

LEIDER: (*To Hopkins*) There's sumpin' up, Peely.

HOPKINS: Ya kin count me out. If it's got anything to do with John Brown, ya kin count me out.

FUGERT: Hell! Who's scared a' John Brown!

O'DRISCOLL: Better men n'you, Killer Tim.

JOHN JUNIOR: (*In a sing-song voice.*) Sherman and Wilkinson and the Doyle's—they said they wasn't. John Brown come on a dark night and they cried like babies when they died.

REVEREND WHITE: (*Going to the side door.*) Well, boys, I think I'll be goin'. (*At the door.*) It maybe we'll need a bit a'help. (*He leaves.*)

FUGERT: (*Staring after him.*) Yeah. Well, not me. No goddamn abolitionist kin scare Killer Tim.

JOHN JUNIOR: John Brown finished with 'em right enough, and when they was killed, him and the others took Bowie knives and cut and slashed at the dead bodies. "And they shall go forth and look upon the carcasses of the men that have transgressed against me. And they shall be an abhorring unto all flesh."

FUGERT: Gimme that chain! (*He goes over to the bar and seizes the chain. The others murmur excitedly.*)

HOPKINS: God! Killer, what a'ya gain' to do?

FUGERT: (*Rolling up his sleeves*) Figgerin' to make whiskey mash outta that Free Soiler half-wit!

O'DRISCOLL: (*Backing up the stairs and onto the Porch.*) Don't do it, Killer, there'll be hell to pay fur!

JOHN JUNIOR: (*Laughing softly.*) The vengeance of the Lord.

FUGERT: Yeah. We'll see about that. (*He makes a start at John Junior, but Kagi intervenes, coming between the two and restraining Fugert's hand.*)

KAGI: Hold on a minute Fugert, you can't do this! (*John Junior stops laughing.*)

FUGERT: Oh, can't I?

KAGI: The boy's defenseless, it's murder! (*Fugert swings the chain and hits Kagi full in the face. The young abolitionist falls to the ground, senseless. Pandemonium. Men shout and plead with Fugert. Curses.*)

FUGERT: (*Standing over John Junior, his hand raised to crush him with the great chain, shrieking.*) Murder? Christ! I'll drink his heart's blood! (*At this Red Emery, who has been out on the porch comes rushing back into the room.*)

O'DRISCOLL: (*Shouting at Fugert.*) Drop that Killer! (*There is instant silence. The men turn to look at him.*)

FUGERT: (*His arm falls, but the chain remains in his hand. Wheeling about—*) What the hell!?

O'DRISCOLL: (*In a tense voice.*) Git yer guns men! (*The others catch the note of danger and hurry to the place where they have left their rifles, picking them up and leveling them at the center doorway through which Red Emery has come. Fugert stands his ground making no move towards his gun, the chain still clasped defiantly in his hand.*)

O'DRISCOLL: (*Rifle in hand, shouting hoarsely at Fugert.*) Git yer gun, I tell ya! (*The men start like frightened children as Red Emery yells—*) It's John Brown! (*For a terrible moment nothing happens. Then the silence is broken by the sound of a footfall on the porch outside, and there appears in the doorway an old man, bearded—grey. He sweeps the room with a glance and then fixes Fugert with wide glittering eyes, a great eagle, you think, an eagle in homespun. There is something about him, his bearing perhaps—something—but there is no doubt that Red Emery was right. This man certainly is John Brown.*)

JOHN BROWN: (*After a pause—quietly.*) Well, boys—put down your guns. (*For a moment they make no move. Brown takes his eye from Fugert and glares dangerously at the others.*) Put down your guns! (*There is a note in his voice that makes refusal impossible, and, after a bit, the rifles are lowered, one by one. Red Emery is the last, but a look from the old man is enough and he obeys. Descending the steps, John Brown returns his gaze to Killer Tim. Slowly he approaches him. The terrified Fugert waits, silent and still, as some bird charmed motionless by a snake.*)

JOHN BROWN: (*Standing close to him.*) Killer Tim Fugert, you're the man I want. (*Brown's gaze travels to Kagi who turns a bit on the floor and moans, and then back to Fugert. Suddenly, he seizes the chain out of the Border Ruffian's grasp, holds it for a moment, and then slings it away*) And I've come to get you!

FUGERT: (*Panic-stricken*) Mr., Mr. Brown? What a'ya want me fur?

JOHN BROWN: Murder. I want you for murder.

FUGERT: Murder? What a'ya talkin' about? I ain't done nothin'!

JOHN BROWN: On the contrary, Killer Tim, you've done—too much. Three weeks ago, you cut off the scalp of a man called William Hoppe and left him—to die. That's what I want you for!

FUGERT: I'm innocent, I tell ya! Honest, I am! Judge Lecompte said so! He said I was innocent!

JOHN BROWN: There's only one Judge, Killer Tim, and He says that yer guilty. (*Dutch Lieder and Red Emery who are standing behind John Brown have begun raising their rifles, pointing them at him.*)

JOHN BROWN: (*Sharply, without turning.*) Drop those guns! All of ya! Drop 'em on the floor! (*The rifles rattle and crash to the floor. Red Emery keeps his; he is well out of Brown's line of vision.*)

JOHN BROWN: You, too, Red Emery. (*Red Emery lets go of his gun; it drops noisily.*)

JOHN BROWN: (*Still looking intently into Fugert's face.*) I think if the Lord had delivered Judge Lecompte into my hands, it would have taken the Lord to get him out again. If every court that ever judged on earth had called you innocent, you'd still be guilty—guilty in your soul and before God.

FUGERT: (*Terrified*) I don't know what yer talkin' about, Mr. Brown! What's it all about?

JOHN BROWN: You'll know very shortly—Tim Fugert, in the name of God Almighty, I sentence you to death!

(*Red Emery is the only man among the Border Ruffians who is not completely intimidated. Immediately after dropping his rifle, he began edging his way to the bar, now he has seized a bottle and is just raising it above Brown's head, ready to strike, when suddenly the side door flies open and John Edwin Cook, pistol in hand, jumps in and shoots the bottle out of Red Emery's grasp. It shatters into a thousand pieces, but John Brown, unruffled, goes on staring at the unhappy Fugert.*)

RED EMERY: (*Looking first at the bottleneck, still in his hand, then wildly about the room.*) Who the Hell did that?

COOK: (*Dramatically*) John Edwin Cook! The second best shot east of the Rockies! (*He strikes an attitude. There is a loud cheer at this from just outside and cheering and laughing heartily, a small group of Brown's men enter behind Cook from the side door. Aaron Dwight Stevens first, a heroic figure, a huge bearded man with kindly bright eyes, and after him Jerry Anderson, the happy-faced Albert Hazlett, Billy Leeman, a slim handsome boy with a dazzling smile, and finally the dark-visaged, ugly Charles Plummer Tidd.*)

STEVENS: (*Laughing*) Good work, Johnny!

HAZLETT: (*Laughing*) Pretty good! (*General laughter from the Brown men. Cook, chuckling happily, walks across the room brandishing his pistol, herding Red Emery and the other Border Ruffians into the comer.*)

COOK: (*Good-humoredly*) Now get over there, all of you!

JOHN BROWN: (*Gravely—still looking at Fugert.*) Thank you, Cook. Call in my sons from the front there, somebody.

HAZLETT: (*Stepping to the door and calling out.*) Hey, there, you Brown boys! The Old Man wants you! (*He steps aside to allow them to come in, Oliver, Owen, and Fredrick. There is a pause; the men wait silently for the next orders. John Brown continues to look at Fugert who is terribly frightened, finally—*)

JOHN BROWN: Fredrick! (*Fredrick steps forward.*) Oliver! (*Oliver steps forward. Looking away from Fugert for the first time, facing forward and speaking slowly*) Take this man out and shoot him. (*Oliver and Fredrick come up and take Fugert's arms.*)

FUGERT: (*Hysterical*) Oh God, Brown! You don't mean that! It's murder! This is murder! Cold-blooded murder!

JOHN BROWN: (*Calmly*) "Without the shedding of blood there is no remission of sin."

FUGERT: Oh God! God! Oh, my God! Ain't y'got no heart, Brown? Mercy, in God's name, Mercy!

JOHN BROWN: (*With cold insistence.*) Take that man out and shoot him. (*Fredrick and Oliver lead the sobbing Fugert across the room and up the steps to the doorway. There they stop, Fredrick, turning to Hazlett, his face ashen.*)

FREDERICK BROWN: Gimme yer pistol, Bert.

(*Hazlett hands it to him and Fredrick, stuffing it into his pocket, grabs Fugert's arm again and he and Oliver lead him out. The condemned man breaks into a violent fit of weeping and can be heard for some time outside as he is carried away. Finally, when there is silence, John Brown walks over to the remaining Border Ruffians and confronts them—*)

JOHN BROWN: You—you, I forgive. That man was your leader and you only followed. As was said of old, you being without knowledge "you know not what you do." You're fighting for slavery. You want to make or keep other people slaves. You come here to make Kansas a slave state! Why you're fighting against liberty—the liberty your fathers fought for, died for, in the Revolution. Your fathers died to establish a republic, a real republic where all men should be free and equal, with the inalienable rights of life, liberty and the pursuit of happiness. And you—you're traitors, traitors to Liberty and to your country, and you deserve to be hung to the nearest tree! But this time you're forgiven. You're free; you can go back to your homes and tell your friends and your neighbors about your mistake. Go back across the border and, if you're wise, and you value your skins, you'll stay there! Now, let's pray. (*The Brown men fall upon their knees instantly, but the others remain standing.*)

JOHN BROWN: (*Angrily, to the Border Ruffians.*) I said let's pray! (*The men move uneasily. Brown draws out a pistol and brandishes it at them.*) Down on your knees and pray to the Lord! Get down on your knees! (*Reluctantly, they kneel; only John Brown remains standing.*)

JOHN BROWN: (*After a moment, praying fervently, his head upraised, the pistol still leveled at his prisoners.*) I will lift up mine eyes unto the hills, from whence cometh my help. My help cometh even from the Lord who hath made heaven and earth. Blessed be the Lord, my Strength, who teacheth my hands to war and my fingers to fight. My heart showeth me the wickedness of the ungodly, that there is no fear of the Lord in his heart. For he flattereth himself in his own sight until his abominable sin be found out. The words of his mouth are unrighteous and full of deceit . . . Blessed is he who is upright in the sight of God. . . . The Lord is his keeper. The Lord shall preserve his going out and his coming in, from this time forth—(*Bang! The report of a pistol from outside followed by—an awful silence. Then John Brown continues.*) As for the transgressor, he shall perish. For thine enemies, O Lord, they shall perish! The workers of iniquity shall be scattered. The ungodly shall be rooted out. (*As he goes on praying the lights dim off, his voice trailing away in the darkness.*) But the salvation of the righteous cometh of the Lord! He shall deliver them from the ungodly and shall save them, because they put their trust—(*His voice becomes undistinguishable—The Scene ends.*)

Scene IV

Scene—The interior of the Empire House, late afternoon. There is practically no wait between this and the preceding scene, simply a moment of darkness and then the sound of shooting, growing desultory as the lights come on. The half-doors on the main entrance and the shutters outside the windows have been partially closed. Before these the men, Aaron Dwight Stevens, Albert Hazlett, Charles Plummer Tidd, Jerry Anderson, Billy Leeman, Owen, and Oliver Brown are ranged, rifle in hand, exchanging shots with an invisible army outside. All the furniture except one chair is in use as a barricade; on this, the still unconscious Kagi has been propped. Cook and Little Chick are ministering to his needs. The old Indian, his pipe in his mouth, holds a pail of water for Cook who is sponging the injured man's face and head. John Junior has his chain again and is in the corner beating out his rhythm on

Inside the Empire. Set by Todd Troupers.

the floor; John Brown stands over him looking sadly down at his son. The prisoners, the Border Ruffians, have gone.

TAWKY: *(During a lull in the shooting.)* It don't take much to drive p'um crazy in this country. *(Cook dips his rag in the pail, wrings it out, and goes on sponging Kagi's head.)* Now me, I don't think either one's wuth dyin' fur, slavery or freedom.

COOK: Kagi's not badly hurt, he won't die.

TAWKY: Mebbe not, but he will purty soon if he sticks around here. They all get killed in this country—sooner or later.

COOK: *(Laughing)* You've managed, little Chick.

TAWKY: Well, I do git tired a'be'n shot at, but a' wun't be druv out. *(The men fire a rapid volley.)*

OWEN BROWN: *(Leaving his station after the firing has finished and going up to John Brown.)* They've stopped firing, father.

JOHN BROWN: Good. Don't waste any more ammunition than you have to.

OWEN BROWN: Yes, sir. *(Just as he starts to go, John Junior begins to laugh. His father and brother turn to look at him.)*

JOHN JUNIOR: Marching feet . . . ! Marching feet . . . ! Marching feet . . . ! One foot is chained down and the other is free . . . marching . . . marching . . . *(Suddenly, he slams the chain down on the floor. It makes a terrific noise and the men at the windows turn to look at him.)* Sometimes I think it's the spirits—the spirits of them that has been killed in this fighting. Marching

. . . Marching . . . (*Hoarsely*) Like now, seems I can hear Fugert's footstep and Hoppe's. (*Giggles*) Those two! Chained together . . . tied to the same chain! Marching on. (*He presses his hands tightly against his temples and speaks slowly, almost rationally, in an elaborately matter-of-fact-tone.*) But that's just my imagination. I don't know what is real—'m crazy, you see, and I can't think—straight. (*After a minute he laughs again, hysterical laughter that ends in a sob.*)

JOHN BROWN: (*Turning away—bravely.*) It will pass. (*The men turn back to their posts. John Brown stands silent for a moment and then walks over to Kagi.*)

JOHN BROWN: (*To Cook, as he comes up.*) How's this fella Kagi? Conscious?

COOK: Not quite. He's coming to.

JOHN BROWN: (*Examining Kagi's head.*) Should have bandages—

COOK: Yes, he should. (*He and Brown look hopefully at Little Chick. The old Indian takes the pipe out of his mouth, chews reflectively for a moment and then putting the pail down on the floor, he spits into it with an air of finality. Cook looks discouraged. Without a word, John Brown rolls up his coat sleeve to the elbow and tears off the shirt sleeve at that point. Ripping it down the center, he begins bandaging Kagi's head with it as the young man opens his eyes.*)

KAGI: (*After a pause, looking vaguely at Brown.*) Hello, Mr. Brown.

JOHN BROWN: Hello Kagi. How you feeling?

KAGI: (*Frowning*) I know you were here when I went after Fugert. (*Looking around.*) What happened to Fugert? Where is he now?

JOHN BROWN: (*Quietly*) Fugert is dead.

KAGI (*Incredulously*) What?

JOHN BROWN: Oliver and Frederick, two of my sons, they—took care of him.

KAGI: (*Staring at Brown uncomprehendingly.*) Say, how long have I been unconscious?

JOHN BROWN: About two hours. (*Smiling*) You got a nasty clip.

KAGI: So, it seems. (*Hazlett and Tidd discharge their rifles. It startles Kagi who leaps to his feet, drawing his pistol and wheeling about to face them.*)

TIDD: (*Turning to Stevens; his back to Kagi.*) I got him.

STEVENS: You sure finished him off. That was Red Emery, one of the O'Driscolls.

KAGI: (*Looking first at the row of armed men at the windows and then at Cook.*) Hey, what's all this about? There's Whipple. (*Then to Cook*) What are *you* doing here? (*Cook laughs—Turning to Brown.*) Captain Brown, explain this. What's going on here, a war?

JOHN BROWN: You sit down and take it quiet. That injury isn't anything to joke about. (*He turns slightly away.*)

KAGI: (*Sinking back into the chair.*) Yes, I know, but—

COOK: Old Preacher White has dug up a crowd of Border Ruffians and Missourians. The High Sheriff is here, too, with a big posse. They've surrounded the house.

KAGI: (*Alarmed*) That sounds like several hundred men!

COOK: (*Casually*) Oh, it is.

KAGI: And they're all armed and surrounding us? (*To Brown*) What are you going to do, Captain?

JOHN BROWN: Do? Chase 'em away.

KAGI: You've only half a dozen men in the building! When do you expect reinforcements?

JOHN BROWN: I don't.

KAGI: No reinforcements?! You can't hold back an army with six men!

JOHN BROWN: I certainly can, sir, an army of bullies. I could hold back six such armies. A handful of men strategically placed, who respect themselves and fear God too much to fear anything human—can resist the universe.

TAWNY: (*To Brown—spitting into the pail again and picking it up.*) Them pro fellas has bin jest achin' to get ya cornered, un now they have. They're scared as hell of ya, but they're mad too, sumpin' awful. It ain't just the price on yer head neither; they're out fur yer scalp.

JOHN BROWN: (*Simply*) Sir, the Angel of the Lord will camp round about me.

TAWKY: Mebbe so, Ole Brown, mebbe so. Yer a great fighter, that's certain, I reckon the greatest fighter that'll ever be. N'mabe ye kin fight or bluff yer way out a'this. But your time'll come. The pro-slavery men'll get ya, mark my wurds, they'll have ya yit.

JOHN BROWN: (*Calmly*) That was decided in the beginning, Tawky, before the world was made. (*A sudden volley of shots from outside is returned by the men within. Little Chick hurries behind the bar with his pail and John Brown walks to the center entrance, opens the door wider and stands looking out, oblivious to the firing.*)

KAGI: (*With a look in Brown's direction, to Cook.*) Doesn't anything worry that man?

COOK: He's worried now, worried sick about Oliver and Fredrick.

KAGI: His sons?

COOK: (*In a low voice.*) Two of them, there are lots more. Fredrick is the favorite, little funny in the head, but he's a great fellow and a real hero, too. Really won the Battle of Black Jack.

KAGI: Why, I thought—

COOK: Sure, he did. Things were looking pretty bad for the Old Man. He was out-numbered about a hundred to one when up rode Fredrick, right into the midst of Pate's company, waving his hat and shouting, "Come on, boys, we have 'em surrounded! You're all right, father, the reinforcements are here, and we've cut off all communication!" He did that absolutely alone, right in the midst of all that firing, and bluffed the enemy into surrender!

KAGI: *(Laughing)* That sounds almost too wonderful! Where's Fredrick, now?

COOK: That's just it, where's Fredrick now? That's what's worrying John Brown.

KAGI: When was he last seen?

COOK: Two hours ago, he and Oliver went out with Fugert.

KAGI: Fugert? Why Fugert?

COOK: *(Gravely)* John Brown sent them out—to kill him.

KAGI: *(Sharply, not believing his ears.)* What?

COOK: It was—well, a kind of execution. This Fugert was a murderer of the worst kind and according to John Brown, God—required his death.

KAGI: *(Incredulous)* God? God?

COOK: *(Simply)* Yes. Old Brown—well, he—communicates with Him. He claims his authority from—God. *(At the window, John Brown levels his rifle, takes careful aim, and just as Cook finishes speaking, fires. Then he lowers his gun and continues calmly with his vigil.)*

HAZLETT: *(Looking over his shoulder at Cook.)* There's one better shot east of the Rockies!

COOK: Dear boy, I've always admitted it! *(They both laugh and Hazlett turns back to his post.)*

KAGI: *(Quietly, continuing his conversation with Cook.)* Direct from God— and you believe that?

COOK: *(Very quickly)* I don't know what I believe. I'm not a religious man. But if you believe anything, you believe that! I don't know, I—I believe in John Brown and what he stands for, and I think I believe in God. . . . If you knew John Brown and loved him like I do, you'd know what I mean. If there is a God, reigning in heaven, he's picked that man from among men. John Brown is—well, he's chosen, that's the word. The things he does—the way he draws men to him. Look into that man's eyes and you'll know that there's a power behind them that isn't human. He's in touch I tell you, he's inspired by something—something we can't even conceive.

KAGI: Inspired?—Nonsense, Cook. This is the nineteenth century. There's no such thing as—inspiration.

JOHN JUNIOR: (*Slamming his chain suddenly on the floor and shouting.*) Inspiration! Inspiration! You don't understand! You don't know what inspiration means! I've been inspired. . . . I can tell you about it. . . . It ain't nonsense, and inspiration don't mean being crazy—not—not exactly. (*Ecstatically*) Inspiration is a kind of happy song, it's like a spring rain shower falling soft and sudden on young leaves, it's like a ray of dawn sunshine smiling, and pointing at the mountain-tops. And mostly—mostly it's like my dreams—the dreams I have I can't tell about—or understand— (*Several of the men have turned to listen, after a bit he continues.*) take that marching, now—the sound of that marching. That's—that's inspiration. It's like the ray of sunshine really because it's beautiful and very terrible and mainly because it means something. You think I hear that sound just because I've marched in a chain-gang and gone simple doing it, and I've got chains and marching on my crazy mind. Well, maybe you're right. Maybe that's why. But believe me, that sound isn't crazy. Other men hear it, too, sane men—and it hurts them, little stabbing pains in the heart. And for a few—the great men that hear it, the really great—it's a fine, wild kind of music. A Call, sort of a great call to arms. (*With sudden ferocity, sensing Kagi's incredulity.*) It ain't insane, I tell you! It ain't crazy! (*His face suddenly lights.*) It's the footsteps of a whole nation, marching in the chains they was born in! That's what it is! You don't have to be simple to hear that echoing and echoing in your heart, do you? John Brown hears it and he knows what it means! (*A prolonged volley of shots from outside. The men at the windows take aim and prepare to answer it.*)

JOHN BROWN: (*Closing the door and turning to the men.*) You needn't reply to that, it's a waste of bullets. Shoot only when you have to. (*In answer to this, there is a murmured "yes sir" from several of the men. John Brown comes down the steps and walks over to Kagi. As he approaches, John Junior crawls quickly back to his corner. Pleasantly to Kagi.*) Well, how's your head feeling?

KAGI: (*Smiling up at him.*) Better, thanks. (*Cook starts for the doorway to fill Brown's post.*)

JOHN BROWN: (*Handing Cook his rifle, smiling—*) Here, John. My Beecher's Bible.

COOK: (*Taking it; laughingly to Kagi.*) I'll read 'em a sermon or two out of this, all right, and they'll be a long time forgetting the text. (*Kagi laughs.*)

JOHN BROWN: (*Smiling, to Cook.*) I'm glad you and Mr. Kagi are making friends; you'll see a lot of each other in the next few years.

COOK: Why? Is he joining us?

JOHN BROWN: (*Nodding*) In the big fight.

COOK: At Harpers Ferry? (*To Kagi*) Why didn't you tell me so in the first place? I'm going down there pretty soon to live. (*Shoots off.*) That is if I live through this! Got to get a job and settle down there as a kind of spy. When are you going?

JOHN BROWN: Kagi doesn't really know anything about it; just that we're going to free the slaves. He heard me hint of the plan in Concord and volunteered his services. He has a splendid record fighting with Stevens here in the west, and he's a scholar. We're very happy to have him.

COOK: I should say so. (*Another volley of musketry from outside. He turns to go.*)

JOHN BROWN: (*To Cook*) When this clears up you must introduce Mr. Kagi to the boys. (*Another volley.*)

COOK: (*Over his shoulder, hurrying to his post.*) Yes, Sir! (*Another volley louder than the rest.*)

OWEN BROWN: (*Tensely*) Can't we answer that, father?

JOHN BROWN: Where's the enemy? Are they approaching? (*Another volley.*)

HAZLETT: Coming nearer, sir, but they're still stickin' to the brush.

JOHN BROWN: Don't fire till they begin crossing the creek again. It ain't worthwhile.

HAZLETT: (*After a pause, tersely.*) Yes, sir.

JOHN BROWN: (*Coming closer to Kagi, pleasantly.*) Well, Mr. Kagi, I didn't expect you so soon. Since you're here, perhaps you'd better remain with us 'til we're ready to strike. (*More shooting in the distance.*)

HAZLETT: Them's the Sheriff's men. Makin' for the hickory. (*A few scattered shots.*)

JOHN BROWN: (*Continuing to Kagi.*) I have a few minutes now. If it doesn't tire you, I'll outline the plan. (*The cracking of rifles during all this.*)

KAGI: Which? The plan to get out of here?

JOHN BROWN: Certainly not. The plan you've come thousands of miles to take part in, the plan for which we are all of us dedicating our lives: The liberation of God's despised poor; the slaves. (*A heavy round of musketry. It sounds closer than before—he continues calmly.*) In Concord, it was impossible for me to be specific. In fact, all over the East, I have had to exercise a great deal of caution. These jack-daw politicians, these so-called abolitionists are very difficult people. They make beautiful speeches, but they refuse to take any definite stand, they won't act. (*More rifle shots.*) Great cry and little wool, all talk and no cider. I believe in action. Talk is a national institution, but it does no good for the slaves!

STEVENS: (*Quietly, after a slight pause.*) The Lampson Boys are crossin' the creek.

JOHN BROWN: (*Coolly*) Let 'em have it. (*The sound is deafening as the entire body of men guarding the windows fire their rifles. Kagi, startled, turns to look at them, but John Brown remains perfectly composed.*)

JOHN BROWN: (*Speaking quietly, his voice thrilling in the silence of the shadowy little room.*) I believe in the Golden Rule, sir, and in the Declaration of Independence. I think they both mean the same thing, and it is better that a whole generation should pass off the face of the earth—men, women, and children—by violent death—than that one jot of either should fail in this country. I mean exactly so—, sir! (*There follows a pause.*)

LEEMAN: (*In a tense voice.*) 'Don't think we got Brud. Looks like he's still movin' over there in the grass. (*For a moment no one replies, then Jerry Anderson speaks.*)

ANDRSON: (*Slowly*) He's dead.

TAWKY: (*At the windows with the rest.*) Reckon so. (*The tension is broken. The men move and relax. There are knocking and clicking sounds, heavy breathing, and then shuffle of feet as rifles are reloaded. John Junior laughs softly to himself.*)

KAGI: (*Slowly, looking up into John Brown's face.*) I'm a cynic, John Brown, and I haven't a belief to my name. But damn it, you've only got to look at me and say the word, and I'll follow you into the ocean, over a cliff . . . anywhere! (*Quietly*) What is it this time? Death? (*John Junior begins again, beating out his weird rhythm, pounding the floor with his fist and slapping it with his chain. John Brown turns from Kagi to watch his son.*)

JOHN JUNIOR: (*Chanting in time to his drumming.*) Marching feet . . . ! Marching feet . . . ! Marching feet . . . ! Marching feet . . . ! One foot is chained and the other is free. . . . Marching feet . . . ! Marching feet . . . marching feet . . . ! (*He goes on pounding the floor.*)

JOHN BROWN: (*Speaking above it to Kagi.*) How we shall come out of the furnace, God only knows. But we're ready to be offered. (*The pounding continues.*)

KAGI: But we're finished, aren't we? We can't get out of here. This is the end.

JOHN BROWN: (*Ecstatically looking upward as John Junior pounds louder and louder with his chain.*) This is only—the beginning! I hold a commission from God Almighty to act against slavery—and I'm going to act! We're going to carry the war into Africa! (*A resounding crash of musketry; John Junior drops his chain and, covering his face with his hands, begins to sob hysterically. John Brown moves closer to Kagi, speaking earnestly, intensely, completely oblivious to the shooting—round after round of which is shot off as he speaks.*)

JOHN BROWN: The plans are carefully laid, more so than I could give you in New England. The attack is to be widespread. We'll strike at different points and at different times. At first, the movement will attract little attention, but as it increases in magnitude and the perfection of our organization becomes apparent, the slave-holders will be terrorized. Eventually, they will band together. There'll be Civil War. But, by the time the South can take concerted action, we'll be in a position to resist the Universe.

KAGI: But where are your men? Why doesn't this army of yours come to our assistance now?

JOHN BROWN: I have no army. The first company of men with which I shall liberate the Negroes are only in part recruited. You see them here.

KAGI: How many do you propose to have?

JOHN BROWN: In good time—twenty men.

KAGI: Twenty men? You think you can end slavery with twenty men?

JOHN BROWN: I do, sir. Twenty highly efficient fighters will strike the first blow. The Negroes will flock to them and will be given arms. Later, there will be reinforcements from Canada.

KAGI: You have confidence in the Negroes themselves?

JOHN BROWN: Give a slave a pike and you make a man of him. When the bondmen stand like men, the nation will respect them. Of course, it's necessary to teach them this.

KAGI: But you can't make soldiers of the slaves by simply arming them.

JOHN BROWN: Of course not. They'll be placed in companies under experienced militarists and will only be given rifles when they have proved themselves capable of managing them.

KAGI: But where will you move the slaves for this drilling? Into Canada?

JOHN BROWN: No. The purpose is not the extradition of one or a thousand slaves, but their liberation in the states wherein they were born and are now held in bondage. We will free large companies of Negroes from different points. In Virginia, first of all, and later in Mississippi and Tennessee, Alabama, Georgia, and the Carolinas. These attacks will be made at different times and in widely different places. On each occasion, the slaves will be hurried into retreats prepared for them. Inaccessible wildernesses and rocky places where a good military defense can be set up. The country abounds with such places. The mountains and swamps of the Southland were established by God from the foundation of the world that they might someday be a refuge for fugitive slaves.

KAGI: (*Looking at John Brown, after a silence.*) It's a good plan. It's almost logical, really, from the military point of view, and it's so daring. I—I don't know how it could fail!

JOHN BROWN: I've studied warfare abroad, Kagi. I've studied battles and the science and history of battles all over Europe. I've given forty years of my life to the preparation of this plan. Of course, it can't fail! It was ordained at the beginning of all time. It has the sanction of God!

KAGI: I believe you. That's the most wonderful part of it! I believe you! (A *terrific crash of discharging arms; the men in the room pause to reload but the firing continues at a furious rate outside.*)

JOHN BROWN: (*Above the din.*) Our first point of attack is the United States Arsenal at Harpers Ferry—

KAGI: In Virginia?!

JOHN BROWN: Certainly. Rich plantation country and Harpers Ferry, remember, is right at the foot of the mountains. The slaves will flock to us immediately. They can be organized into small companies during the night and hurried away under escort to various camps of ours up in the Alleghenies.

KAGI: But, Captain Brown, a government arsenal?

JOHN BROWN: Certainly. Our Eastern friends will supply us with arms, but we'll need a great deal more at first. The southern armories are well stocked; Jefferson Davis has seen to that, but they're badly guarded. The arsenal at Harpers Ferry in particular. Twenty men can take it easily. (*The rattle of ammunition has grown still louder during this. Now the men at the windows fire another volley.*)

OWEN BROWN: They're pretty close, Father!

COOK: Looks like Preacher White and the Sheriff's men are making for the corral. (*They fire another round through the windows.*)

JOHN BROWN: (*To Kagi, continuing, paying no attention to the others.*) Cook here is going ahead to reconnoiter the territory and locate Washington's sword.

KAGI: Washington's sword?

JOHN BROWN: Cook is acquainted with a Colonel Washington who lives near there—nephew of George Washington. It is with George Washington's sword, the sword presented to him by Frederick the Great, that I shall lead this new battle for freedom. In due time, our twenty men, selected and tried, will begin to assemble. Shipments of ammunition will be run into headquarters, a farm a few miles out of town. We'll gather there, secretly, one by one, and await the hour when God—(*An excited murmur from the men interrupts him.*)

HAZLETT: That's a white flag they're carrying!

COOK: (*Turning to John Brown.*) The sheriff and old Reverend White come with a flag of truce, sir. Will you go out to meet them?

JOHN BROWN: (*Calmly*) I will not. If Preacher White has got anything to say for himself, he can come here to me. (*Cook with a "yes sir" puts up his gun and goes out.*)

TAWKY: Sheriff's likely fixin' to serve that warrant, John Brown. The president's got a price on yer head and so's the guvner of Missouri—More 'n three thousand dollars. That's a pow'r a' money.

JOHN BROWN: (*Quietly*) I should hate to spoil your carpets, Mr. Tawky, but you know—I shall never be taken alive. (*After a pause, Preacher White and the Sheriff, a large dark-faced man, carrying a rifle with a white shirt tied to it, appear in the doorway followed by Cook.*)

REVEREND WHITE: (*After an uncomfortable silence—laughing faintly.*) Why—hello—Captain Brown.

JOHN BROWN: (*Ignoring him*) Stack your rifles, boys. (*They do.*)

SHERIFF: (*Covering his timidity with an aggressive manner.*) Are you John Brown?

JOHN BROWN: I am.

SHERIFF: Well, I'm the High Sheriff of this county. I hold a warrant for your arrest.

JOHN BROWN: So, you're here to claim the president's reward under a white flag? (*The Sheriff can think of nothing to say. After a silence—*) Get out of here!

SHERIFF: What's say?

JOHN BROWN: Get out of here. You and your dirty shirt. Get out!

SHERIFF: I represent the President of the United States!

JOHN BROWN: My business is with Preacher White, not with the President. Goodbye. (*After an uncomfortable pause, Preacher White gives the sheriff a significant nod towards the door.*)

SHERIFF: Well, perhaps it would be better if you handled this thing alone, Reverend. (*He goes out, uncertain of himself.*)

JOHN BROWN: Well, now, Preacher White, what are you up to, you and the rest of your pro-slavery bullies?

REVEREND WHITE: (*Smirking foolishly, he comes down the steps into the room.*) We all have our opinions, Captain. You can't say I'm no gentleman.

JOHN BROWN: I don't say you are no gentleman. I say more than that, sir.

REVEREND WHITE: (*Sharply*) What's that!

JOHN BROWN: I say, sir, it would take as many men like you to make a gentleman as it would take hens to make a cock turkey.

REVEREND WHITE: (*With bravado.*) Now look here, Captain, I'll have you understand that I—

JOHN BROWN: I understand exactly what you are and I don't want to hear any more about it. Have you any propositions to make?

REVEREND WHITE: Well, not exactly; that is—

JOHN BROWN: Very well, White, I have one to make to you—your unconditional surrender.

REVEREND WHITE: (*Gulping*) Surrender? Unconditional?

JOHN BROWN: (*Quickly, businesslike.*) I won't bother to take prisoners. Your army will forfeit a percentage of its arms. I consider that sufficient. Of course, you will evacuate at once. Every man jack in your company must be out of the country and across the border by nightfall, with the understanding that he stays there. That's all.

REVEREND WHITE: (*Laughing suddenly.*) Oh, that's all is it? Well, that's enough! (*Laughs again, heartily.*) The joke is on you, John Brown! I hold the trump card! (*Approaching the bar.*) Gimme a small one, Little Chick, (*He throws the money on the bar-top.*) I got to celebrate!

COOK: (*Threateningly coming down the steps towards him.*) What'a ya' celebrating?

REVEREND WHITE: (*Wheeling around, facing Cook and the others, suddenly serious.*) Oliver hasn't come back yet, has he? (*The men look at one another in silence.*)

COOK: No. No, he hasn't.

REVEREND WHITE: (*Laughing*) Good! (*Laughs louder*) Good! I didn't think he had. (*Little Chick shoves his drink towards him across the bar-top. Taking it in his hand, Reverend White raises it aloft, still laughing.*) Gentlemen! A toast! (*For a moment he pauses, holding his glass high in the air, squinting at Brown and the others with little blue eyes. Then he speaks.*) To Fredrick! (*The effect is instantaneous. There is a roar of angry and surprised voices. Only John Brown is silent.*)

OWEN BROWN: (*Louder than the rest.*) Fredrick?! (*He has seized the hand with which Preacher White was drinking his toast; now the glass falls out of it and tinkles to bits on the floor. The men are silent.*)

REVEREND WHITE: (*With venom.*) Yes, Fredrick. The favorite son—(*Going up to John Brown.*) You'd better watch out, Old Brown, if you ever want to see him again—alive!

JOHN BROWN: (*Sharply*) What's this?

REVEREND WHITE: Some of the boys nabbed him when you wasn't lookin,' right by the house here, along with Oliver, that's another one of your promisin' young sons, ain't it?

JOHN BROWN: Where are they now?

REVEREND WHITE: Oliver escaped, most probably layin' low somewheres to keep out of the fightin'. (*Owen makes a movement in Reverend White's direction and is restrained.*) But we got Fredrick safe enough, and we'll keep him safe, 'til you come to reason.

JOHN BROWN: (*Thoughtfully*) You got Fredrick in hostage?

REVEREND WHITE: You're damn right! We got him in hostage. What a'ya say to that Captain John Brown? (*A pause.*) Just how much is Fredrick's life worth to you?

JOHN BROWN: (*Quietly*) Everything in the world—

REVEREND WHITE: (*Quickly*) Well, then—

JOHN BROWN: (*Loudly*) But neither his life nor mine is worth so much to me that I would—buy it—at your price.

REVEREND WHITE: But I only ask—

JOHN BROWN: (*Furious*) I won't trade and barter with the devil, Reverend!

REVEREND WHITE: Not even for Fredrick?

JOHN BROWN: No, By Heaven! (*Turning away*) I won't give in to slavery—not an inch!

REVEREND WHITE: (*Coming up behind him, fawning on his shoulder.*) Just give us a chance to get away, Captain, that's all we ask. (*Insinuatingly*) If not—if not—we'll take care of this Fredrick of yours. I'll deliver him myself to your doorstep—dead. (*John Brown clenches his fists and draws in his breath sharply.*) Dead—he'll be stone dead!

JOHN BROWN: (*Fiercely, to himself.*) God! (*After a long pause, quietly, to Reverend White.*) What's your price?

REVEREND WHITE: We don't like your ideas, John Brown. I'll return Fredrick on one condition. That you get out of the country and stay there.

JOHN BROWN: (*With decision.*) I won't do it! My sentiments ain't worth it. Why, I'll string you up, every last one of you to the same tree before moonrise! What d'ya think of that Preacher White?! You can't mollycoddle me out of my purpose. I'm not a father; I'm an instrument of God!

REVEREND WHITE: All right then. All right! Name your own price.

JOHN BROWN: I'll get out of Pine City and stay out for forty-eight hours. That's my price. (*A pause.*)

REVEREND WHITE: (*Finally, extending his hand.*) You're on—

OLIVER BROWN: (*Outside*) Father! (*Appearing on the porch.*) Father! (*In an instant John Brown is on the porch at Oliver's side, supporting him.*)

OLIVER BROWN: Father!

JOHN BROWN: Yes, son, what it is?

OLIVER BROWN: (*Hysterically*) Preacher White! Preacher White! Where's Preacher White?

JOHN BROWN: (*Quietly*) He's in here, son. (*Bitterly*) Bargaining with us, for Fredrick's life.

OLIVER BROWN: (*Horribly shocked.*) What? (*The old man doesn't reply.*) Listen to me, Father! (*He whispers into his ear. John Brown stiffens, fixes Reverend White for a moment with a vengeful eye, and then hurries off. Supporting himself on the edge of the doorway stares about the room until he locates the terrified Reverend White, then with a roar, he is upon him.*) You damned rat! (*Reverend White rushes to the side door, but Oliver is upon him just as he opens it. Seizing the old man by the neck, he begins beating him terribly. Several of the men attempt to restrain him.*)

OWEN BROWN: Here Oliver, stop it! He's under the white flag!

OLIVER BROWN: (*Furiously*) White flag! (*Both hands on the preacher's neck. Oliver shakes him as a dog shakes a rat.*) Truce, eh?! Bargaining for Fredrick's life! (*To others.*) Fredrick's dead I tell you! AND HE KILLED HIM! (*He begins choking White, snarling into his face.*) Lined him up against the wall, White and a bunch of the others—they shot him down in cold blood! (*Suddenly, the men, sensing their leader's presence, turn to the doorway. John Brown towers above them carrying the dead Fredrick, tenderly, like a sleeping child. A tragic silhouette against the sunset sky. Oliver stares up at his Father, his hands relaxing their grip on White's throat.*)

JOHN BROWN: (*To Oliver, quietly, after an awful silence.*) Let him be. (*Oliver relinquishes his hold and White sinks to the floor.*)

JOHN BROWN: (*Very simply.*) We're not fighting slave-holders, Oliver, we're fighting slavery. (*Reverend White, still badly frightened, scrambles to his feet.*)

JOHN BROWN: (*Comes slowly down the steps and confronts White. After a pause, with terrific restraint.*) I think you'd better go now Reverend. (*Silently, Reverend White stumbles up the steps and hurries away. John Brown remains in the center of the room, the corpse hanging limply in his arms. There is absolute silence save for the torturing sound of his breath. No one moves. Finally, John Junior, with a convulsive movement crawls up to Kagi.*)

JOHN JUNIOR: (*His finger to his lips—whispering.*) Shh! (*Kagi looks down at him.*) Listen! (*After a moment, Kagi becomes aware of a strange sound. The ominous pulsing and pounding of numberless feet—marching—in chains. It grows louder as the Scene ends.*)

Scene V

Scene—Before Colonel Washington's home on the Washington Estate in Virginia, about five miles from Harpers Ferry. The picture is joyous and colorful.

About the house, a gracious colonial mansion, bloom genial gardens, and beyond the abundance of plantation, fields shine gold against the distant purple of Virginia Mountains. The scene opens with a rousing song. Four of the Colonel's slaves are celebrating their noonday rest. The leader, Jeff, plays a banjo, another jigs on occasion, and the quartet sings. John Edwin Cook approaches and raises his hand in salutation.

COOK: *(As theatrical as ever, but in this scene deeply sincere.)* Brothers! *(The Negroes fail to notice him and the music continues.)*

COOK: *(Louder)* Brothers! *(This time they hear and the singing stops, abruptly. The slaves turn and regard the white man, open-mouthed.)*

JEFF: *(Stepping forward, respectfully.)* Yes, suh?

COOK: *(Impressively)* Prepare!

JEFF: *(Uncomprehendingly.)* What's dat, suh?

COOK: *(With more emphasis.)* Prepare!

JEFF: Prepare? *(He looks to his companions for explanation and finding none. back to Cook.)* Prepare for what, suh?

COOK: For war! Prepare to take up arms and fight! Nearby a holy man prepares to help you, to array you for battle and put the sword of vengeance in your hands. Almighty God has invested this man with authority. He will put down Pharaoh and lead you out of Egypt to the Promised Land. *(With an abrupt change of tone.)* Is Colonel Washington at home?

JEFF: *(Completely bewildered, responds vaguely.)* Yes, suh. My master, he's at home. Yes, suh.

COOK: *(Looking at him. After a slight pause.)* Count no man your master, friend.

JEFF: No, suh.

COOK: Is this the way?

JEFF: To de master's, suh? Yes, suh. Dat's de Washington Mansion up on de hill. You kin cut across de lawn, but de regular road is right ovah dere *(Pointing.)* Do you see suh? At de end ob de bridal path. Dat'll take yo all right to de front doh.

COOK: *(Stares absent-mindedly at the little group of Negroes for a moment and then resuming grandiloquently.)* The hour is at hand! Your shackles shall be struck from off you and you shall stand up, men among men, in a nation emancipated, a new republic rededicated to equality. A land without masters and without slaves! *(Cook looks at the others with the intense expression of a man half swept away by his own eloquence and half desirous of knowing how it has affected his audience. Finally, he raises his finger to his lips in a command of silence, and with a little wave of his hand strides off toward the house.*

The Negroes stare after him and then look blankly at one another. Finally, Jeff begins to laugh and the others join him, heartily, as the scene ends.)

Scene VI

Scene—Colonel Washington's study, a delightful old room, dominated by great French windows, their lace curtains glowing with the sunshine of early afternoon. A delicate little table stands in the center and, on either side of it, a chair of the same

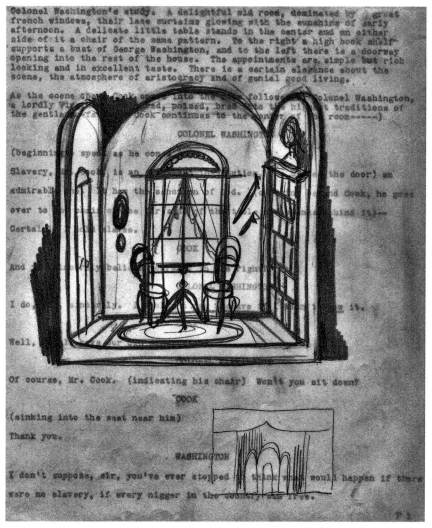

Inside George Washington's study. Sketch by Orson Welles.

pattern. To the right, a high bookshelf supports a bust of George Washington, and, to the left, there is a doorway opening into the rest of the house. The appointments are simple but rich and in excellent taste. There is certain elegance, an atmosphere of aristocracy and of genial good living. As the scene opens, Cook comes into the room followed by Colonel Washington, a lordly Virginian, cultured, poised, bred into the highest traditions of the gentlemen-farmer. Cook continues to the center of the room.

COLONEL WASHINGTON: (*Beginning to speak as he comes in.*) Slavery, Mr. Cook, is an excellent institution, (*He closes the door.*) an admirable one. It has the sanction of God. (*Crossing behind Cook, he goes over to the chair on the far side of the table and stands behind it.*) Certainly, I hold slaves.

COOK: And you sincerely believe yourself in the right?

COLONEL WASHINGTON: I do, sir, sincerely. I wouldn't own a slave if I didn't know it.

COOK: Well, we all have our own convictions.

COLONEL WASHINGTON: Of course, Mr. Cook. (*Indicating his chair.*) Won't you sit down?

COOK: (*Sinking into the seat near him.*) Thank you.

WASHINGTON: I don't suppose, sir, you've ever stopped to think what would happen if there were no slavery; if every nigger in the country was free.

COOK: Oh, yes, I have Colonel—

WASHINGTON: A disastrous thought, sir. A direct challenge to the laws of God! The black man was created a savage. He was brought into the world that he might serve. Now—

COOK: But he's a man just the same. He's constituted just like you. He functions exactly as you do! (*Washington clutches the back of his chair, for an icy moment fighting fiercely for his self-control.*)

WASHINGTON: (*Very quietly.*) There is a certain—difference, sir. (*After a moment, he speaks again, in his normal tone.*) Your nigger is a sort of child, Mr. Cook. He requires guidance. I presume you've had no intimate associations with the race?

COOK: (*Pleasantly*) Please, Colonel Washington, I'm not a "damn Yankee."

WASHINGTON: (*Laughing.*) But you are my guest. It wouldn't matter if you were an abolitionist!

COOK: (*Wistfully.*) Bad lot, aren't they?

WASHINGTON: (*seriously*) Oh, dreadful, sir, dreadful. I'm told the Northerners hate 'em as much as we do.

COOK: (*quietly*) I guess you're right, Colonel, everybody hates an abolitionist.

WASHINGTON: Even the niggers.

COOK: (*quickly*) What's that? (*The Negro quartet is heard on the lawn, the happy lilt of their song growing in volume as they approach the house.*)

WASHINGTON: You look a bit pale Mr. Cook, but we'll soon fix that up. What will you drink? (*He pulls the bell-rope as he speaks.*) I have an excellent whiskey. (*Cook rises, listening intently to the singing outside. The Colonel is about to press his question when he notices his guest's interest.*) Good, isn't it? Those are the slaves we were speaking of, the ones you met at the gate.

COOK: You're very kind to your slaves, aren't you, Colonel?

WASHINGTON: (*gently*) I try to be, Mr. Cook. We're like a big family here on the plantation, and I'm what you might call the father. (*chuckling*) I'll grant you I enjoy the part! (*The door opens and a liveried butler appears, a gigantic Negro.*)

THE BUTLER: Yes, suh?

WASHINGTON: Some of that whiskey, Mr. Cook?

COOK: Yes—yes, if you please.

WASHINGTON: (*to the butler*) Our best Bourbon, Tom, and be quick about it. I'm sure Mr. Cook is thirsty.

THE BUTLER: Yes, suh! (*He leaves.*)

WASHINGTON: So, you've come all the way from Harpers Ferry on foot? That's a long walk in the heat of the day.

COOK: (*smiling*) Further yet, across the river. I'm a lock-tender now, you know, on the old canal.

WASHINGTON: Really? You will forgive my saying so, Mr. Cook, but I wonder what we have here in this dull old Virginia of ours to attract a man of your parts. You've been with us now—what is it—nearly a year?

COOK: (*bitterly*) More than that, Colonel. (*With a change of tone, by way of explanation.*) Oh, I have ties, you know, family ones.

WASHINGTON: Oh, of course, how stupid of me! I'd forgotten that there's another—Virginia besides the state. And how is she, and the little fellow?

COOK: Fine, thank you, sir, my wife sends you her regards. So, do all the Kennedy's.

WASHINGTON: (*with a bow*) Return mine. Oh, speaking of the Kennedy's—do sit down sir, (*They both sit.*) Do you know anything about these strangers who've rented old Doctor Kennedy's farm, up Maryland way?

COOK: (*starting*) No, I—No, I don't, Colonel.

WASHINGTON: (*laughing*) That's very strange. Farmer Unseld told me he'd seen you visiting there.

COOK: (*testily*) Farmer Unseld was mistaken!

WASHINGTON: Of course, he was. And I hope he's just as mistaken in his suspicions regarding these—new tenants.

COOK: *(apprehensively)* What does he suspect?

WASHINGTON: Oh, I don't think his ideas are very tangible. These Eastern Dutch people are naturally suspicious, slow-moving races always are. As far as I can gather, this—this Isaac Smith is a cattle buyer of some sort, although I heard somewhere he's a mineralogist. At any rate, he appears to be just an unsociable sort of old man with a number of sons and a long white beard, it doesn't sound very alarming to me. *(He laughs and Cook joins him with an effort.)*

WASHINGTON: *(Pushing a cigar case across the table to Cook.)* Have a cigar, Mr. Cook?

COOK: No, thanks.

WASHINGTON: Anything else?

COOK: Well, frankly, yes. It's really what I've come over here for. I'd—I'd like to examine your famous relics.

WASHINGTON: The historical sword and pistol? *(rises)* With pleasure, sir. *(He goes to the wall and unhooks the sword and pistol which have been hanging there. He hands the pistol, a giant-flint-lock to Cook, who has risen to examine it.)*

WASHINGTON: George Washington's Pistol, sir, given to him by Lafayette.

COOK: *(Taking the pistol reverently and examining it, then with a glance at the bust above the bookcase.)* General Washington was an ancestor of yours, was he not?

WASHINGTON: *(proudly)* A great-grand-uncle, sir. *(With a twinkle in his eye.)* And like myself, a slave-owner.

Inside George Washington's study. Set by Hascy Tarbox.

COOK: Lafayette didn't know that when he gave this to your great-grand-uncle because later he said, "I never would have drawn my sword in the cause of America if I could have conceived that thereby I was helping to found a nation of slaves." (*He hands the pistol to Washington.*)

WASHINGTON: (*Taking it—after an icy moment.*) Lafayette was a Frenchman, sir. (*After a moment, handing him the sword.*) Here's the real treasure, Mr. Cook. But, of course, you've heard of it. A gift to the General from Frederick the Great.

COOK: (*Seizing the scabbard in his right hand he draws out the blade with his left and flourishes it before him.*) This is—a treasure, Colonel.

WASHINGTON: You collect this sort of thing?

COOK: No, not really, I—(*A sudden burst of laughter from the slaves outside followed by the hum of happy conversation. Cook looks up quickly, and then turns and walks slowly to the window. He stands there behind the little table and stares out. There is a silence.*)

WASHINGTON: Does that disturb you, sir? I'll have it stopped—

COOK: No—no don't, please. Those Negroes out there, your slaves—they seem so—so happy.

WASHINGTON: (*laughing*) Why not? Nothing to do today. Jeff has the new banjo I gave him. It doesn't take much to make a nigger happy, and they have everything they want.

COOK: (*turning suddenly*) I don't believe it!

WASHINGTON: Why, what do you mean?

COOK: They can't be really happy. They're men; they must want to be free. (*For a long minute, Colonel Washington regards his guest, and then—*)

WASHINGTON:—I'll tell you what I'll do, Mr. Cook. Tom, the butler, is due in here any minute now, with the drinks. I'll offer him anything in the world.

COOK: His freedom, anything?

WASHINGTON: Anything and we'll see what he wants. Is it a go? (*Cook takes his outstretched hand in silence just as Tom comes in carrying a decanter and glasses on a tray.*) Oh, here he is now. Just a minute, Tom. (*Tom stops and Washington crosses over to him in front of the table. Cook moving to the Colonel's former place.*)

TOM: Yes, suh?

WASHINGTON: (*lounging on the chair-back*) Tom, what do you want most?

TOM: Wha's say, suh?

WASHINGTON: What is it you want, Tom, more than anything else in the world?

TOM: (*grinning*) They ain't much, suh ah doan know's ah kin think of any thin' straight off.

WASHINGTON: (quietly) Would you like your freedom, Tom? Would you like to be free?

TOM: (scarcely believing his ears) Would ah like to be free? (Tom stops and the other two hang on his next words, finally they come.) Lawsy no, Marse Washington, ah doan want to be free. Ah likes it heah.

WASHINGTON: (softly) Well, I'm glad of that, Tom. (He looks back at Cook, a twinkle in his eye. To Tom again—) Oh, but surely Tom there's something, something in this wide world that you want? (Tom shakes his head and scratches it.) I've promised Mr. Cook that whatever it is, I'll get it for you so you'd better think hard. (There follows another pause during which Tom visibly cudgels his brain.) Come on, Tom, think of something!

COOK: Remember, you can have anything, anything you ask for, your— your master, has promised me that, and he won't break his word.

TOM: (Suddenly brightening, and then growing glum again, obviously thinking better of the idea.) No, dat won't do—

WASHINGTON: Tell us, Tom, what is it?

TOM: (timidly) Well, Marse Washington, Ah knows it's askin' a lot, but— since you all tells me ah kin have just what Ah wants—

WASHINGTON: Well, Tom? What is it?

TOM: (brightly) A watch-chain, suh. A watch-chain like de Governah's.

WASHINGTON: (laughing) How about the watch?

TOM: Ah doan care 'bout no watch, Marse Washington, Alls ah wants is de chain.

WASHINGTON: Well, Tom, it is bad for the morale, but you shall have it.

TOM: (deeply grateful) Thank you, suh. (Tom carries his tray to the table, and standing behind it, unloads the decanter and glasses. Washington turns and regards Cook, highly amused.)

COOK: (Going up to Tom, earnestly.) I don't think you understand, Tom. Colonel Washington made a bet with me; he swore he'd give you whatever you asked. Don't you want anything except a watch-chain? (Washington is pouring drinks.)

TOM: No, suh, Ah cain't think a nuthin'. (scratches his head) 'Cept maybe— well ah reckon Ah would kinda like a watch. (Outside the music strikes up again, the quartet singing a joyful "Oh Susanna." The effect on Cook of Tom's reply and this last burst of music amuses the Colonel vastly. Chuckling he hands him a glass.)

WASHINGTON: (His eyes twinkling he raises his glass.) Mr. Cook, may I propose a toast—To Slavery!

COOK: (Raising his glass) To the slaves!

Unconsciously they form a picture, these three, Tom in the center behind the table, and the two white men on either side of him their glasses raised in salutation. In the *other hand, each holds a weapon: Washington, a pistol. Cook, a naked sword. The orchestra takes up the strain and it grows louder, as the scene ends.*

Scene VII

Scene—The parlor, kitchen, and back-porch of Kennedy Farm, John Brown's headquarters near Harpers Ferry, on the Maryland side. The little kitchen is well stocked with a stove, a cupboard full of dishes, and a small table. A door to the right opens onto the porch, a platform with steps leading to the ground. Another door in the left wall connects with the sparsely furnished parlor. There are but two simple chairs, and lining the rough-hewn walls, row after row of packing-boxes, marked

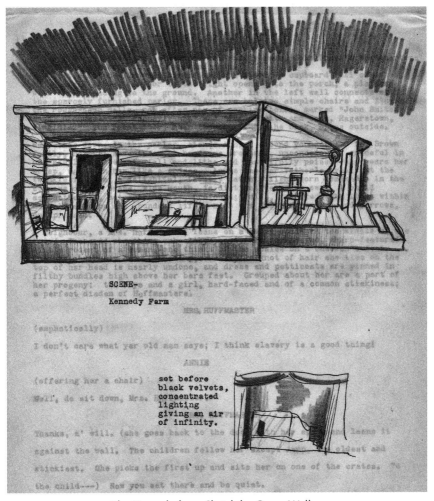

The Kennedy farm. Sketch by Orson Welles.

"John Smith and sons, Chambersburg, Pennsylvania" and "Issac Smith and sons, Hagerstown, Virginia." The front door, near the center of the back, opens outside.

Near this door, in the parlor, stands Annie, second youngest of the Brown family, not yet seventeen. A handsome creature, unconsciously graceful in her simplest movement, tall and lithe and beautifully poised—she wears her crisp, ugly gingham like a goddess. Annie has her father's eyes, but the twinkle in them, a delightful, faintly satanic light born somewhere in the corners of her brave, wide mouth, is distinctively her own. A child aesthetically, not spiritually, profound; quiet, reserved, she lives within herself a happy and abundant life. Hers is a life full of deep joys and sorrows, unexpressed.

A neighbor, a Mrs. Huffmaster, leans on a muddy spade in the middle of the room. There is something about this sharp-eyed, sharp-featured little rodent of a woman, one thinks of the scales on a chicken's feet. She has obviously been gardening, the little knot of hair she ties on the top of her head is nearly undone. Dress and petticoats are pinned in filthy bundles high above her bare feet. Grouped about her are a part of her progeny: two boys and a girl, hard-faced and of a common stickiness: a perfect diadem of Huffmasters.

MRS. HUFFMASTER: *(emphatically)* I don't care what yer old man says; I think slavery is a good thing!

ANNIE: *(Offering her a chair.)* Well, do sit down, Mrs. Huffmaster.

MRS. HUFFMASTER: Thanks, a' will. *(She goes back to the door with her spade and leans it against the wall. The children follow her except Jepp, the oldest and stickiest. She picks the first up and sits her on one of the crates. To the child—)* Now you sit there and be quiet.

ANNIE: I'm sorry we can't offer you anything very comfortable, but we're— we're not settled as yet.

MRS. HUFFMASTER: *(putting another child on the crate)* Why don't you ever unpack these boxes, Miss Smith? Jepp! Come here to yer Ma! *(Puts Jepp on the crate next to his brother and sister.)* I'd s'pose you'd be sick a' the sight of 'em litterin' up yer parlor.

ANNIE: We are really. But you see—these are my mother's things, and she wants to do the unpacking herself when she comes.

MRS. HUFFMASTER: *(doubtfully)* That's a lot of unpackin' for one woman.

ANNIE: Yes, it is, but she's written us strict instructions that we're not to touch any of it 'til she arrives.

MRS. HUFFMASTER: Yes, a' know. That's what you told me three months ago. Seems yer ma is a long time arrivin'.

ANNIE: *(coldly)* Yes, she is, Mrs. Huffmaster.

MRS. HUFFMASTER: Well—(*Walks over to the chair Annie offered her and sits down on it.*) As I was sayin', slavery is a good thing.

ANNIE: (*Bringing up a chair and standing behind it. With forced politeness.*) Do you think so, Mrs. Huffmaster?

MRS. HUFFMASTER: Sure, it's a good thing. Keeps them niggers in their fittin' place. (*Turning around, speaking to Jepp who has started to descend from his perch.*) You stay where y'are, Jepp! Do you hear me? (*to Annie*) They gives me the shivers. I wouldn't trust a nigger out a' my sight, and neither would Franc, not for a minute. (*to Jepp*) Now, Jepp you heard what I said! (*to Annie*) Yep, they gives me the shivers. They're a lot a' low down ignorant savages that's what they are, and they ought 'a be kept where they belongs. (*laughs shrilly*) They was a (*laughs again*)—they was a free nigger down in Charles Town where I used to live. He had store-clothes and patent leather shoes. Cocky? You'd think he was white! (*laughs again at the recollection.*) I'll never forget the time he tipped his hat to me, friendly-like. It was Saturday night and Franc was in town; he was courtin' me in them days. Well, you oughta seen what he done to that nigger, him and a bunch of the boys. (*Cackles softly.*) Now mind you, I don't think that nigger meant to be unrespectful, and they're them as says Franc and the boys was drunk and outn't to have been so cruel. But all the same, he had it comin' to him. It was a good lesson for the other niggers. They gotta be kept in their place.

ANNIE: (*quietly*) Well, you see, we don't feel quite that way about it—

MRS. HUFFMASTER: (*Menacingly*) You know—I'd hate to think you was abolitionists. Franc is death on abolitionists. He sez they ain't no better than the niggers they wants to set free! If he should ever get it into his head that you was inclined that way, he'd never let me visit you again.

ANNIE: (*with that smile of hers*) Oh, Mrs. Huffmaster!

MRS. HUFFMASTER: No, he wouldn't. I wouldn't darst to come a hundred yards a' this farm if I didn't want my hide tanned. (*Turning to Jepp who has crawled down from the box again and is trying to open it.*) Jepp! Come away from that. Get back up there where y'ma set ya! (*Annie in desperation goes over to him and lifts him back on top of the box. Examining the lock carefully to see that it's fast. Mrs. Huffmaster drones on.*) What he's really dead ag'in is this here slave-runnin'. A boy's a right to his own opinions, that's what Franc sez, but when it comes to stealin' other folk belongins and meddlin' with other folk's affairs, he draws the line. Franc won't have nary at all to do with them anti-slavery men and their underground railroad. He's death on 'em that's what he is.

ANNIE: Yes. I'm sure he is. But a great deal of the slave-running is carried on simply to liberate free-Negroes who've been kidnapped and sold into slavery.

MRS. HUFFMASTER: Yes, and a great deal of it ain't. A great deal of it's plain piracy! (*insinuatingly*) Y'know, I think that right here—here in these parts I mean, there's a station for the underground railway!

ANNIE: (*innocently*) There have been a few slaves in the valley who've escaped, and I s'pose a few pass through the mountains during the night-time, runaways from the Gulf States following the North Star.

MRS. HUFFMASTER: I'm thinkin' it's more than a few, Miss Smith, that are followin' the North Star through this country. The hill people are noticin' things, markins, and queer signs. Yer old man sez it's the Indians, but there are them as think different, there are them as thinks the savages ain't red skinned.

ANNIE: (*A trifle apprehensive, she has caught the meaning in Mrs. Huffmaster's voice.*) Of course, it's difficult to say—

MRS. HUFFMASTER: I don't think so. Everybody knows the anti-slavery people have a station at Chambersburg. Now, where's the next one south? The runaways move more in the Alleghenies than they does in the Blue Ridge don't they? So, it ain't likely this here station's east a' Harpers Ferry. Where is it then? I sez it's here—here! (*Jepp got down again and this time he has succeeded in forcing the lock, he is just about to open the lid, in fact, just started to, when Annie sees him.*)

ANNIE: (*quickly*) Jepp! (*Jepp, momentarily petrified, drops the lid. Annie rushes up to him, grabs him by one hand and attempts to drag him into the kitchen. Quickly, nervously—*) Jepp! How would you like a nice slice of bread? A big thick one? Miss Martha is an extra good light bread maker. She baked a fresh loaf just before she left.

JEPP: (*Doubtfully, still straining to get at the box.*) Kin I have salt on it?

ANNIE: (*Enthusiastically, pulling him into the kitchen.*) 'Course you may! (*Sitting Jepp on the table and calling into the other room.*) Come on into the kitchen. Mrs. Huffmaster! Oh, and bring the children. (*Mrs. Huffmaster, her arms folded sits grim and silent in her chair. Annie gets out a loaf and begins slicing it at the cupboard calling over her shoulder.*) Do come into the kitchen, Mrs. Huffmaster! It's much warmer in here. You miss a stove up on the mountains! (*shouting desperately*) Specially in this weather! (*Mrs. Huffmaster rises with a sigh.*)

MRS. HUFFMASTER: Well—A' don't mind if a' do. (*Goes to the kitchen door.*)

ANNIE: *(Her back turned to Mrs. Huffmaster. She's at the table, slicing bread.)* And bring in the children, Mrs. Huffmaster; there'll be a nice thick slice for everybody! *(The children are crowded about their mother in the doorway. They wait in silence.)*

MRS. HUFFMASTER: *(suddenly)* Did you ever hear tell of a fella called— John Henri Kagi? *(Annie stops slicing with a start and remains motionless, her back still turned, listening.)* He's a famous Kansas Free-Stater and anti-Slavery fighter. They do say as he's Osawatomie Brown's right-hand man Well, we know him down here, he's really a Keagey. That's a Virginia Family, Swiss Mennonites. He used to teach down to Hawkinstown before they run him out. Well, just a piece ago they was several hereabouts as swore they seen him! Growed older a' course and all a' that, but the same Kagi—slinkin' about Harpers Ferry after daylight. *(Annie finishes cutting the bread and gives a piece to one of the children.)* A lot a' folks around here has got their suspicions up, like Farmer Unsold and my Franc. They just got a' be put on the right track. *(Annie gives a slice to another child. As Annie hands her a piece of bread, looking into her eyes and speaking slowly and with emphasis.)* Now me, I keep my eyes open and there ain't much I miss. *(Annie returns her look with the cool, steady eyes of her father. Mrs. Huffmaster weakens and tries another approach. Picking up the shaker from the cupboard, she devotes her attention to salting her bread.)* Niggers gives me the shivers. *(The slice of bread posed at her mouth, studying it.)* I don't know why, but they does. *(She takes an immense bite and speaks with her mouth full.)* I guess it's account of them bein' so black and all. It ain't healthy. *(There is an unpleasant pause while the Huffmasters eat. Mrs. Huffmaster finishes all but the last bite and then, with a sudden and passionate meaning—)* That's why I got such a start when I seed that nigger, that nigger on your porch yesterday! *(Annie drops the bread-knife. It clatters to the floor.)*

ANNIE: *(After an infinitesimal, but thoroughly dreadful pause.)* Why, what do you mean Mrs. Huffmaster?

MRS. HUFFMASTER: You heard what I said. A strange nigger, standin' out there on your kitchen porch in broad daylight. Had a big ugly face as black as soot. It nearly scared the daylights out a'me!

ANNIE: I—I don't understand, Mrs. Huffmaster. A Negro? On this porch?

MRS. HUFFMASTER: When he saw me, he run to the door and ducked inside here, I waited a couple a' minutes to see what would happen. Well, a bit afterwards, you come out to this same doorway and set down there with your knittin'. *(Annie looks at her for a minute and then stoops down and picks up the bread-knife.)* Aw, you ain't foolin' me a bit, with your covered mule wagon a' rattlin' along the roads b'night and yer niggers and free-state men bobbin' up and down in the hills b'day,—not a bit. The folks around here may swallow your cock and bull stories, but not them on the border. Not me either. I keeps my eyes open and I seen a thing or two. (*She takes another bite out of the bread.*) "Isaac Smith and Sons," a minin' firm—that don't mine. (*Takes another bite.*) "John Smith and Sons," cattle buyers that doesn't buy cattle. It don't sound right. Even that "John Smith" don't sound right, not to me anyways. When I lived in Charles Town, I worked in a hotel—(*She takes the last bite.*)

ANNIE: Just what are you getting at?

MRS. HUFFMASTER: You know what I'm getting at, and you needn't pretend you don't. This ain't no farm, they ain't no twenty men livin' on a farm, not even if they are "a' studyin' minerals."

ANNIE: What do you mean by twenty men?

MRS. HUFFMASTER: I tell ya, I keeps my eyes open! They's strange goin's on in this house. I know 'cause I seen things. Like that nigger for instance, and I can guess a lot more. (*insinuatingly*) I should judge you keeps a pack of 'em in here sometimes, don't you? Though a' course you keeps movin' 'em up North, I suppose as soon as you can make connections with Chambersburg.

ANNIE: Stop beating about the bush, Mrs. Huffmaster. What kind of a family do you think we are? What kind of a home do you think this is?

MRS. HUFFMASTER: I think you're a lot a' crazy abolitionists and slave-runners and I don't think this is a home, I think it's a station, a station for the underground railway!

ANNIE: Well, you're wrong. You're absolutely wrong, Mrs. Huffmaster. You may be very observing, but those sharp eyes of yours have been deceiving you this time. You may take my word for it; we're not slave-runners here!

MRS. HUFFMASTER: (*After a pause, with her aggravating drawl.*) Yer men folks has a right smart lot a' laundry. There's enough hangin' out there on your line to fit up an army. (*Another pause, then the drawl again, still more aggravating.*) And there's a site a' silverware and crockery in this cupboard. Y' could begin a hotel almost with what you got here.

ANNIE: The silverware and the laundry is—extra stuff.

MRS. HUFFMASTER: Oh, I see it's, extra stuff. (*whining*) I'm a poor woman, Miss Smith. I ain't near got the clothes and crockery I'd like to have. Now if you got so much extra stuff, why don't you give some of it to me? I'd appreciate it a whole lot.

ANNIE: (*deeply shocked*) Oh! Oh, Mrs. Huffmaster! I'm sorry.

MRS. HUFFMASTER: They's a lot a' folks 'ud be powerful interested to hear about that nigger, and about a few other things, too. I'd hate to think what Franc and the boys would do if I let anything slip. *(Annie looks at her, too hurt to speak. There is a pause, then with a sudden burst of passion.)* You kin tell me all the tall stories you likes, but I'm thinkin' you wouldn't like it if they was an investigation! *(insinuatingly)* Now if the Bordermen get on yer trail.

ANNIE: *(With the cold fury of disgust.)* Take what you want!

MRS. HUFFMASTER: *(Looks at her for a minute)* You needn't fly up in the air about it. I ain't goin' to tell the Bordermen.

ANNIE: *(At the end of her string.)* Take it! Take all you want! Only get out of here! And don't come nosing around here with those little brats of yours anymore!

MRS. HUFFMASTER: *(whining again)* I can't take it all in one trip. The tea-pot and this bakin' pan is about all I can manage. *(Annie's eyes are flashing dangerously.)* Come along children!

(The Huffmasters hurry into the parlor, and are nearly at the door when Jepp remembers the box and goes back to it. At the doorway, his mother notices what he is up to, and is struck with a similar curiosity. She tiptoes to the kitchen entrance. Annie stands where Mrs. Huffmaster has left her, transfixed with rage. Reassured, the little woman trots up to the box and, with the help of Jepp and her two youngest, she has nearly lifted the lid when the front door opens revealing a Negro, Dangerfield Newby. Mrs. Huffmaster is thrown into a state of "shivers." The box-lid bangs shut, the tea-pot and baking pan rattle to the floor, and Huffmasters run screaming through the kitchen and bounce out of the back-door. Dangerfield Newby steps into the room followed by Kagi. Newby is an extraordinarily handsome man, bearded, beautifully proportioned; he stands six-foot-two, the Scotch half of his lineage showing clearly in his fine mulatto face. He is carefully, almost elegantly, dressed. There is a slight pause; the two men look about the room in bewilderment and then at one another. There is something magnificent about Newby's embarrassment. It amuses Kagi who laughs quietly in his rich, resonant baritone and then steps into the kitchen. Annie, completely dumbfounded by the strange deportment of the Huffmasters, has gone to the door and is looking out. Kagi comes up behind her and laughs again.)

KAGI: Good Lord, look at the Huffmasters! What are they running for? They look as though they'd seen a ghost!

ANNIE: *(startled, turning)* John! So, it was you that scared her!

KAGI: Me? Good Heavens! Do I look like a ghost?

ANNIE: *(For a moment, charmed out of her indignation, reproving him with an unmistakable inflection.)* Oh, worse yet! Johnnie, don't you ever shave?

KAGI: Not anymore. I'm growing a beard. Really, I am.

ANNIE: *(earnestly)* Oh, John, I wish you'd stay in Chambersburg where you belong. You've been recognized again. Old Mrs. Huffmaster said so just before she left.

KAGI: *(dryly)* By the way, why did she leave?

ANNIE: On account of you. She's probably making for the sheriff's now as fast as she can get. She saw Shields Green on the porch yesterday, and she thinks we're running slaves. Now you've bobbed up. We're bound to have an investigation! Oh, Johnnie, Father's told you to stay at your post!

KAGI: *(wistfully)* It's been three weeks since I've seen you.

ANNIE: I know it, John, but supposing the Bordermen get after us. Suppose—suppose they lynch you! Father said—

KAGI: I'm acting on Captain's Brown's instructions. *(Goes to door and speaks to Newby who has been waiting patiently in the parlor.)* Oh, come in Mr. Newby, I'm afraid I've been rather rude.

NEWBY: *(Coming to the door.)* Not at all, sir.

KAGI: Mr. Newby, this is Miss Annie Brown.

NEWBY: *(Bowing as he comes into the kitchen.)* How do you do, Miss?

KAGI: Mr. Newby got into Chambersburg two days ago and my instructions were to see him here. Naturally, we were to travel only by night, but we ran into a little trouble at the river, and it was imperative we keep moving.

ANNIE: Oh, John, the Pennsylvanians! Are they still after you?

KAGI: *(smiling)* Yes, and I suppose they will be for quite some time.

ANNIE: Johnnie, this is awful! What are you goin' to do?

KAGI: Lay quiet here awhile and wait for a very dark night. Why, don't you want me around?

ANNIE: I don't understand it at all. You're usually so level-headed.

KAGI: And now?

ANNIE: I don't know how you could be any less with Mrs. Huffmaster and her investigations hanging over our heads like a sword of—the sword of—

KAGI: Damocles.

ANNIE: Like the sword of Damocles. Any minute now they may be swooping down on us.

KAGI: They won't swoop darling. There isn't the remotest chance of it.

ANNIE: I don't know what you mean by that. Those sheriffs and slave-catchers are as bad as any Kansas pro-slavery men. They'd do anything in the world for a little money. *(Kagi looks at Newby with a despairing shrug.)*

NEWBY: Yes, Miss, but you see, they is headed in the wrong direction.

KAGI: We were mistaken for runaways, so our pursuers are chasing due North; they probably won't turn back 'til they reach Canada.

ANNIE: *(Annie and Kagi laugh)* Oh, I'm sorry, John. I've been unreasonable, I know, but I'm terribly upset. It's that Huffmaster woman. *(Kagi reassures her.)*

NEWBY: If you're speaking of the little lady who was snoopin' in your boxes, I'm afraid I give her quite a scare when I come in.

ANNIE: "Shivers" is the word. Well, never mind. She'll come back for her tea-pot. You must forgive me fussing, Mr. Newby, but you see it's my job. Father keeps me here just to watch out for raiders and Sheriff's men and to entertain curious neighbors. *(laughs)* It's a hard job.

(The front door in the parlor opens and Martha comes in. She's a truly beautiful girl with gold-brown hair and serious baby-wide blue-grey eyes. She is childishly earnest, and erratic as a child in moods and emotions. There is something puckish and youthfully impish about her, but she lacks Annie's mature sense of humor and perspective. Born in the shadow of tragedy, despite her breezy manner, she is a little girl trying to be grown up, trying to look and act like a wife, a woman of responsibilities. Her big questioning eyes mirror the wonder and bewilderment that is in her soul. In her passionate and undisciplined heart, she loves her husband, Oliver, deeply, almost wildly, but she also loves Edwin Cook and many others. There is something of the real mother, the essential mother impulse, beating in that little child heart of hers. Now, she is loaded with parcels. She kicks the door shut.)

ANNIE: That's Martha. She's been shopping down at Harpers Ferry.

MARTHA: *(calling)* Somebody give me a hand. Yoo! Hoo! Annie!

ANNIE: Hello, Martha! *(Kagi goes into the parlor and relieves her of her bundles one by one. These are piled so high as to cover her face at first.)*

MARTHA: *(recognizing him)* Hello, John Henri! What are you doin' away from Chambersburg? I thought you was supposed to lay low up at Mrs. Rittners. *(He starts to answer, but she interrupts him.)* Never mind we're all crazy to see you, particularly Annie. And I'm dying to have a nice long talk with you. How are you?

ANNIE: *(At the kitchen door.)* Just a minute, Martha, give the poor fella a chance. Johnnie, bring those groceries in here to me. Oh, and introduce Martha to Mr. Newby. Mr. Newby go out and be introduced. *(A greatly embarrassed Newby goes into the parlor.)*

KAGI: *(Doing the honors, his voice somewhat muffled by the groceries.)* Mr. Newby, I'd like you to meet Martha Evelyn, Oliver Brown's wife. *(Going into the kitchen and unloading the bundles. Calling into the next room.)* Mrs. Brown is the youngest of our "household." Aren't you, Martha?

MARTHA: *(To Newby, smiling.)* Yes, I'm still fifteen—Anne has me beaten by a year.

NEWBY: I'm pleased to meet y—(*Newby puts out his hand and Martha puts a package in it.*)

MARTHA: I'm very glad to meet you, Mr. Newby. We've been expecting you for some time now. You're the man with the wife and children in slavery, aren't you? I'm just dying to have a long talk with you. Your first name is Dangerfield, isn't it? Yes. Well, you can call me Martha. (*With one of her sudden changes of mood.*) I do hope you won't think me disrespectful, but I'm just a kind of mother to all the boys here.

NEWBY: (*Smiling down at the little mother.*) Oh, no Madam. It's very gracious of you, I'm sure.

MARTHA: (*Very seriously, slowly, after a slight pause.*) I think you're awfully nice. (*Suddenly businesslike, giving him her last package*) Now, you take that into Annie, Dangerfield. (*Dangerfield does. Martha calling after him.*) Be careful, it's eggs!

(*In the kitchen, Kagi has unloaded his packages onto the table and has come into the parlor just before Dangerfield leaves it. Annie helps Dangerfield unload and then goes to the door while Martha is speaking. Dangerfield standing behind her.*)

MARTHA: (*Hanging up her shawl on a peg near the door.*) Oliver! Oliver! John Henri, where's Oliver?

KAGI: Don't know. I thought he and Owen were away bringing in the last shipment of rifles.

MARTHA: Yes, but—

ANNIE: They haven't got back yet, Martha.

MARTHA: Well they ought to be. Where are the boys? Where are the invisibles?

ANNIE: (*laughing*) Oh, how stupid of me—Poor boys!

MARTHA: What's so funny?

ANNIE: (*laughing*) I don't suppose it's so funny really. I hid them away when Mrs. Huffmaster came and I'd forgotten all about them! (*laughs*)

MARTHA: I should say it isn't so funny! Why Annie Brown, they'll catch their death a' cold down there, in this weather. And what'll happen to Barclay Coppoc! I'll bet he's dead of pneumonia by this time! (*She stoops down and picks up a ring at her feet, opening a trap door. Calling down.*) Invisibles! Invisibles! Come on up boys, it's all right!

WILLIAM THOMPSON: (*From below, he appears in the trap towards the end of this line.*) Is the coast clear'? (*sees Kagi*) Hello, Kagi! How are ya? (*He steps up on to the ground level, a large-featured, ruddy-faced, rustic looking man with good-humored eyes.*)

KAGI: (*As they clasp hands.*) Fine thanks, Thompson.

HAZLETT: (*Coming up out of the trap immediately after Thompson.*) Seems to me Mrs. Huffmaster paid a devil of a long visit.

ANNIE: (*coldly*) She did!

KAGI: Thompson, shake hands with Dangerfield Newby, our latest recruit,—Mr. William Thompson.

HAZLETT: Well, Johnnie. How long you been here?

KAGI: (*Patting Hazlett on the back and introducing him.*) Bert, this is Dangerfield Newby. (*Barclay Coppoc comes up the trap right behind Hazlett.*)

HAZLETT: (*Heartily, his handsome young face wreathed in smiles.*) Glad to know you, Newby.

NEWBY: Glad to know you, Sir.

HAZLETT: I suppose Annie kept us locked down there, just so's she could tell you all about us and you'd know what to expect. Didn't you Annie?

THOMPSON: (*To Newby*) And, Billy Leeman. (*Leeman who has come up just behind Hazlett takes the proffered hand with a "Howdy."*)

NEWBY: How do you do.

MARTHA: Barclay Coppoc, you have caught cold!

BARCLAY COPPOC: (*An audacious adventurous spirit; bold-eyed, big featured, and consumptive.*) No, Martha, I've been—

MARTHA: (*To Osborne Perry Anderson, who followed Barclay Coppoc.*) Mr. Osborne Perry Anderson, this is Dangerfield Newby, the new "invisible." (*The conversation is broken by the rich, wonderful laughter of Aaron Dwight Stevens who has come up in time to witness the last introduction.*)

STEVENS: Don't look so worried, Mr. Newby, being an "invisible" ain't nearly as bad as it sounds.

HAZLETT: (*Leaving Martha to do the introducing he, Kagi, and the Thompsons have retired to an extreme corner of the room with a look at Annie.*) Oh, no it just means sitting down in that ice-cold cellar while Annie entertains her friends for tea! (*Annie disdains to answer; goes into the kitchen.*)

MARTHA: It's just an expression of ours, Dangerfield, for the men-folks the neighbors don't know about, they have to stay in the house always, and be hidden away when we have visitors.

NEWBY: I see. (*Kagi goes to the kitchen door, knocks, calls Annie's name and enters. Behind the closed door, the lovers embrace. Leeman and the rustic, athletic Edwin Coppoc have come up during this, and now Jerry Anderson appears.*)

STEVENS: Jerry Anderson—Dangerfield Newby.

MARTHA: (*laughing*) And this is Aaron Dwight Stevens 'case you'd like to know. (*Newby and Stevens shake. Steward Taylor, stocky, heavily-built, large-jeweled, dreamy-eyes,—come up quietly without being introduced.*)

STEVENS: We invisibles—we ain't really a bad lot of fellows when you get to know us. (*Watson Brown appears, a quiet, thoughtful young man.*) Here's a fella that don't even have to hide away, but he does, just 'cuz he likes our company. Mr. Newby, may I present Watson Brown, the fourth of the Brown boys. (*As he speaks Dauphin Thompson, a blonde-blue-eyed, almost girlish country boy comes up from below closing the trap-door.*)

WATSON BROWN: Hello, Newby, father's told me about you. Glad you've come.

MARTHA: Well, have you met everybody now, Dangerfield?

NEWBY: I think so, thank you, ma'am.

STEVENS: I don't. (*looks at Taylor*) There was some that slipped by since I've come up, and I'm certain-sure they're more yet.

NEWBY: Oh, please don't put the gentlemen out, on my account.

STEVENS: Aw—you gotta get the names straight. Attention! (*In an instant the entire roomful, with the exception of Newby and Martha and, of course, Stevens, is drawn up in military formation across the room.*) Salute! (*They do. There is a slight pause. Stevens watching them closely and with not a small degree of pride at his pupils' work walks slowly towards the end of the row somewhat dramatically.*) That's for you. Mr. Newby.

NEWBY: (*His embarrassment increased. Very simply*) Thank you, gentlemen!

MARTHA: (*To Newby*) Isn't it wonderful? Only a few of the boys are real army men. They've picked it all up drilling with Aaron Stevens.

HAZLETT: (*Sarcastically from the ranks.*) This is nothing! You oughta' see us do figure dancin'—

STEVENS: Silence! Hands down! And now, Mr. Newby, since I don't know which ones you've met, I'm afraid we'll have to do it all over again. (*Stevens, twenty-eight years old, bearded, buoyant and bright-eyed, a heroic figure,—nearly six feet three inches of him—strides along with his regiment introducing its members as he comes to them. Behind Jerry Anderson at the end of the line.*) This is Jerry Anderson, an old trooper. No, don't bother to shake hands. They're a lot more to come. I just want you to get the names straight. (*Indicating the dignified but unassuming mulatto, next in line.*) This is another Anderson, Osborne Perry.

HAZLETT: (*With mock gravity.*) But they're not related. (*The Andersons grin a bit foolishly and there is general laughter.*)

STEVENS: (*Indicating the two Thompsons.*) But the Thompsons really are. (*Laying a hand on each as he mentions them.*) Little Brother Dauphin and Big Brother William. Watson here is the only Brown boy present, but we have three of them, and of course there's the Cuppocs: Edwin (*Stepping to each as he names them.*) And Barclay. The bad boy: William Henry

Leeman, our youngest member, but an old trooper and finally—the old free-state campaigner: Mr. Albert Hazlett. (*At this point the door, in front of which the men are regimented opens and Cook and Tidd enter.*)

COOK: (*Coming in right after Steven's final introduction. Dramatically—*) And last but not least ladies and gentlemen—(*The line breaks, the men falling to either side of the room, giving the center of the stage to Cook. There are cries of "Hello, Cook." "Hello, Tidd." "glad to see you back", etc. Cook's voice, rings out above the greetings.*)—Last, but not least: your introducer: Mr. Aaron Dwight Stevens (*Points at him with the flourish of a ringmaster.*) Alias: Colonel Charles Whipple, an escaped prisoner, an ex-Delaware Indian, the terror of Mexico, the scourge of Kansas, and the Defender of the Faith! (*Cheers and a round of applause from the gayer spirits.*) And furthermore, furthermore ladies and gentlemen—last, but not least—our good friend and Mr. Steven's particular good friend: Mr. Charles Plummer Tidd! (*Another round, Tidd steps up to Stevens and takes him by the hand.*

MARTHA: (*introducing them*) Mr. Newby, I'd like you to meet another "visible". Captain Cook.

COOK: (*With many flourishes and a courtly bow.*) Captain John Edwin Cook the Kansas warrior, sir. Knight Errant in the cause of freedom and the second best shot east of the Rockies.

NEWBY: Happy to know you, sir.

COOK: And I'm happy to know you, sir! (*Mounting a chair.*) We are all of us, all of us happy to know you, sir! Three rousing cheers for Mr. Newby! But make them easy or the neighbors'll hear! (*During the cheering Martha introduces Newby to Tidd and in the kitchen, Annie, who is worried by the noise, starts up.*)

ANNIE: Oh, Johnnie, they oughtn't to do that! (*She goes to the parlor door and opens it.*)

HAZLETT: (*Who is standing near, speaks good-naturedly just as the cheering ends.*) Well, Annie. Come to scold us for making all this racket? (*Angered, Annie slams the door in his face.*)

ANNIE: (*To Kagi*) Bert Hazlett makes me so angry! He's forever teasing, or else making advances.

KAGI: (*Angrily, starting toward the door.*) Advances! (*Annie puts her hand to restrain him. Kagi is about to answer, but is quiet as Cook begins to speak—they both listen at the door.*)

COOK: (*Still on the chair; speaking as he has all along with a genial, friendly theatricality.*) It has been the custom here at headquarters since we first assembled that on the occasion of his first arrival every neophyte addresses the assemblage with a few appropriate and beautifully chosen words. Mr.

Dangerfield Newby, will you honor us? (*A round of hearty applause. Newby stands near the center of the room looking nervously at the floor. The applause stops and there is an expectant hush.*)

KAGI: (*At the kitchen-door, to Annie.*) Listen. Newby's going to make a speech.

ANNIE: Poor fellow, he's dreadfully embarrassed at it all. I hope he doesn't think the boys are making fun of him.

NEWBY: (*very simply*) You gentlemen—you all been mighty nice—I'm sure I ain't got all this fuss comin' but—but thank you. You know, I never had this happen to me before. Nothin' like this. Why, you're—you're makin' me feel like I was really welcome—almost like I belonged—and that ain't goin' to happen often to niggers—not for a hundred years. I said I felt like I belonged. But that ain't right. That's all the way you made it seem to me. I don't belong. And that isn't all because I'm black. You see, you gentlemen is heroes. I mean that—kind of martyrs—like, and I'm well, I'm not. You're goin' to fight and maybe die for what you call a cause. You're willin' to give up your life jest because you think something is right and something else is wrong. That makes you heroes.—Well, I ain't a hero—I'm a father. A'course I believe in my people, more maybe than you do, and I'm goin' to fight to make 'em free, but they're my people. And what's more, I ain't fightin' just for them. I'm more selfish. I'm fightin' to free my wife and my children. I'm married to a fine woman, and I got seven of the finest little baby children you ever seen. The youngest has jest commenced to crawl. If I had the money, I could buy my family, and then—then I might have a chance of bein' a hero at Harpers Ferry. But as it is, the finer feelings don't get much of a chance. The finer feelings gets crowded out when I think about my babies goin' to be auctioned off, and my wife sold South, and all of us—scattered all over the land. I jest can't help but think of that. (*After a minute he says very quietly.*) I guess that's all, gentlemen. (*A murmur sweeps over the little room. Hazlett starts to applaud but thinks better of it. Cook, still standing on the chair feels suddenly ridiculous. He steps down and goes over to Newby putting his hand on his back.*)

COOK: Thanks—thanks a lot, Newby. The old man will read you the constitution and give you the oath when he comes back. (*Leaving Newby with a little group on one side of the room, Cook goes over to the kitchen door and opens it. In the kitchen, Annie and Kagi have been very affected by Newby's speech to which they have listened attentively. At its conclusion, they embrace.*)

COOK: (*Opening the door; seeing his blunder, he is greatly embarrassed.*) Oh, oh! I'm awfully sorry! (*He beats a hasty retreat. Near the doorway in the parlor. Martha stands, sniffling quietly into her handkerchief. Cook takes her little face in his hands, looks at her gravely at some length and then bestows a solemn kiss on her lips.)*

MARTHA: Why, Edwin Cook! I'm a married woman!

COOK: *(very solemnly)* And I'm a married man. With a baby that's "just commenced to crawl." That's just it.

MARTHA: *(Falling tearfully into his arms.)* Oh, Edwin! *(The silence is suddenly shattered by a lusty snore. Everyone in the parlor starts. Leeman draws his revolver.)*

MARTHA: Heavens, what was that?

STEVENS: Did you hear something?

TIDD: I did.

STEVENS: Thank God! *(After a tense moment the snore is repeated, louder.)*

THOMPSON: *(Stepping quickly to the trap-door and opening it as he speaks.)* I knew somebody was missing! *(He goes back into the trap. Stevens has a fit of his wonderful laughter and some of the others relax and smile.)*

LEEMAN: *(Still a little nervous.)* What's so funny?

TAYLOR: What was that strange sound?

STEVENS: It's Shields Green. That's the noise he makes when he's asleep!

LEEMAN: *(Putting his pistol back in its holster.)* Damn—

EDWIN COPPOC: *(quietly to Leeman)* Shut up, Leeman.

MARTHA: Bill Leeman, you watch your tongue! *(There is a terrific crash from below. Martha jumps and falls back into Cook's arms.)* Oh, my goodness!

COOK: That'll be Thompson prying the Emperor out of the arms of Morpheus.

ANDERSON: *(explaining to Newby)* Shields Green is a member of our despised race. I don't know why, but he's referred to here as The Emperor.

TIDD: *(Leaning on the door of the trap and peering down.)* Come on up, sleeping-beauty! There's a new gentleman above who wants to be presented. *(The head and shoulders of Shields Green, a young black with a big Congo face appears in the trap.)*

THE EMPEROR: What's de mattah?

COOK: *(Leaving Martha and going over to the trap.)* Ascend Emperor, let us look upon all of you at once!

THE EMPEROR: S'pose I 'scends, den what?

COOK: Dangerfield Newby, our newest recruit, is dying to meet you socially. Do you think we could arrange an introduction? *(A lengthy pause. The Emperor stares blankly at Cook. Finally—)*

THE EMPEROR: What? *(laughter)*

COOK: *(patiently)* A new man arrived during the course of your majesty's slumber and is wanting to meet you.

The Kennedy farm. Set by Hascy Tarbox.

THE EMPEROR: If dis is anudder one o' yo practical tricks, I tells de ole' man. (*Without a word Cook and Tidd reach down, grab the Emperor and precipitately lift him out of the trap and onto the floor level.*)

TIDD: Newby, meet the Emperor!

NEWBY: (*Pleasantly, but without any appreciation of the humor of the situation.*) How do you do?

COOK: Well, Emperor, what have you to say?

EMPEROR: A speech? (*Groans from Leeman, Tidd, and the Coppocs.*) No, ah ain't goin' make no speech. Ah suggests that Mistah Taylor get out de fiddle, and we all sings.

WILLIAM THOMPSON: Fair enough!

COOK: Bravo, good idea! Watson, where's that mandolin?

WATSON BROWN: (*producing it*) Here, but there's only three strings.

COOK: All right, I'll pick at it somehow. 'Long's I have Taylor to follow. I will have you to follow won't I, Steward?

TAYLOR: (*Getting a battered violin case from behind one of the boxes.*) I'm afraid so.

DAUPHIN THOMPSON: Do you sing, Mr. Newby?

NEWBY: Why no, sir, not very well.

EDWIN COPPOC: That's all right. We none of us do, really, except Stevens and Tidd. They're honest-to-goodness musicians.

HAZLETT: Martha here ain't to be sneezed at, neither.

MARTHA: (*giggling*) Bert you fool! Neither's Cook.

COOK: Oh, we're all good, Newby! (*He and Taylor have been tuning their instruments. The men have settled themselves in comfortable positions—some on the floor—some on the boxes and crates which line the walls. Now they begin to sing.*)

ANNIE: (*In the kitchen—looks up apprehensively.*) They oughtn't to sing. We've aroused enough suspicion—

KAGI: Who's suspicious?

ANNIE: The neighbors. My, what a time I had with the little hen and chickens today!

KAGI: Mrs. Huffmaster?

ANNIE: (*nods*) She's been blackmailing me for kitchen utensils.

KAGI: Blackmailing? You don't mean she's on the right track!

ANNIE: Near enough to start an investigation, and you know what that would mean. I must say you and Newby didn't help matters—popping up that way.

KAGI: We? You'll have to grant we popped opportunely. Pandora had one of those boxes nearly opened.

ANNIE: Honestly? You know she's just bursting to know what we keep in them.

KAGI: Do you think she suspects?

ANNIE: Hardly. She isn't looking for pikes and Sharps rifles. (*laughs*) What she expects is tracks and switches from the Underground Railway! She knows this isn't a house, but she hasn't an inkling it's an arsenal.

KAGI: I hope you're right.

ANNIE: Oh, Johnnie, so do I! I've been so stupid! I feel almost as though I'd betrayed father's trust.

KAGI: Nonsense, Annie. He can't expect any more than what you've done.

ANNIE: But he does, and he has every right to. I was brought here all the way from North Elba to be his—his "watch-dog." It isn't much of a job.

KAGI: You've done everything possible! If anything goes wrong, it couldn't be your fault.

ANNIE: You know father, Johnnie, and you know that, with him, it's a question of principle. I've been assigned my work and, well—I must do it.

KAGI: (*Looking at her for a moment before he speaks.*) I know what you mean.—Osawatomie Brown wasn't born to fail. It isn't woven in the pattern of his life.—Well, you've been faithful. This watching business must be hard on the nerves.

ANNIE: It's lonely. (*Kagi kisses her.*) But I like the evenings. (*Smilingly Kagi goes to the door and opens it.*)

KAGI: (*quoting*) "For the night shows stars and women in a better light."

ANNIE: (*Going to the door and standing next to Kagi, looking out.*) The moon'll be coming up most any time now. I love the moon.

KAGI: (*Taking her face in his hands and looking long and gravely into her eyes.*) Darling, I love you. (*They go out on the porch together. The moon has not yet risen and they are almost in darkness. In the parlor, the singing continues for a bit. Jerry Anderson is telling Leeman his fortune with cards.)*

LEEMAN: *(Impetuously, but not so loud as to drown out the music.)* You're a liar, Anderson. You're faking.

ANDERSON: *(calmly)* Here's your card.

LEEMAN: *(Stares at the card for a moment and then leaps up, drawing his revolver. The board on which they have been playing crashes noisily to the floor. The music ceases abruptly and everyone turns. After a moment Leeman speaks—)* Why you, why you God damned—

STEVENS: *(fiercely)* Leeman!

LEEMAN: *(to Stevens)* Go to Hell! *(Stevens with one long stride reaches Leeman and with the passionless science of an executioner cracks him a terrific blow on the face. Leeman falls to the floor.)*

STEVENS: *(quietly)* Watson, take your sister into the kitchen. *(Watson goes out with a very frightened Martha. They close the kitchen door behind them and stand there, silent and listening.)* *(Quietly)* Get up, Leeman! *(Roaring)* Get up, Leeman! *(Leeman, terrified, scrambles to his feet.)*

TIDD: *(to Stevens)* Shall I give it to him?

STEVENS: *(Shakes his head to Tidd's question and then speaks to Leeman.)* Gimme that gun. *(After a tense moment, Leeman slinks up to Stevens and hands him his revolver. Stevens takes it, looks at it, and then to Leeman. Instead of exploding as we had expected him to, he speaks in a quiet, reproachful voice—)* Why, Billy, I'm surprised at you. Ain't ya got no manners? *(He begins to unload the revolver, very slowly and deliberately. The other men watch him in silence. In the kitchen, Martha looks anxiously at Watson.)*

MARTHA: What'll he do to him, Watson?

WATSON BROWN: Nothin' much, I don't think.

STEVENS: It isn't enough that you smoke cigarettes and get drunk agin' the ole man's orders, but you have to carry on and curse in front of his son's wife, a little girl, even younger than you are.

LEEMAN: Listen, Stevens, Anderson can't pull that stuff with me. Nobody can and get by with it.

STEVENS: What happened, Jerry?

ANDERSON: I was predicting Bill's future. The reading was unfortunate.

LEEMAN: He said I'd die at Harpers Ferry. That I'd be the first to fall.

STEVENS: The trouble with you, Billy, is you're too quick on the draw. This ain't Kansas.

LEEMAN: *(under his breath)* I know it ain't. It's Hell!

STEVENS: *(angered)* What d'ya mean by that?

LEEMAN: *(loudly)* I said—Hell. Ed Coppoc and Dauphin may like it—waitin' round for months on end, hidin' away in a cellar and singin' hymns, but I don't. I'm a fighter, I ain't a little girl.

STEVENS: We ain't none of us little girls, Leeman. Maybe you're a little baby. *(Leeman makes a start for him, but Cook holds his arms from behind.)* I mean that Billy! As a fighter, you're a cracker-jack, but the man in ya ain't growed up, I guess. You're too young.

LEEMAN: A man I s'pose is a fella who can squat in a farm-house for two months, and talk big about military tactics!

STEVENS; No, a man is a fella who can take his medicine.

LEEMAN: By medicine, you mean waitin'? *(Stevens doesn't reply.)* Aw, it's easy enough for you to talk high and mighty, but you don't know what I go through.

STEVENS: Oh, don't I? *(A murmur from the others, laughing bitterly.)* Do you think you're the only one of the lot of us that gets tired of waitin'? I'm just as bad off as you are, worse. I'm bred on deserts and prairies. I wasn't born for book-reading and fortune-telling and roofs. I gotta' have sunshine and starlight—distance miles in front of me and behind. I wasn't brought into the world to stay screwed in one spot like a toadstool.

LEEMAN: What's keepin' ya screwed? *(Stevens with a sound of disgust turns away.)*

THOMPSON: *(In his kindly, fatherly tone.)* Same as what's keepin' you, Billy, and all of us—an idea. That idea says men hide in a cold cellar for half a year. We gotta' collect money and ammunition. So, we hides.

TIDD: Some of us keep cool and some of us don't. But we all hide.

LEEMAN: You're a fine one to talk. You lose yer temper, but you don't hide. 'Less it's away from your friend Stevens down at the Ferry! *(Tidd makes an angry pass at Leeman, but he is restrained.)*

STEVENS: *(A little pettishly—coming quickly to Tidd's defense.)* Well, Tidd didn't pull a gun! *(Then, realizing his own smallness.)* Oh, I know, we're all pretty bad, Billy. This waitin' is powerful hard on all of us and we don't bear up so well under the strain. But we all got this—this idea, and we gotta stick by it.

LEEMAN: Whata' ya talkin' about?

COOK: *(ecstatically)* That idea, Bill. That wonderful, splendid thing—it brings us here, it keeps us here. It puts the sword in our hands.

LEEMAN: *(coldly)* Name it. *(Cook stares at him blankly.)* Cook, you're talkin' through yer hat. Name it!

COOK: *(bewildered)* Why, I—what do you mean?

LEEMAN: Go ahead, name it! Just what is this splendid idea that can send me to my death?

COOK: Well, you see it's—

LEEMAN: *(shouting)* NAME IT!

COOK: I—I can't—*(Leeman fixes Cook with a contemptuous gaze.)*

LEEMAN: *(After a pause—speaking very quietly.)* Well, I can—*(shouting)* I CAN! *(He turns on his heels and stalks gravely over to Anderson offering his hand—speaking very quietly.)* I'm sorry, Anderson. *(Anderson takes Leeman's hand silently—a kind, but a typically impersonal smile on his face. Leeman turns around and notices Cook again, who stands staring at him, hurt and bewildered.)* Play yer damned fiddle, Cook! Let's have some music. *(Cook looks at him stupidly, his fingers twitching nervously over the strings of his guitar. Taylor picks up his violin and begins to play. Cook joins him, and, in a bit, there is singing. Leeman retires to a corner laughing to himself hysterically.)*

MARTHA: *(In the kitchen turns away from the door after the singing has begun.)* Well, I'm glad they've fixed it up. Billy Leeman has a wicked temper, but he means well.

WATSON BROWN: *(Getting paper, pen, and ink from the cupboard.)* We're all short-tempered these days. It's the waiting and the close confinement. *(Goes to the little table, puts down his supplies, and sits down on a chair.)* It must be terrible on the Kansas men.

MARTHA: It's just as hard on you what with Bella and the baby.

WATSON BROWN: Nonsense, every man in there has somebody waiting for him. Even Aaron Stevens has a sweetheart, though he doesn't talk much about her.

MARTHA: Her name is Jennie Dunbar. He talks to me about her.

WATSON BROWN: *(smiling)* I know, everybody confides in you, Martha. What a mother you'll make!

MARTHA: *(ecstatically)* Oh! I hope so Watson! *(pause)*—I hope so. *(Watson begins writing. The quill scratches on the paper and awakes Martha from her reverie.)* What are you writing? *(She goes around behind him)* A letter to Isabella?

WATSON BROWN: *(Nodding, without looking up.)* Mm—mm.

MARTHA: *(Looking over his shoulder. Watson stops writing, as she reads aloud—)* "My dearest Bella—" *(Watson resumes writing.)* You're very much in love aren't you, Watson?

WATSON BROWN: *(Stops, looking up earnestly.)* Oh, very much!

MARTHA: *(thoughtfully)* We're fortunate, we couples who can stay near to one another. It doesn't usually work out that way with your father's plans. When he calls, the men folks just has to pick up and go. *(She turns away, her voice strained with repressed emotion.)* I wonder what's happened to Oliver—he's never been this late.

WATSON BROWN: Running another shipment of arms with Owen. Anything might happen to them. *(Martha starts apprehensively. Watson, seeing he has frightened her, speaks with an assumed indifference, rapidly.)* I mean, well, you know they might have met up with Father, and been sent on another errand. There's a million things might have delayed them.

MARTHA: *(soberly)* I know it. *(She goes into the parlor. Her destination is one of the crates into which the supper dishes have been dumped just before Mrs. Huffermaster's arrival. Jerry Anderson is seated on the crate next to it. His cards are arranged in a strange pattern in front of him on the board which he and Leeman were using. Jerry has taken no part in the singing but has brooded silently over his game, occasionally changing a card or shuffling the pack. Now Martha goes up to the box beside him, unlocks it, opens the lid and drags out an immense tablecloth, knotted at the ends to form a bag which is full of dishes. She drops it in front of her to get a breath as the song ends.)*

ANDERSON: *(Looking—not at her—but at his cards.)* You are worried, Miss Martha. You have been thinking of Oliver Brown.

MARTHA: He's a whole day late. Naturally, I worry.

ANDERSON: *(In his kind, but impersonal voice.)* Naturally. *(He turns over a card.)*

THOMPSON: *(Who is sitting nearby and has overheard this conversation.)* Naturally's right. They've only been married a couple a' months. *(Martha looks at him. Jerry gravely turns over another card.)*

ANDERSON: Your husband is safe, Miss Martha, and will return from the venture.

MARTHA: Of course, he will.

ANDERSON: *(Putting the last card on top of another.)* Oliver is your life a—necessity? *(There is a faint note of polite questioning in his voice. Enough to keep his words from sounding rude.)*

MARTHA: *(As Jerry turns over another card.)* I'd die without him. *(Jerry looks at his cards and then gravely at Martha, fixing her with his deep, far-seeing gaze. Misunderstanding his look.)* Well, I would—

ANDERSON: *(With quiet sadness.)* My dear—you will. *(Martha stares at him for a moment and then picks up the tablecloth full of crockery and goes into the kitchen.)*

MARTHA: *(After a pause during which she has stood motionless at the door with her arms full of dishes.)* Watson—

WATSON BROWN: *(writing)* Yes, dear?

MARTHA: You said everybody here has a wife or a sweetheart.

WATSON BROWN: *(still writing)* Mm—yes—

MARTHA: Well, I don't think Jerry Anderson has. *(Watson smiles and goes on writing.)* You know, he says the funniest things. I don't blame Billy a bit. *(In the parlor, Steward Taylor has begun a violin solo.)*

WATSON BROWN: *(For the first time since Martha's re-entrance, he looks up from his writing.)* Listen! Steward Taylor's playing that piece Father likes so much—"Serenade" by Schubert.

MARTHA: Steward Taylor's a spiritualist, too.

WATSON BROWN: What?

MARTHA: And so's Aaron Stevens, but he doesn't show it.

WATSON BROWN: What?!

MARTHA: They're all crazy. They must be.

WATSON BROWN: What on earth are you talking about?

MARTHA: Spiritualism, occult science, and boogey-boogey. He and Jerry held a séance the other night while you was in Chambersburg. They said they "got" Nat Turner. Isn't that nonsense?

WATSON BROWN: Maybe not.

MARTHA: It's pure heathenism. Nat Turner, my sakes! T'ain't Christian.

(Watson shrugs and goes back to his writing. Martha begins to wash dishes; filling a tub with warm water that has been heating on the stove and plunging the dishes in, wiping them, and putting them in place. The moon has been rising during latter-half of this last scene and now the two lovers, Kagi and Annie, are revealed sharply in its yellow light.)

KAGI: "The stars are forth, the moon above the tops
  Of the snow-shining mountains.—Beautiful!
  I linger yet with Nature, for the night
  Hath been to me a more familiar face
  Than that of man; and in her starry shade
  Of dim and solitary loveliness
  I learn'd the language of another world."

ANNIE: The language of another world—Father knows that language. He goes off by himself, and something in the night talks to him. He says that the stars have a song, a kind of anthem and that if I listened long enough, I could hear it. It must be very beautiful. *(Kagi is silent.)* I believe that. You don't believe in anything, do you, Johnnie?

KAGI: No, dearest.

ANNIE: Not anything at all?

KAGI: No, dearest.

ANNIE: Don't you even believe in me?

KAGI: *"Wenn ich dich lieb habe, was geht's dich an?"*

ANNIE: (*awed*) You're very clever, aren't you, Johnnie?

KAGI: No, Annie, it's the moon.

ANNIE: What do you mean—the moon?

KAGI: Dogs bark at it, young people make love under it, and other people go crazy. It shines down on poets and they write verses. It shines down on me and I recite them.

ANNIE: How can you help doing those other things?

KAGI: What for instance—barking?

ANNIE: No, making love.

KAGI: *"Omnia vincit amor nos et cedamus amori."* (*He takes her in his arms. The music stops.*)

ANNIE: That was an unhappy kind of kiss. (*Looking at him thoughtfully.*) It's goin' to look splendid when it grows longer.

KAGI: Darling, what?

ANNIE: Your beard, silly. (*a pause*) Hear the trees whispering together and the little creatures crying in the tall grass. Do you suppose they're talking about us! (*Kagi doesn't reply. He is rapt in his own thoughts.*) Johnnie!

KAGI: Yes, dear.

ANNIE: Do you suppose they're talking about us?

KAGI: Good Heavens! Who?

ANNIE: The little creatures, you know the crickets.

KAGI: I hardly think so. They're probably discussing the next presidential election.

ANNIE: Why should they be doing that?

KAGI: Crickets are devoted to big, weighty questions. They haven't any time for love.

ANNIE: Do you suppose if they ever get around to thinking about it, they'd say we were wicked to be in love?

KAGI: (*Testy, quite suddenly—*) Why the devil should you say that?

ANNIE: (*Misinterpreting the nervous note in his voice, impishly—*) I just wondered. (*Kagi stares at her for a long moment and then turns away.*)

KAGI: Darling, don't reproach me, I'm miserable enough as it is.

ANNIE: Johnnie—what do you mean? I'm not reproaching you!

KAGI: Maybe you're not, Annie. Maybe it's just my imagination. But God knows you ought to. I deserve to be horse-whipped! Leaving Chambersburg, deserting my post to come down here and visit you—doing that time and time again—that was enough!

ANNIE: Well, if I'm not worth a sacrifice to your precious sense of duty—

KAGI: I'm a soldier, Annie.

ANNIE: I know that, but—well, if you don't love me—

KAGI: That's just it, Annie, I do love you. Love, don't you understand, not just desire. I've told you dozens of times I have no religion, well I lied, I have a religion. *(ecstatically)* A deity presides over it, a great and powerful God. His word is in no holy books, its abiding place is in no tabernacle either of bricks or stars, neither is it extolled in astral harmonies or in the clashing of comets. He is unnamed in the firmament and his word—his word—is enshrined, in the high places of my heart.

ANNIE: You mean a great—conviction.

KAGI: *(bitterly)* John Brown has a great conviction. He's a great man—I have only an urge.

ANNIE: *(Shocked at the idea which has occurred to her.)* Johnnie! You don't mean that—our love—is in some way—against your beliefs?

KAGI: *(patiently)* I tell you I have no belief. I have only opinion. *(In the same tone as before.)* "And at the right hand of the Lord there stands an Archangel—"

ANNIE: You're crazy, Johnnie! You're talking crazy!

KAGI: Sure, I am. I'm insane. I've—I've heard it! Do you know what I mean? *(Annie doesn't reply.)* There's a rhythm we all hear—you and I and those people in the house—a rhythm as insistent and as undeniable as your own pulse-beats.—The great tramp of marching feet, the heavy, chained footsteps of a captive race. That's why we're here—because we hear it.

ANNIE: *(slowly)* Yes, I know—

KAGI: *(At once ironic and dreadfully earnest.)* Someday, at the proper conjunction of Mars and Venus and the exchequer, we're going to arise, all of us, and gird up our loins and attempt to halt that hideous procession. We'll die—

ANNIE: Johnnie! You mustn't—

KAGI: We'll die. As others have died before us and as others will die in the years to come. We'll die, most of us, like martyrs. The skies will shine at our passing, and the Heavenly Gates will swing open to receive us, and a divine military band will play something impressive as we go to join the great army of the Lord. That's all very fine. But how about that other army of the Lord, that little broken, wretched army we'll leave behind us, on earth—an army of ruined lives—mothers and sweethearts and sixteen-year-old widows with fatherless children. Oh God, no! Martyrdom isn't worth it! I have a few things to sacrifice, my life, for instance—my future, and a little honor among men. I'm giving all that to John Brown—everything except your happiness. He can't have that!

ANNIE: I think I begin to understand. We're to be like the crickets. We're to "devote our lives to big, weighty questions." We haven't any time for love. (*The sound of horse's hooves growing rapidly louder.*)

KAGI: Sounds like they're coming this way. (*He opens the door and speaks into the kitchen.*) Watson! Somebody coming up! Quiet the boys. Quick! (*Watson jumps up from his writing and runs into the parlor.*)

WATSON BROWN: Hey quiet! Shut up that music! (*The music stops instantly.*)

DAUPHIN THOMPSON: What's wrong?

TIDD: (*roughly*) Lay low! (*Sudden silence—everyone standing absolutely still, not daring to move, waiting. Martha is in the kitchen, a little frightened, and on the porch, Annie and Kagi are straining their eyes trying to make out their visitors in the darkness. There is the sound of dismounting, the jingle of harnesses, and then the approaching footsteps of two men.*)

ANNIE: (*Recognizing them with a little cry of relief.*) It's Oliver and Owen, I might have known! (*They come into the light.*)

OWEN BROWN: Hello, John Henri! Hello, Annie! (*He kisses her.*)

KAGI: Hello how's everything!

OLIVER BROWN: (*Shaking hands with Kagi.*) I reckoned you'd be back to Chambersburg by this time.

KAGI: I should be right enough.

OLIVER BROWN: Sure, I know. (*To Annie*) Where's Martha? In the kitchen?

ANNIE: (*nods assent*) Mm—mm.

OLIVER BROWN: (*Speaking to Kagi.*) Say, we've got bad news for you—

MARTHA: (*Overhearing his voice and grabbing him just as he backs into the kitchen.*) Oliver!

OLIVER BROWN: Martha, My sweet! (*They embrace.*)

KAGI: (*To Owen*) What's the news? What does he mean? (*Owen with an apprehensive glance at the two in the kitchen whispers something to Kagi and Annie. They are shocked at what he says and stand on the porch stunned as Owen steps into the kitchen past Oliver and Martha to the parlor doorway, smiling at Watson who stands near it.*)

OWEN BROWN: Hello, Watson. Give me a hand outside with this gear. (*Starting to go into the Parlor.*) Come on—let's go through this way.

(*Watson follows, closing the door behind him. In the kitchen, Martha and Oliver embrace and on the porch, Kagi gives Annie's hand a reassuring little pat. The men, who have been crouching uneasily waiting for something to happen, expecting almost anything, are respectively amused, annoyed, irritated, or relieved at discovering the cause of the alarm. There is a general murmur. Cries of "Owen!" "So, it's you." "Hello, Owen," etc.*)

OWEN BROWN: 'Lo, boys! (*Noticing Newby, and going up to him.*) You're Dangerfield Newby, aren't you? My name's Owen Brown. (*Newby and Owen shake hands. The men murmur during all of this.*)

STEVENS: Have you got that last shipment, Owen?

OWEN BROWN: Yes, but we had a lot of trouble over it.

HAZLETT: (*This line overlapping Owen's.*) You certainly gave us a start. What did Annie take you for anyway?

COOK: Personally, I expected anything from a bomb to a Huffmaster!

STEVENS: It'll be a great relief now, to have a real belly-laugh.

OWEN BROWN: Well, you'll just have to get along without it. Oliver and I met up with father a piece back. He stopped at the cabin, but you can expect him in here any time now. You know what he thinks about noise-making here at headquarters. So, shut up—if only for Annie's sake. (*He turns to go out.*) Come along, Bill, we need another hand. (*Owen, Bill Thompson and Watson go out, shutting the door behind them.*)

MARTHA: (*In the kitchen.*) Oliver, I've worried so. Why are you late?

OLIVER BROWN: I—Dearest, I have something to tell you.

MARTHA: (*Burying her head in his arms—in a small happy voice.*) And I have something to tell you. Something awful important—

OLIVER BROWN: You'd better let me finish what I have to say. It's bad news.

MARTHA: Oh, Oliver!

OLIVER BROWN: Father's due here any minute. Owen and I have just been talking to him—he—well, he gave us orders—

MARTHA: Yes?

OLIVER BROWN: You see—now we've brought in the last lot of rifles. We'll be ready to strike most any time. (*Oliver looks at Martha; there is no understanding in her face.*) You and Annie'd better start packing—you're to leave for North Elba in the morning.

MARTHA: (*After a long and dreadful silence; too stunned to speak. Finally, with difficulty—*) in—the—morning—? (*Oliver nods gravely.*)

OLIVER BROWN: That's orders—

MARTHA: Oliver, I can't—I can't go. (*pause*) I just can't—tomorrow—it's—tomorrow's baking-day. (*Suddenly she is in tears, hysterical, Oliver comforting her.*)

ANNIE: (*On the porch, bravely.*) Of course, it—it has to be.

KAGI: Of course, dear.

ANNIE: (*Brave, still, but the note of tragedy creeps into her voice.*) I think it was—worthwhile.

STEVENS: (*In the parlor, speaking very quietly.*) So, the old man is back—

TIDD: Where's he been?

STEVENS: Up in the mountains. You know, getting inspiration!

COOK: Having—visions—

HAZLETT: (*under his breath*) Nonsense.

STEVENS: (*Who has overheard Hazlett.*) It ain't nonsense, and don't you go talkin' that way about John Brown. He has vision. It's a great thing. (*Sobs from Martha in the kitchen all during this.*)

THE EMPEROR: I had a vision visit me once, when I was a slave. (*Tidd and a few others laugh.*)

COOK: (*politely*) Tell us about it, Emperor. What was the vision?

THE EMPEROR: Oh, it were jes' like every vision, I reckon.

COOK: I've never had a vision, Emperor. Tell me, who was in it?

THE EMPEROR: De Lord.

COOK: (*awed*) "The Lord!"

ANDERSON: (*Reciting in the sing-song cadence of a minister.*) "Now it came to pass as I was amongst the captives, the heavens were opened and I saw visions of God."

COOK: Tell me, what was it like, could you—describe it!

ANDERSON: (*Still reciting, a touch, very slight, of irony in his voice.*) "As the appearance of the bow that is in the cloud in the day of rain, so was the appearance of the brightness around about. This was the appearance of the likeness of the glory of the lord."

COOK: Shut up, Anderson! Emperor, please tell me about it!

ANDERSON: "And when I saw it, I fell upon my face, and I heard a voice of one that spake. And he said unto me—"

COOK: (*furious*) Damn it all, will you shut up!

ANDERSON: (*After a moment—coldly.*) You're a strange man to be worrying about visions.

COOK: (*fiercely*) Why shouldn't I? (*With a sudden change of mood, he turns aside and speaks quietly, pitifully to himself.*) All my life I've waited and prayed for—inspiration—for, well—for a vision. It's hard to feel, or-dained—chosen—without something. Ego isn't enough.

TAYLOR: (*gravely*) What did your vision say to you, Emperor?

THE EMPEROR: Ah was a slave den, you know. De Lord raised his hand an' pointed at de North star. "Emperor," say de Lord—"git outa dis mess," So ah got.

COOK: (*eagerly*) How did the Lord look? What was he like?

THE EMPEROR: (*Scratching his head.*) Well—(*The others wait for his reply. Finally, after a considerable pause.*) As ah remembers it, he looked a power-ful like—John Brown. (*The men in the parlor are silent at this. There is not the sense of relaxation; they remain tense as when waiting for the Emperor to speak. In the kitchen, Martha is tense, still weeping, and her head on her husband's shoulder.)*

OLIVER BROWN: Martha, Martha—we must be brave. It's father's orders.

MARTHA: Oh, no, Oliver, no! He can't send me away. He mustn't separate us. Jerry Anderson was right. I'll die without you.

OLIVER BROWN: Martha! We've all got to sacrifice something—look at Annie—

MARTHA: *(The idea suddenly striking her.)* And look at your mother—the mother of John Brown's children. There's the hero.

OLIVER BROWN: So are you, sweetheart.

MARTHA: No, I'm not, I'm not, Oliver. I don't come from your stock. My folks is just plain common people. I ain't a Brown. I'm a Brewster. Sacrifice! It ain't in my blood!

OLIVER BROWN: What a' you talkin' about Martha?

MARTHA: *(wonderingly)* You don't know do you? *(Oliver looks at her and then understands.)*

OLIVER BROWN: *(Pressing her close to him.)* Sacrifice—I sometimes think that's what we came into the world for—

COOK: *(awed)* It's—it's wonderful.

TIDD: *(gruffly)* What is?

COOK: The Emperor's vision. I wish I could understand—

STEWARD TAYLOR: *(very earnestly)* There's nothing wonderful about a vision.

LEEMAN: *(sneering)* There's nothing wonderful about corn likker!

COOK: No, seriously—

LEEMAN: *(curtly)* I don't believe in visions—

STEVENS: *(Quickly, but not assertively.)* Neither do I, you see—

COOK: Of course, you don't. Neither do the Coppocs or the Thompsons, I'll bet. But they believe in God. We all have differences of opinion. Jerry Anderson's a Universalist, Perry Anderson's a Christian, and when nobody's around Steward Taylor and Stevens turn out the lights and hold long conversations with Nat Turner! Nobody believes alike. Dangerfield Newby believes in his wife and children, Hazlett and I believe in John Brown, John Kagi is a rationalist and he doesn't believe in anything. But that's belief. We all of us think different things, and those thoughts differ—widely, but I say there's something we all believe. Some one thing—I can't describe it quite, but I know what it is—some one thing we all have in common. We maybe react individually, according to our natures and opinions, and for some, I'm sure this light—this belief—must seem much brighter and clearer, they must understand it better, than—than the rest of us.

STEVENS: We all know what you're talkin' about Edwin.

ANDERSON: *(to Cook)* But you don't.

COOK: What's that?

ANDERSON: You're hiding that light under a bushel called John Edwin Cook. You talk about beliefs; you say you and Hazlett believe in John Brown. How can you? How can you possibly believe in anything except yourself?

HAZLETT: *(coldly)* I don't believe in John Brown.

STEVENS: Shut up, Hazlett!

HAZLETT: Well, I don't. I believe in the man—but I don't believe in his ideas.

STEVENS: Just what do you mean by that?

HAZLETT: What I said. His ideas are wrong. His tactics. His whole plan's wrong.

STEVENS: John Brown is the best tactician on the face of the globe! He was studyin' tactics in Europe before you was born!

HAZLETT: Well, as Cook says, we all of us think different things.

STEVENS: *(furious)* Why, I'm a better tactician than you are! And I say, the Harpers Ferry plan is right. I know it is. I'm a soldier.

HAZLETT: Yeah, a soldier! You was given a death sentence that it took the President of the United States to get you out of. High Treason, wasn't it, or something like that. Interferin' with a higher officer in the exercise of his duty, beatin' him on the head with your soldier's bugle—

STEVENS: *(Starting towards him.)* I'll beat you on the head with my soldier's fist.

TIDD: *(Threateningly to Hazlett.)* Yeah—*(There is a sudden confusion. Men restrain the fighters, shouting, angry, murmuring, bedlam. Cook has been sitting well to the front away from the others, brooding over what Jerry Anderson has said to him. In the midst of the noise, he looks up, an expression of wonder, ecstasy on his boyish face. He starts up, shouting wildly.)*

COOK: LISTEN! *(The confusion diminishes at this and many of the men turn to look at him, but some of the brawling continues.)* LISTEN! GOD DAMN YOU! LISTEN!!

(At this all noise stops abruptly. Everyone stands where they are and for a moment there is absolute silence. Then little by little a sound insinuates itself into their ears, growing rapidly louder and louder until the close of the act. It is the "rhythm" Kagi has spoken about. The ominous, pulsing and pounding of numberless feet, marching in chains. As the sound grows louder, everyone faces forward raising their heads and staring upward with a common look of religious joy. The lights brighten in the

kitchen as Oliver steps away from Martha and with head uplifted, stands practically at attention in a sort of tribute. Martha hears the marching, but for her, it lacks meaning. She looks wonderingly before her, dazed and confused.

Then the moonlight grows brighter on the porch. Annie is about to enter the kitchen, her hand on the knob when "the marching" begins. She looks up with the rest as does Kagi, then her eyes meet his. With a grave smile, they clasp hands. She is on the porch and Kagi on the steps looking up at her.)

COOK: *(Relaxing his tense position and turning to the others.)* That's it! That's what I mean! Isn't it wonderful! *(There is no reply to this. The sound of the marching increases.)* I heard it! I heard it first! I heard it before any of you! I heard it in the midst of all that noise, while you were fighting among yourselves! My light's under a bushel is it? *(There is not a movement from anyone in the house. None indicates in any way that he is aware of Cook's existence. All are motionless as statues—after a moment Cook continues.)* I hear it plain. Plainer'n I ever hoped I could hear it. Glory-be-to-God. Hallelujah—it's a vision! I'm chosen, I tell you. You're not the only ones! I'm chosen, too! I'm ordained!

(Suddenly, with one accord the men turn to the center door. It opens slowly and the sound of the marching grows louder as John Brown enters the room. The scene ends.)

Scene VIII

Scene—The Engine House in the United States Arsenal at Harpers Ferry, an uninteresting brick structure, barren and impersonal, stone-paved and full of echoes. Three great doors topped by many-paned half-circular windows take up an entire side of the building. The hose and fire apparatus have been moved away and the doors, still opened, reveal a great expanse of the luminous outside. The whole picture is brilliant with autumnal moonlight.

In the center doorway, silhouetted against the sky, is John Brown. For a while, he stands there, in silence, triumphant and alone until, as the sound of marching dies away, there appear in the other portals, certain of his men. Cook, followed by William and Dauphin Thompson and the Coppoc brothers, Barclay and Edwin, with Leeman, Newby, Jerry Anderson, Hazlett and Stewart Taylor, march by their general, heavily armed. The other marching merges into the sound of theirs and, as they stop, turning about to face John Brown in a long line stretching completely across the doorways, there is absolute silence.

JOHN BROWN: *(After a pause.)* Harpers Ferry is ours, gentlemen.
COOK: Hallelujah!

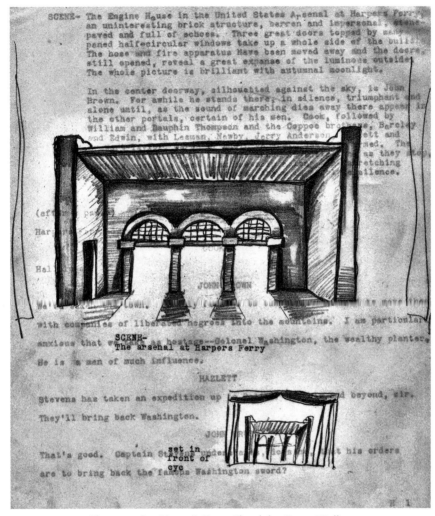

The arsenal at Harper's Ferry. Sketch by Orson Welles.

JOHN BROWN: We've taken the town. It only remains to take prisoners and to move them, with companies of liberated Negroes, into the mountains. I am particularly anxious that we take as hostage—Colonel Washington, the wealthy planter. He is a man of much influence.

HAZLETT: Stevens has taken an expedition up to Bolivar Heights and beyond, sir. They'll bring back Washington.

JOHN BROWN: That's good. Captain Stevens understands, does he, that his orders are to bring back the famous Washington sword?

HAZLETT: *(doubtfully)* I don't know, sir.

COOK: Well, he'd better!

JOHN BROWN: It would be fitting that the first blow in this new battle for freedom should be struck with the sword of George Washington. It was something I had planned. *(quickly)* It's not dawn yet, you'd better rest for a minute. —Company dismissed! *(The men unshoulder their rifles and move into the building, grouping at the right portal.)*

DAUPHIN THOMPSON: Judas Priest, it's cold!

LEEMAN: *(Laughing nervously.)* Well, Jerry, I'm not dead yet!

ANDERSON: *(quietly)* Not yet.

COOK: *(To himself, with suppressed hysteria.)* Canaan! That's it! We're at the threshold of Canaan!

THOMPSON: *(To Hazlett)* Where's he gonna' collect the prisoners, here in the Engine House?

HAZLETT: Maybe at the rolling-mills. I don't know.

LEEMAN: I notice Stewart Taylor ain't dead neither. God, you spiritualists is bluffs!

STEWART TAYLOR: *(Under his breath.)* Shut up, Leeman!

EDWIN COPPOC: *(To William Thompson and Hazlett.)* So, this is the "Engine House?"

COOK: *(ecstatically)* This is the River Jordan. The far bank is Canaan! Canaan! The Promised Land!

KAGI: *(Appearing in the left door, a lantern in one hand.)* The Promised Land! *(He comes inside and sets his lantern on the stone floor. It is bright and the whole building is lighted by its presence. Even John Brown in the center doorway is no longer a silhouette. Kagi speaks sarcastically.)* A wonderful land flowing with milk and honey!

JOHN BROWN: Well, Kagi, the slaves are free. We've struck the first blow.

COOK: Hallelujah!

KAGI: *(Imitating Cook)* Hallelujah! *(He fixes Cook with a grave glance and there follows a silence.)* You're right, the first blow has been struck, an unfortunate one. I should consider the blood we have so far shed, unpropitious—to say the very least.

JOHN BROWN: Blood, sir? We've taken the town without a loss.

KAGI: On the contrary, General Brown, there has been a loss—a tragic loss. One man, at least, tonight, has been wantonly or foolishly slaughtered.

JOHN BROWN: What man?

KAGI: A porter at the railway station. A man of comfortable circumstances and high repute in his community. A FREE NEGRO! *(Bitterly, looking intently at Cook.)* He offered no resistance, simply failed to understand a command. He was shot in the back. (*John Brown is too hurt to speak. After a silence—*) A good omen, that, for emancipation! (*Disgusted, he tosses his rifle to the floor. Cook sobs aloud. All turn to look at him.*)

JOHN BROWN: (*Looking away from Cook.*) This thing was decided at the beginning of the world, Kagi. It's not for us to question.

KAGI: (*testily*) There isn't any blunder, is there General, you can't fit into your neat little theory of predestination?

JOHN BROWN: Let's not argue, Kagi. We're not blundering—this is God's work.

COOK: (*Still sobbing a little to himself.*) Amen.

KAGI: (*furiously*) Holy! Holy! Holy! Jesus Christ Lord God! Won't you listen to reason?

OWEN BROWN: All right, Kagi, watch your tongue!

KAGI: I'm sorry, Owen, but can't you see with your eyes what a mess you're making of this? All of you, can't you think! Are you letting John Brown and a lot of Dark Age superstitions hypnotize you into thinking you're acting like men?

HAZLETT: Who's making a mess of this?

KAGI: You are! We all are! John Brown is making a mess of this, a mess!

JOHN BROWN: You'd better explain yourself, Kagi.

KAGI: I think you'd better do the explaining, General! I used to think you were incapable of failure—damn it, I still do! But what in hell is this?!

JOHN BROWN: This is war, Kagi. The beginning of the war to end slavery.

KAGI: I know all that! But why now?

JOHN BROWN: The hour is at hand! I've waited forty years for this!

KAGI: Well, if you've waited forty years for this, why can't you wait another two weeks? The mountain camps aren't ready yet! The Canadian armies aren't prepared! They don't know anything about this! The blow isn't scheduled for fourteen days!—Why ruin everything?

COOK: He hasn't, we can't fail!

KAGI: I know it! I know it! (*After a short silence—turning again to John Brown.*) But why blunder? Why upset our carefully planned schedule and deliberately weaken our position?

COOK: We'll succeed, I tell you! He isn't blundering!

KAGI: He is! We'll succeed, of course, we'll succeed. But tactically, from my point of view, this whole thing is a blunder.

JOHN BROWN: Gentlemen: I've studied abroad for nearly a whole lifetime in preparation for this thing which we are beginning tonight. But I ask you, all of you, not to believe in what I am doing as a tactician nor as a warrior, but as an administrator of the Divine word of God. You have all come to me that you might serve under me in the Holy War. If any of you wish to retire now you may, or, if now, that the sword has been drawn, you should, any of you, feel that another General should carry it—you have only to name him. No one will follow more cheerfully than I! If, on the other hand, I am to continue as your leader, I must require that you follow—and just as cheerfully, I must insist that you believe in me; devoutly, as you believe in the Bible; for I swear to you solemnly, gentlemen, that the Bible is no more inspired! There are only a few amongst you, who deny the existence of the Lord. You might just as well go over to the other side of the Mason and Dixon Line and deny that I exist. Perhaps, you'd better, for when I tell you that yesterday I stood on a mountain with the Lord of Hosts—with Jehovah—and that He spoke to me, just as He spoke to Moses on the mountain of Sinai, and dictated a plan of battle just as He dictated to Gideon—when I tell you that and you don't believe me, then there's no place for you here, and there's nothing else for you to do! (*A silence—and then—with finality.*) I'm not striking two weeks from now, I'm striking tonight! And I'm striking to-night because yesterday God told me to! (*At this moment, a little contingent of men carrying lanterns and rifles come in through the left door. Stevens is at the head, and after him come Tidd and Anderson leading the captive Colonel Washington. The Emperor brings up the rear.*)

STEVENS: (*saluting*) We've taken the prisoners, sir. The Allstadts, Byrne, and the others. They're under guard in the watch-room next door. This here is Colonel Washington. I brung him in 'cause I thought y' might wanta' talk to him.

COLONEL WASHINGTON: This is an outrage, suh—

JOHN BROWN: How d'ya do, Colonel Washington?

COLONEL WASHINGTON: (*Recognizing him.*) Isaac Smith!

JOHN BROWN: (*quietly*) My name is John Brown.

COLONEL WASHINGTON: John Brown!? You don't mean *the* John Brown? Osawatomie Brown?

JOHN BROWN: (*simply*) I tried to do my duty there. (*to Tidd*) Let the gentleman go. (*Washington is released.*)

COLONEL WASHINGTON: What are you doing here? What do you and your brigands want in Virginia? Money? (*An angry snarl at this, from the men.*)

JOHN BROWN: (*patiently*) There are many thousands of dollars in deposit here in the arsenal. None of it will be touched. We will take possession of a part of the government arms, but our principal object is to liberate the slaves.

COLONEL WASHINGTON: Insurrection!

JOHN BROWN: This is the first of a long series of attacks we shall make all over the South. I shall take leading white citizens as hostages and—

COLONEL WASHINGTON: The Blazes, suh! You can't take me prisoner! The people of Virginia won't stand for it suh!

JOHN BROWN: (*His eyes twinkling.*) I'm sure they won't like it. You're an Aide of Henry Wise, aren't you? And he's the Governor of the State.

COLONEL WASHINGTON: This is kidnapping! You'll hang for this!

JOHN BROWN: (*impatiently*) I advise you to be quiet, Colonel, and not make any trouble. You'll be treated with every kindness as long as you're in my hands. (*To Cook near to whom Washington has moved without noticing him.*) Take him away, Johnny. Put him in the watch-room with the other prisoners.

COOK: (*saluting*) Yes, sir. (*At the sound of his voice, Colonel Washington turns and his jaw drops as he recognizes him.*)

COOK: (*Humorously, taking Colonel Washington's arm and leading him off.*) Come along, Colonel!

ANDERSON: (*reciting*) "Do I not hate them, O, Lord, that hate thee, and am I not grieved with those that rise up against Thee. I hate them with perfected hatred. I count them mine enemies—"

JOHN BROWN: Where's that sword? (*No one replies.*) Where's that sword?!

STEVENS: Which sword, sir?

JOHN BROWN: You know what sword. You were detailed to get it from the man's house. The sword Fredrick the Great gave to George Washington.

STEVENS: (*After a moment's pause.*) I forgot, sir. I recollect you once said you wanted it—to use in the new revolution. But I had no orders, sir.

JOHN BROWN: (*furiously*) You had no orders?! I've got to have that sword, I tell ya! We can't go on without it!

O.P. ANDERSON: (*Stepping forward quietly.*) Excuse me, sir, but I remembered it. I took it off the wall when the others were over in the slave's quarters—freeing them.

JOHN BROWN: Where is it?

O.P. ANDERSON: I left it in care of some Negroes stationed in the component department.

JOHN BROWN: Go get it, Stevens.

STEVENS: Yes sir. (*He goes out.*)

(*John Brown turns away. His hands behind his back, he stares out into the night. There follows a very short silence.*)

THE EMPEROR: (*Plaintively, to himself.*) Golly, my legs is weary—

TIDD: (*His heartiness a little forced.*) Guess I'll sit down for a minute. It's been a hard night. (*He does, his action breaking a little of the tension. Several follow his example and there is general movement and noise as they settle themselves on the stone floor.)*

WATSON BROWN: *(In a half-whisper to Oliver.)* Everything's going fine as far as I can see.

OWEN BROWN: Sure, it is, but what are we waiting for?

HAZLETT: *(Mumbling to himself, disgustedly.)* That damn sword!

OLIVER BROWN: The sword is important.

THOMPSON: Anyway, we need a few minutes rest. It'll be daybreak pretty soon.

NEWBY: *(Coming to the door.)* Mr. Brown?

JOHN BROWN: Yes, Newby.

NEWBY: It's about the liberated slaves, sir. The ones stationed at the bridge.

JOHN BROWN: Well?

NEWBY: I can't keep them together, sir. They jest don't seem to want to fight.

JOHN BROWN: Have you impressed them with what they're fighting for? Their own liberty?

NEWBY: Yes, sir, I have, but it don't make any difference. A lot of 'em have deserted already. I think they're frightened, sir.

JOHN BROWN: *(after a moment)* Well—Go back and see what you can do.

NEWBY: Yes sir. *(He leaves.)*

JOHN BROWN: *(without turning)* How did the Washington slaves respond, Perry Anderson?

O.P. ANDERSON: They won't be much use to us, sir. They were given pikes and told they were free, but it doesn't seem to mean much to them. A few actually refused to come.

JOHN BROWN: The Negroes haven't acquitted themselves very well, have they, Anderson?

O.P. ANDERSON: No, sir, they haven't.

JOHN BROWN: A few, at least, seem enthusiastic?

O.P. ANDERSON: Sorry, sir, I don't think any are to be relied upon.

JOHN BROWN: *(After a moment's silence.)* Of course, it was to be expected. This is simple farm country and the slaves are underworked and over-fed. They're fairly well satisfied with their lot; some are even devoted to their master. We'll have better luck in the big cotton plantations further south.

O.P. ANDERSON: Yes sir.

ANDERSON: "This day will the Lord deliver thee unto my hands: and I will smite thee, and take thine head from thee; and I will give the carcasses of the host of the Philistines this day unto the fowls of the air and to the wild beasts of the earth, that all the earth may know that there is a God in Israel." (*Cook and Stevens carrying the famous Washington sword have appeared in the doorway.*)

STEVENS: (*Approaching John Brown and handing the sword to him.*) Here's the sword, sir. (*John Brown takes it and Stevens goes over to the other men. There is a hint of daylight outside.*)

ANDERSON: (*Still reciting.*) "Vengeance is mine saith the Lord—"

JOHN BROWN: (*Suddenly unsheathing the sword, exultantly.*) Gentlemen! Gentlemen! Rise up! (*The men scramble to their feet, expectantly. John Brown speaks the minute there is silence.*) The dawn is breaking! This is the hour ordained by God! Take up your arms! Be ready to march! Leeman, you and Taylor, and Perry Anderson will rejoin Copeland at the rifle works, Oliver and William Thompson will wait at the bridge with Leary and Dangerfield Newby, Owen you will go to the schoolhouse, you'd better take Tidd and Barclay Coppoc. The rest of you will return to your regular stations and await further orders. Hold yourself in readiness to leave at daybreak. We'll be in the mountains before noon. March, Gentlemen! March!

(*John Brown, still framed in the doorway, raises his sword aloft as the men march out and away into the early morning. Jerry Anderson, Kagi, and Cook remain. The sound of the marching dies away in the distance.*)

JOHN BROWN: THE SWORD OF THE LORD AND OF GIDEON! (*Suddenly a great unearthly light falls full upon him. He is transfigured. After a tremendous moment, the sword drops out of his hand and clatters to the floor. His arms have been stretched sideways in triumph and now a strange thing happens to them, they are momentarily paralyzed. Only the fingers of the hands clutch and writhe, and, with a shock, we realize that the attitude is no longer that of triumph but of crucifixion! In awful agony, unconscious that he is quoting, he speaks directly from the depth of his tortured soul.*) "O my Father, if this cup may not pass away from me, except I drink it. Thy will be done."

KAGI: My God! Look! (*Crossing himself, Cook sinks to his knees.*)

ANDERSON: (*breathlessly*) "And as he prayed, the fashion of his countenance was altered and his raiment was white and glistening." (*Kagi, after a moment, sinks to the ground.*)

JOHN BROWN: (*Pleading intensely, his plaintiveness almost childlike.*) O my Father, if it be possible, let this cup pass from me. (*Then with heroic resignation.*) Nevertheless, not what I will, but what Thou wilt. (*With a great cry, he wrenches his hands from the invisible nails that have held them, and, as he does so, a part of the light diminished—faintly to himself—*) Amen.

ANDERSON: (*Awed, half-whispering.*) He's discovered it! He's been shown the New Testament!

COOK: (*Like a little child.*) Dear God, I believe. . . . I believe. . . . (*The sun rises in the silence behind John Brown. The old man straightens and speaks bravely—*)
JOHN BROWN: We are now to fight this battle. We are to give our lives for it. (*Kagi starts to his feet.*)
COOK: I believe. I believe. . . .
JOHN BROWN: (*simply*) You will go to your posts and hold them—indefinitely.
KAGI: Do you realize that you're sentencing every one of us, your own sons—to death? (*Cook and Anderson get to their feet.*)
JOHN BROWN: Yes, Kagi, we are to die. (*After a moment.*) "For whosoever will save his life shall lose it, but whosoever will lose his life for my sake, the same shall save it." Now go!
(*After a pause, the three men go silently out of the building. Fist clenched, head upraised, John Brown stands alone—his back to the breaking day. The scene ends.*)

Scene IX

Scene—The interior of the Engine House early on the last morning. The great doorways have been closed and except for three small areas lit by shafts of sunlight pouring through the broken panes of the windows and an open lookout glowing in the paneling of the right-hand door, the scene is in darkness and deep-shadow. Stevens, Edwin Coppoc, and Dauphin Thompson are guarding the left and center doors, pressing their rifles to the chinks; the Emperor is sitting despondently on the floor; to the left, in a shadow huddled, are the prisoners; and in the middle, Jerry Anderson stands in a little patch of sunlight leaning on his gun, near his feet the prostrate bodies of Stewart Taylor, dead, and Oliver and Watson, dying. John Brown is at the look-out. Outside there is bedlam.

A huge mob of frenzied civilians and drink-crazed militia cheer wildly and howl for blood. There is a long pause. Oliver turns over and groans. Finally, the Emperor speaks—

THE EMPEROR: Lordy, but it's wicked cold in heah. Ain't been to sleep in sixty hours.
EDWIN COPPOC: None of us have. Not even that mob outside.
DAUPHIN THOMPSON: (*near hysteria*) Why do they keep howling, and shooting, and screaming like that? They've got us locked in here. What else are they yelling for?
OLIVER BROWN: (*in agony*) Blood. That's what they're yelling for. Blood!
DAUPHIN THOMPSON: Blood? Haven't they had enough?! (*A louder cry from outside, desultory shooting, and a furious howling.*)

ANDERSON: (*After a moment.*) And the mob cried out the more, crucify him!

STEVENS: They've had a bad scare and they're drunk. Mainly they're drunk. The saloons have been doing a lot of business.

OLIVER BROWN: I don't know why they have to cut up our bodies after they've finished with us. (*With a sharp intake of breath at the pain of his wound.*) You can't feel anything—after you're dead. Do you know—do you know what they did to Dangerfield Newby, Watson, after they were finished killing him? (*Watson only groans faintly. Oliver continues.*) They drove stakes into all of his wounds! They got him pinned to the ground right out there under the window, fixed up so's they can dance around him and spit in his face and curse at him. (*He starts painfully to his feet.*)

WATSON BROWN: (*with difficulty*) I wonder about his wife. Harriet is her name—and the little children. He told us he wasn't a hero—

OLIVER BROWN: (*Looking through a door-chink.*) God, Dauphin, gimme that gun! (*He attempts to wrest Dauphin's rifle from him, but the other holds it firmly and fixes him with a steady eye.*)

DAUPHIN THOMPSON: (*Slowly, looking quietly at Oliver.*) We've got to keep sane. They're using my brother William's corpse as a rifle target. (*Oliver falls to the floor, sobbing wildly.*)

OLIVER BROWN: Savages! They're not humans! Oh, God, I'll soon be dead. I'm dying—I wonder if they'll do that to me!

THE EMPEROR: What's de mattah?

OLIVER BROWN: (*In a delirium.*) Martha won't recognize me. She may never know what happened.

WATSON BROWN: What's wrong, Oliver?

OLIVER BROWN: (*Almost too horrified to speak.*) Newby—Dangerfield Newby—

THE EMPEROR: Yeah?

OLIVER BROWN: Oh, God! Those fiends out there, they've brought out a couple of pigs, some old sows—They're eating his guts! (*A sudden very loud round of musketry, and then renewed cheering and noise.*)

COLONEL WASHINGTON: (*Distinguishable in the dark mass that is the prisoners.*) I can only apologize, gentlemen, as a citizen of the land you have come to outrage. The atrocities of the past twenty-four hours are worse than a disgrace. Believe me, gentlemen, this—this trash outside is in no way representative of either Virginia or the South. (*Dauphin Thompson and the Emperor and Edwin Coppoc turn to look at him. The others have paid no attention whatever.*)

DAUPHIN THOMPSON: There's an awful lotta' "trash" out there.

EDWIN COPPOC: The whole militia is out—troops from Martinsburg, Hagerstown, Charles Town, and Shepherdstown. And there're thousands of others. Looks like every able-bodied man in Virginia and Maryland is out after our necks. It's a mighty representative group. (*The noise grows louder.*)

STEVENS: They're drunk and they're badly frightened. Nobody's responsible in that condition.

EDWIN COPPOC: Frightened? What have they to be frightened about? All our men have been killed, we're trapped in here without any way to get out, we haven't eaten or slept for three days and we're out-numbered ten thousand to one. I can't see why they should be frightened.

STEVENS: They think we got reinforcements in the hills. You don't 'spose we could have held this place so long, if they didn't, do ya? They're scared of a general uprisin' among the Negroes.

THE EMPEROR: (*mournfully*) They ain't much danger a' that. (*The noise outside rises to the crescendo, and, for a moment, it is deafening. Then it subsides and there follows a silence. We are aware of Jerry Anderson, leaning on his rifle in thought. At length, he turns and speaks to John Brown.*)

ANDERSON: All of our men, all of our brave little army, except those of us who are still alive in this room are either killed or unaccounted for. Kagi is dead. He died horribly. So did Leeman and William Thompson and the others. They fought like heroes and now they're gone. I suppose they may be considered martyrs. But there's nothing exalted about any of this butchering. That, I suppose, is the greatest martyrdom of all. This whole thing has been filthy and indecent, and posterity will hold its nose and say that we have died for what will be called the conviction of a single man. (*John Brown turns and looks at him.*) Will you make every sacrifice? Owen has been offered up with his brothers. Watson and Oliver here are dying. This thing is loathsome. The air is heavy with the stink of rotten bodies. Haven't we been sufficiently sensational? In the name of all that is beautiful and splendid, John Brown, say that we may not die—offensively.

JOHN BROWN: (*coldly*) We are to die.

ANDERSON: No one understands that more profoundly than I. Of course, we must die, we must be killed and offered up, just as the sun rises and sets and the rain falls. But why can't it be done just as beautifully?

JOHN BROWN: (*Regards Jerry Anderson unsympathetically for a moment and then calls.*) Stevens, come here! (*Stevens steps forward. John Brown is down on one knee before the corpse of Stewart Taylor.*) Get me a pike. (*Stevens goes to the darkest corner of the room, where the prisoners are huddled and comes carrying a long pole tipped with a sharp blade like a bayonet, the medieval "pike" with which John Brown dreamed to liberate the slaves. With a sudden movement, the old man rips the shirt off his dead follower's back. Taking the pike from Stevens, he ties the scrap of cloth flag-wise to its tip. This excited the prisoners who move and whisper among themselves.)*

THE EMPEROR: *(Getting up from the floor.)* De White flag!

COLONEL WASHINGTON: *(His voice rising out of the darkness above the murmur of the other prisoners.)* The flag of truce! Are you going to surrender?

JOHN BROWN: Go out there, Stevens, and tell whatever men may be leading these people that in consideration of all my men, either living or dead, or wounded, being soon safely in and delivered up to me at this point with all their arms and ammunition, we will take Colonel Washington and our other prisoners and—after crossing the Potomac bridge, we will set them at liberty.

STEVENS: *(Taking the pike, after a moment's pause.)* Yes, sir. *(He goes bravely to the center door, pauses for a second before opening it and then straightening, goes out.)*

COLONEL WASHINTON: Those terms are impossible. Don't you realize your position, Brown? They won't listen to anything but surrender!

JOHN BROWN: *(quietly)* Of course they won't. *(The interlude of silence is broken by the resounding crash of firearms.)*

DAUPHIN THOMPSON: *(At his post in the door crack.)* They've killed him. He's dead.

EDWIN COPPOC: Shot him down in cold blood! They must have seen that flag. *(John Brown pays no attention, not even turning to look out of his window.)*

ANDERSON: *(Peeking through the center door.)* He's only wounded. They're making him prisoner. *(The sound of distant cheering.)*

WATSON BROWN: *(Weakly, his eyes closed.)* What are they cheering for? Have we given up?

JOHN BROWN: We'll never give up, Watson.

ANDERSON: *(In reply to Watson's first question.)* I don't know; I can't see anything.

COLONEL WASHINGTON: Probably the arrival of the U.S. Troops! It's only a matter of time.

(The cheering diminishes and there follows a silence. Edwin Coppoc, Dauphin, the Emperor, and Jerry Anderson are at the doors looking out. Washington goes back into the darkness and John Brown remains as ever, immobile, his sons dying at his feet. Watson is propped up against the wall, calmly awaiting his fate. Oliver moves on the floor, in agony.)

OLIVER BROWN: Martha . . . Martha . . . Our baby, I'll never see it. I'll never live to see my child. My own child. *(writhes)* Oh, God! The pain!

JOHN BROWN: (*Turning to his window.*) It will pass. (*Oliver goes on groaning.*)

JOHN ALLSTADT: (*one of the prisoners*) Are you men all crazy? This leader of yours is a fanatic. This is the end. You can't hold out against the world! (*Only the Emperor turns to look at him.*) These two boys are dying. They've gotta' have medical attention. If you surrender you may save their lives.

JOHN BROWN: Sit down, Mr. Allstadt, and be quiet.

ALLSTADT: But why—

JOHN BROWN: You heard me! All of you prisoners. (*turning to them*) I want you all to be quiet. You haven't much longer to wait; pretty soon you can do the talking, but right now we're not interested in anything you got to say. (*Oliver screams in agony.*)

OLIVER BROWN: God, the pain! I can't stand it! Anything but this! Oh, God, I can't stand it! (*John Brown turns back to his lookout, his face drawn. Oliver crawls up to him.*) Father, put me out of this! I can't bear it! I can't bear this pain! (*He clutches pitifully at the old man's trousers looking anxiously up into his face. John Brown regards him in silence.*) Father! Father! Please! Take your gun and shoot me, through the head. I'm no good to you anymore. You shoot a horse when he's no good to you when he's in pain. For God's sake put me out of this! I can't stand it! I can't stand it!

JOHN BROWN: (*After a moment, looking away.*) If you've got to die, die like a man. (*A silence; Oliver looks at him pathetically.*)

OLIVER BROWN: (*With pitiful resignation.*) Yes, sir, I'll try to— (*Slowly, painfully, he crawls back to his spot on the floor and lays there struggling valiantly with his pain. The Emperor leaves his place at the door and starts over to the left corner of the building. Colonel Washington appears suddenly out of the shadows and takes his arm.*)

THE EMPEROR: Yes, suh?

COLONEL WASHINGTON: (*His finger on his lips.*) Shh!

THE EMPEROR: (*whispering*) Yes, suh. (*Washington draws him aside and then looks him over.*)

COLONEL WASHINGTON: (*In a quiet voice.*) I've had my eye on you for some time and now I remember—

THE EMPEROR: (*starting*) What's dat, suh? Remembah me?

COLONEL WASHINGTON: From before you ran away. I know your master. (*The Emperor starts in fear, but Washington maintains his grip on his arm.*)

COLONEL WASHINGTON: Don't be alarmed. He'll take you back, and if he doesn't I will. I'm badly short-handed myself.

THE EMPEROR: Back to slavery?

COLONEL WASHINGTON: Certainly, I'm willing to forget all about this. I don't think you have any idea what you're doing. You've been duped into it.

THE EMPEROR: Lordy, what 'ud the ole man say!

COLONEL WASHINGTON: That's just it. It won't make any difference what he says. He's as good as dead now. You are too, unless you listen to reason. And, believe me, I have your own well-being at heart. There's no need for this slaughtering of good, strong, peaceful niggers. It's practically murder.

THE EMPEROR: (Looking furtively about, whispering.) Do you mean, suh, yo kin get me out of this? Clean, scot-free?

COLONEL WASHINGTON: Scot-free! I'll pass you off as my own slave prisoner with the rest of us. It's your only chance. (A pause—the Emperor scratches his head. Finally—)

THE EMPEROR: Ah doan know. I rekon ah stays wid de ole man. (Washington turns away in disgust and, from far in the distance, there comes the sound of rolling drums and cheering.)

ALLSTADT: That's the U.S. Troops! I'm sure it is! You'd better say your prayers, Old Brown!

EDWIN COPPOC: (With an unexpected ferocity.) Will you shut up! (The sound of drumming grows louder.)

WATSON BROWN: (After a short pause, weakly.) I'm dying now, Oliver. This is just about my last minute. Give my love to Bella, will you, Oliver? The Thompsons will take care of her. Tell her I love her and tell her not to resent my death, or to feel hard against father, tell her I died—in a just cause. (The sound of drumming stops.) Someday all this fighting will be over, the North and the South will have had it out, and our little child will grow up in a free country, without slavery. Tell her that, will you Oliver? Oliver. (sharply) Oliver!

JOHN BROWN: (At the note in Watson's voice, he turns quickly from the window. On one knee, feeling Oliver's pulse, speaking slowly after a silence.) I guess he's dead. (There follows a pause. The men strain at their posts. Suddenly, with a jingle and click, all rifles are leveled at the right doorway and, after a moment, it opens and Lieutenant J.E.B. Stuart comes in. The prisoners rise and all look at him except John Brown, who stays at Oliver's side.)

STUART: Mr. John Brown?

JOHN BROWN: (Still on his knees, without turning.) Yes.

STUART: My name is Stuart, sir, Lieutenant J.E.B. Stuart of the First Cavalry, acting as Aide to the Commander of the special United States Forces commissioned yesterday by the President and the Secretary of War to put down this insurrection.

JOHN BROWN: (Still without turning.) Well?

STUART: I bear a communication from my Commander.

JOHN BROWN: (*Rising and drawing himself proudly to his full height.*) I won't give in. Your Commander had better fully understand that. I won't give in. (*For an answer, Stuart holds out to the old man the document he has been carrying. John looks at it look at it for a minute and then takes it.*)

JOHN BROWN: (*Opening it with a look at Stuart, he reads—*) "The Commander of the United States army sent by the President of the United States to suppress the insurrection at this place, demands the immediate and unconditional surrender of the persons now holding the armory buildings." (*He glances up from his reading, encounters Stuart's eye for a moment— then continues.*) "If they will peaceably surrender themselves and restore the pillaged property, they shall be kept in safety to await the orders of the President. It is represented to them in all frankness, that it is impossible for them to escape; that the armory is surrounded on all sides by troops and cannons and that, if the Commander is compelled to take them by force, he cannot answer for their safety. Signed: Colonel Commanding United States Troops, Robert E. Lee." (*John Brown lowers the paper and looks up as—the scene ends.*)

Scene X

Scene—The passageway before John Brown's cell in the Charles Town jail. Leaning against a large undecorated wall, which forms the larger portion of the scene, are the two newspapermen, Choley Archer and Rufus Wentworth. Wentworth is smoking a cigarette and Archer is lighting one as the scene opens. The murmur of an angry crowd, which began at the conclusion of John Brown's speech a minute before diminishes slightly, but continues.

ARCHER: (*Throwing a match away and puffing at the cigarette.*) Still making a damn racket.

WENTWORTH: I can't understand it. John Brown will be hanging from gallows before noon. Why would they want to lynch him now?

ARCHER: You'd understand if you were a southerner, Rufus, instead of a damn Yankee writing for a God Damned Yankee newspaper.

WENTWORTH: But why this heavy guard? You don't need all the cannon and half of the United States Army to protect one man—not even John Brown.

ARCHER: Afraid of escape—the Northern people getting him out.

WENTWORTH: Nonsense, no escape party could get through all this artillery. Every military force in the South, every man with a gun and a uniform is mustered here in this foolish little town. They're even camped in

A passageway in the Charlestown Gaol. Sketch by Orson Welles.

the churches and the cemetery. I'd just love to know what Governor Wise wants with all those men and ammunition. Maybe if I was a Southerner, and a newspaperman of your caliber, I'd know.

ARCHER: I'm surprised at you, Rufus! This is a historical morning. A great hero is going to be martyred in the Northern cause! Do you begrudge Old Brown "the soldiers' music and the rites of war?"

WENTWORTH: Certainly. Three Southern states contributed ropes to hang him, didn't they? Well, I'm sorry to say he can only be hung once and with one rope. Calling out great armies and parading them around the scaffold is just as futile. No civilians will be there to admire it all and the victim will be blindfolded! And may I ask why the cannon?

ARCHER: Probably to safeguard against any attempt on the part of heaven to arrange ascension.

WENTWORTH: (*bitterly*) Probably.

ARCHER: Hello, here comes Captain Avis. (*Avis leading Stevens, appears.*) G'morning, Mr. Jailer.

AVIS: (*sorrowfully*) Hello, boys.

ARCHER: (*Recognizing Stevens and halting the two as they start forward.*) Your name is Stevens, isn't it? You're one of the surviving Brown men?

STEVENS: (*Heavily bandaged, he speaks in a low sad tone, his voice choked with emotion.*) That's right.

ARCHER: (*Drawing out a notebook and pencil and stepping briskly up to him.*) Well, I'm Archer of *The Atlanta Clarion-News*. Got anything for publication? How do you like captivity? Are you badly hurt?

STEVENS: (*patiently*) No, I ain't so bad off. I got a throat wound keeps me from laughing or singing—that's pretty hard.

WENTWORTH: (*Throwing away his cigarette and taking out a pad of paper.*) Mr. Stevens do you consider that John Brown is insane?

STEVENS: If you please, gentlemen, I'm going to visit Captain Brown right now. It's—it's the last chance I'll have of seeing him and I ain't allowed much time. Please let me go.

AVIS: (*In a kindly tone, leading him past the newspapermen and down the hall!*) Come on, Stevens.

WENTWORTH: (*Tipping back his hat and scratching his head.*) Well, I'm damned! (*Avis and Stevens proceed to the door and the jailer, unhooking keys from his belt, begins to unlock it.*) No chance of talking to Old Brown?

AVIS: (*Looks up.*) Not right now, boys. Later, perhaps.

ARCHER: You all better hurry up and make up your mind. It's ten o'clock now. (*Avis opens the door and follows Stevens into the cell, locking the door after him.*)

WENTWORTH: They been allowing visitors all along?

ARCHER: I would say they have! Anybody the old man wanted to see, and that's everybody—everybody except the ministers, he won't talk to them. This jail has been a perfect meeting house for Northern sympathizers and plotters, and a show house for the Southern curiosity seekers. He talked to everybody, lectured to them and delivered his crazy sermons. And he wrote letters, dozens every day, to all his friends, big influential people Down East, some of them, and he wrote to the papers, too. Oh, I tell you, he's accomplished a lot during this last forty days. John Brown has fought a bigger battle right in there, in that cell, than he did in all his Kansas wars put together. A bigger battle than people may ever know.

WENTWORTH: He's caused a good deal of talk, certainly.

ARCHER: A good deal of talk? What's wrong with you up in Boston, are you asleep? Why he's shaken the world! I said this was a historical morning. It's more than that. My God, it's epic. This isn't the end. The execution of John Brown is only the beginning.

WENTWORTH: Well, there're different opinions.

ARCHER: Different opinions! That's exactly it. Very different opinions. And they'll differ more and more as time goes on. Here in the South, we hate him for a miserable old fanatic, and because he fought against us and everything we hold to be right, and up in the North folks have canonized him, even before his death.

WENTWORTH: Canonized him? Nobody's canonized Old Brown unless it's Virginia. You surround the prison and the gallows with an army, armies. To guard against what, fictitious Northern forces and escape? Do you think John Brown would let himself be rescued? I should say not. He wants to be a martyr and the South is willing to play Pilate. Any tuppeny, ha'penny pickpocket is a martyr if you hang him. If all this had happened in Boston, we'd simply have tossed him into a penitentiary or an insane asylum, and that would have been the end to it.

ARCHER: *(gloomily)* And now we've begun something that hasn't any end. Victor Hugo says that in killing Brown the Southern States have committed a crime which will take its place among the calamities of history. He says, "John Brown was an apostle and a hero. The gibbet has only increased his glory." And he says that his assassination will be followed fatally by—by the rupture of the Union.

WENTWORTH: Why Choley Archer you're raving! The Union ruptured? What's a little political prejudice? I don't like you going on like that about "we Southerners" and "you Northerners." You shouldn't talk that way. We're all Americans, aren't we? And you and I are old friends.

ARCHER: You and I are old newspapermen, Rufus. Let's face the facts.

WENTWORTH: Well, what are the facts? Osawatomie Brown is an impressive figure. Very well. And everybody all over the Union admires him. Very well. But in two hours from now he'll be hanging from the end of a rope and two days from now he'll be six feet underground. John Brown was Great on the Missouri border, but he can't be much use in the grave. *(The cell door opens and Stevens and Coppoc, their faces drawn and white come out and walk slowly away at the back. After a moment, Cook, sobbing miserably, staggers out of the cell and hurries after them. Avis follows him after locking the door.)*

ARCHER: These are the Brown men that weren't killed and that didn't escape. There are one or two others. One chap called Hazlett, the Old

Man won't talk to. Thinks he can get him off by pretending he doesn't know him.

WENTWORTH: They're to be hanged later on, aren't they? (*Archer doesn't reply. Avis appears again and goes to the cell door.*)

ARCHER: Anything new, Avis? (*Avis after looking into the cell comes up to them.*)

AVIS: No, Mr. Archer, but you can see him pretty soon, I think.

ARCHER: Good. How is he feeling?

AVIS: (*genuinely affected.*) I think he's the happiest man in Virginia. But the rest of us aren't. The prison guards are in tears.

WENTWORTH: What's he doing now?

AVIS: Writing a letter to his family. Oh, here's a statement he gave me. Maybe you'd like to see it. (*He hands Wentworth a slip of paper.*)

WENTWORTH: (*taking it*) Thank you. (*reading*) "Charles Town, Virginia, the Second of December, 1859. I, John Brown, am now quite certain that the crimes of this guilty land will never be purged away but with blood. I had, as I now think vainly, flattered myself that without very much bloodshed, it might be done." (*Wentworth looks up from his reading. Then slowly hands the paper back to Avis. The jailer takes it in silence and goes off.*)

ARCHER: Well, Rufus, what do you all got to say about that?

WENTWORTH: He's a lunatic, isn't he? We agree, don't we, that he's crazy?

ARCHER: Some Northerners don't think so. Ralph Waldo Emerson called him "that new saint, than whom none purer or more brave was ever led by into conflict and death,—the new saint awaiting his martyrdom, and who, if he shall suffer, will make the gallows glorious like the cross."

WENTWORTH: (*after a moment*) The cross! So Old Brown is another Christ! God, the cheek of the man!

ARCHER: You're a hell of a Yankee, Rufus. I can't make you out.

WENTWORTH: Well, you've got the damned silliest ideas about a Yankee. The North may abhor your "peculiar institution" of slavery, but it doesn't agree with John Brown or his tactics to end it. (*A soldier in the uniform of the Richmond Company comes down the hallway.*)

ARCHER: Nonsense. You condemn John Brown only because he failed.

WENTWORTH: I do not. And the North doesn't. (*To the soldier who is just passing.*) Isn't that true?

JOHN WILKES BOOTH: (*stopping*) What's that?

WENT'NORTH: We don't approve of Brown do we? We Northerners. He hasn't our sanction.

JOHN WILKES BOOTH: (*with dignity*) I am not a Northerner, sir. (*Archer laughs.*)

WENTWORTH: *(embarrassed)* Oh, I'm sorry. I should have known.

ARCHER: My brother journalist here is trying to persuade me of his hatred for John Brown.

JOHN WILKES BOOTH: I reckon everybody hates John Brown. Even the Yankees.

WENTWORTH: *(to Archer)* You see!

JOHN WILKES BOOTH: He's a villainous old assassin, a murderer, that's what he is, and a traitor. I'd like to kill him myself! *(Taking a newspaper out of his pocket and handing it to Archer, pointing to an article.)* Look, look what one anti-slavery man has to say about him, a politician by the name of—*(Looks over Archer's shoulder at the paper.)*—of Abraham Lincoln. Just read there—

ARCHER: *(Reading)* "John Brown's effort was peculiar. It was not a slave insurrection. It was an attempt by white men to get up a revolt among the slaves, in which slaves refused to participate. In fact, it was so absurd that the slaves, with all ignorance, saw plainly enough it could not succeed. The affair, in its philosophy, corresponds with many attempts related in history. An enthusiast broods over the oppression of a people until he fancies himself commissioned by Heaven to liberate them. He ventures the attempt which ends in little else than his own execution." *(Looks up—the sound of marching begins. Very, very distant.)* That's very interesting. *(Handing the paper back to the soldier.)* Thank you. Er—Lieutenant. I didn't catch the name?

JOHN WILKES BOOTH: *(Extending his hand.)* Booth—John Wilkes Booth. *(As Archer and Booth shake hands, the sound of marching grows louder and the lights, which have already begun to dim, go out. Ending the scene.)*

Scene XI

Scene—The Gallows. It stands on a hill, dark against a glowing sky. The sound of marching continues and after a bit, the figure of John Brown appears walking slowly and proudly up the hillside. Suddenly, the air is filled with insane laughter. It silences the sound of feet. The old man halts on his way, a voice ringing in his ears—taunting him. Then the laughter echoes and melts in the silence, and we remember it, it belongs to John Junior, the idiot son. Now the giant pulsing of feet returns. John Brown draws himself up and continues to the highest point, almost directly under the great gibbet. The marching sound is louder and by the stiffening of his posture and the brave upturn of his head, we sense that he hears it—that it throbs into his soul. He stands there on the hilltop, erect and alone, and now his voice is heard above it—victorious—thundering triumphantly above it.

JOHN BROWN: *(The marching becomes quieter as he speaks.)* I have nothing to say except prepare yourselves! I stand here as Old Moses stood upon Nebo, and I see in the distance a new land—a land of freedom which I may not enter, and a Jordan which I may not cross. *(The laugh again, ringing crazily! John Brown silences it with his next words.)* You people of the South, you had better prepare yourselves! Prepare for a settlement of this question that's coming up! The sooner you're prepared the better! You may dispose of me very easily; I am nearly disposed of now, but this question is still to be settled—this Negro question I mean. The end of that—is not yet!

The sound of marching feet grows louder and louder. But the note is gradually changing. The chains are gone and a martial ring has taken their place. The drum and bugle insinuate themselves. The tempo is quickened and the cadence is now that of a great army of free men—Marching, Marching, Marching, Marching. Indomitable. A thunderous, deafening, and triumphant rhythm. Now the bugle sound has melted into a vaster harmony, the full chords a song, a marching song beaten out by hundreds of thousands of feet. The old man still stands, a silent figure on the hill—and as the play ends the whole theatre is filled with the song—

JOHN BROWN'S BODY LIES MOULDERING IN THE GRAVE, BUT HIS SOUL GOES—MARCHING ON!

~

Epilogue

The Social Conscience of Orson Welles

Three decades after his death in 1985, Orson Welles remains a universally recognized creative genius for his considerable contributions to America's cultural and political life. The social conscience that may have been stirred in young Orson by his mentor Hill continued in his work and beyond.

On Broadway, in his early twenties, he was starring in and directing revolutionary plays that dealt with race and prejudice. In early 1936, working with the Federal Theatre Project, under the auspices of the Works Progress Administration (WPA), Orson directed Shakespeare's *Macbeth*, which opened at the Lafayette Theatre in Harlem, New York, on April 14. With an all–African American cast of 150 and set in nineteenth-century Haiti, the play came to be known as *Voodoo Macbeth*.

Nine months later, at the Maxine Theatre in New York, Welles staged *The Tragical History of Doctor Faustus*, another Federal Theatre Project, casting the black actor, Jack Carter—who received rave reviews for his role playing the lead in *Voodoo Macbeth*—as Mephistopheles. Not only was the production lauded by the critics and audiences for its innovative staging and lighting, it was celebrated as well for integrating the Broadway stage.

Welles found time later in 1937 to direct Marc Blitzstein's radical musical *The Cradle Will Rock*, a left-leaning account of corporate cupidity and venality. The theme was so controversial that the WPA padlocked the theater in an attempt to close the play. Not to be deterred, on opening night, Welles, Blitzstein, and the cast moved to another theater and, for months, performed the play to sellout audiences.

In November, Orson starred in and directed another Shakespeare play, *Julius Caesar*, in modern dress on a bare stage, which brought into sharp focus contemporary Nazi Germany and Fascist Italy. Writing in the *New York Times* of his adaptation, Orson remarked, "It's the same mob that hangs and burns Negroes in the South, the same mob that maltreats the Jews in Germany."[1]

While making headlines for his work on the New York stage, Welles found time to star in and direct hundreds of radio programs, mesmerizing national audiences with what he had to say—from championing race relations and commenting on issues of the moment to adapting novels ranging from Victor Hugo's *Les Misérables* to H. G. Wells's *The War of the Worlds*, which terrified millions of listeners and generated more than 12,500 articles within a month of its broadcast.

As a result of Welles's multiple successes in New York, he landed on the May 9, 1938, cover of *Time* magazine, and five months later he signed a contract with RKO Pictures.

With the invaluable assistance of his Mercury Theatre colleagues, whom Welles brought to Hollywood; his co-screenwriter Herman Mankiewicz; cameraman Gregg Toland; and the steadfast support of RKO's head, George Schaefer, Welles—at age twenty-four—brought to the screen *Citizen Kane*.

The five years following *Citizen Kane* were anything but fallow creatively for Welles. He returned to Broadway in 1941 to direct Richard Wright's *Native Son*, a play based on Wright's eponymous novel, co-authored by Wright and Pulitzer Prize–winning playwright Paul Green. The novel, which received expansive praise the year before, chronicles the short, tragic life of a troubled twenty-year-old black man, Bigger Thomas, who grows increasingly restive and resentful of the world in "Black Belt," a ghetto in Chicago during the Depression. While working as a chauffeur, he inadvertently kills the daughter of his philanthropist boss and is sentenced to die in the electric chair.

As was true of all Orson's work on stage and screen, his input to scripts was insightful and considerable as typified in his letter to Green to be mindful as he writes that, at play's end, Welles envisions Bigger Thomas to be "behind the bars standing there with his arms reaching out and up, his hands clinging to the bars—yes, yes, yes, the crucified one, crucified by the Jim Crow world in which he lived."[2]

Reflecting on the play's overarching theme of race relations in 1940s America, Simon Callow in *Orson Welles: The Road to Xanadu* opines, "The production in general marked an enormous breakthrough in the depiction of a black person's life and death."[3]

Native Son opened at the St. James Theatre in New York on March 24, 1941, and ran through June 28 to sellout audiences. Sidney Whipple, drama

Welles speaks with Richard Wright, author of the novel *Native Son. Photofest*

critic of the *New York World-Telegram*, enthused, "Stark drama stamped with genius. *Native Son* proves that Orson Welles, whether you like to admit it or not, is not a boy wonder but actually the greatest theatrical director of the modern stage."[4]

Time magazine wrote, "Playwright Paul Green has helped Negro Novelist Richard Wright turn his best-selling *Native Son* into by all odds the strongest drama of the season."[5]

In 1942, while Welles was in Brazil working on another film documentary sponsored by the Office of the Coordinator of Inter-American Affairs and RKO to promote United States and Latin American relations, his second film, *The Magnificent Ambersons* was released by RKO amid much controversy after the company's executives rejected the film's somber ending and, without Welles's permission, reshot the final scenes to reflect a more optimistic conclusion.

When not in front of or behind a camera in 1942 and 1943, Welles produced, directed, and hosted a CBS Radio series *Hello America*, much like *It's All True* that RKO had canceled. The programs, sponsored by the Office of the Coordinator of Inter-American Affairs, were designed to enhance North and

Welles directing Canada Lee in the stage version of *Native Son*. *Photofest*

South American comity during World War II. Additionally, during this time, CBS aired another Welles program, *Ceiling Unlimited*, bringing to the American public the vital role the U.S. air force was contributing to the war effort.

After the war, Welles maintained a breathless pace in 1946, with his multiple appearances on film, radio, and stage. Decca Records released *No Man Is an Island*, two albums of Welles dramatically declaiming memorable speeches, prose, and poetry celebrating mankind's consanguinity. Selections included John Donne's "For Whom the Bell Tolls"; Thomas Paine's "Tyranny Is Not Easily Conquered"; Patrick Henry's "Liberty or Death"; Abraham Lincoln's Gettysburg Address; and notably, John Brown's "In Behalf of His Despised Poor"—Brown's final address to the court before being found guilty of treason and sentenced to hang.

Orson Welles Commentaries, aired in 1946 on ABC radio, were weekly fifteen-minute forums allowing Orson to ruminate on his times. Topics ranged from the art of bullfighting and the matador Fernando Lopez to Louis Armstrong to the coup in Brazil that removed President Getúlio Vargas from office to the forthcoming atomic testing at Bikini Atoll.

The most powerful and influential Welles commentaries were devoted to Isaac Woodard, a twenty-seven-year-old black Army sergeant who on February 12, 1946, while en route from Camp Gordon, Georgia, where he had just been honorably discharged from the military after serving in the Pacific Theater during World War II, was savagely beaten and blinded by the racist police chief of Batesville, Georgia, Lynwood Shull.

When word of Woodard's bludgeoning came to the attention of the National Association for the Advancement of Colored People (NAACP), knowing Welles's passion for social justice and racial equality, NAACP executives met with Orson, informing him of Woodard's plight. Before their asking if Welles might find time during a commentary to address this outrage, Orson readily volunteered to employ his energy and microphone to apprise America of the injustice Woodard endured and lead a charge to ferret out the perpetrators and bring them to justice.

NAACP representative Ollie Harrington recalls that after the organization's meeting with Welles, "We communicated by phone every Saturday and he would make a broadcast every Sunday evening. They were fascinatingly dramatic programs in which he took the role of somebody out hunting down these men who had committed the crime. As a result, they actually discovered the people who had done this."[6]

On his July 28 program, Welles took to the airwaves and eloquently inveighed against this monstrous attack and the attackers. For the next four Sundays, Welles continued his fervent crusade, relentlessly championing Woodard and inveighing against race hate.

During the course of the programs, Welles broadcast the name of the police chief, Lynwood Shull, who was indicted, tried, and acquitted in a federal court in South Carolina by an all-white jury. However, Orson's prolonged efforts, heard around the country, contributed to President Harry S. Truman creating a National Interracial Commission and sending to Congress the country's first civil rights bill that desegregated the armed forces and the federal government.

To better appreciate Welles' sentiments on race—sentiments shared in equal fervor by his mentor and co-author—which prompted him as a teenager to co-author Marching Song thirteen years before, the five weekly Woodard commentaries provide invaluable insight on the subject dear to Welles and Hill, written ninety-six years after John Brown was hanged for espousing similar ends though employing far more incendiary and debatable means.

~

July 28, 1946
Good morning, this is Orson Welles speaking.
    I'd like to read to you an affidavit.

I, Isaac Woodard Jr., being duly sworn to depose and state as follows: that I am twenty-seven years old and a veteran of the United States Army, having served fifteen months in the South Pacific, and having earned one battle star. I was honorably discharged on February 12, 1946, at Camp Gordon, Georgia, at 8:30 p.m. at the Greyhound terminal at Atlanta, Georgia. While I was in uniform I purchased a ticket to Winnsboro, South Carolina, and took the bus headed there to pick up my wife to come to New York to see my father and mother. About one hour out of Atlanta, the bus driver stopped at a small drug store, as he stopped I asked if he had time to wait for me until I had the chance to go to the restroom. He cursed and said no. When he cursed me, I cursed him back. When the bus got to Aiken, he got off and went and got the police. They didn't give me a chance to explain. The policeman struck me across the head with a billy and told me to shut up. After that, the policeman grabbed me by my left arm and twisted it behind my back. I figured he was trying to make me resist. I did not resist against him. He asked me, "Was I discharged?" and I told him, "Yes"; when I said "Yes," that was when he started beating me with a billy, hitting me across the top of the head; after that I grabbed his billy and wrung it out of his hand. Another policeman came up and threw his gun on me and told me to drop the billy or he'd drop me, so I dropped the billy. After I dropped the billy, the second policeman held his gun on me while the other one was beating me. He knocked me unconscious. After I commenced to recover myself, he yelled "Get up!" I started to get up; he started punching me in my eyes with the end of the billy. When I finally got up he pushed me inside the jailhouse and locked me up. I woke up next morning and could not see.

A policeman said, "Let's go up here and see what the judge says." I told him that I could not see or come out; I was blind. He said, "Feel your way out." He said I be all right after I washed my face. He led me to the judge, and after I told the judge what happened, he said, "We don't have that kind of stuff down here." Then the policeman said: "He wrung the billy out of my hand, and I told him if he didn't drop it, I'd drop him." That's how I know it was the same policeman that beat my eyes out. After that the judge spoke and said, "I fine you $50 or thirty days in the row." And I said I'd pay the fifty dollars, but I did not have the fifty dollars at the time, so the policeman said, "You have some money there in your wallet." He took my wallet and took out all I had, it was a total of forty dollars, and took four dollars from my watch pocket. I had a cheque for six hundred and ninety-four dollars and seventy-three cents, which was my mustering out and soldiers' deposit. He said to me, "Can you see how to sign this check? You have a government check." I told him, "No, sir." So he gave it back to me after that. Took me back, locked me up in the jail, the policeman did, I stayed in there for a while, and after a few minutes, he came and asked me if I wanted a drink of whiskey. If I took a drink of whiskey, I'd feel better. I told him, "No, sir." I didn't care for any.

At 5:30 that evening they took me to the veterans' hospital, in Columbia, South Carolina; one of the contact men came around one day and said to me they were going to take out a pension for me. I believe that the doctor who cared for me was named Dr. Clarence. I told him what had happened to me; he made no comment. But told me I should join a blind school.

Sworn to me, on this 23rd day of April 1946.

Well, ladies and gentlemen, I had that affidavit in my pocket a few hours before dawn when I left off worrying about this broadcast long enough for coffee at an all-night restaurant. I found myself joined at the table by a stranger. A nice, soft-spoken, well-meaning, well-mannered stranger. He told me a joke. He thinks it's a joke. I'm going to repeat it, but not for your amusement; I earnestly hope that nobody listening will laugh. This is the joke.

Seems there's a white man who came on business to a southern town, it could be Aiken, South Carolina, and found he couldn't get a bed in any of the good hotels. He went to the bad hotels and finally the flophouses, but there was no room for him in any of the inns reserved for white folks, in that southern city, so at last, in desperation, he applied to a Negro hotel where he was accepted with the proviso that he would consent to share a double room with another guest. In rueful gratitude, this white man paid his bill, left a call for early in the morning, he rested well, quite undisturbed by the proximity of the sleeping colored man beside him, and he was awakened at the hour of his request. After breakfast, he left for the railway station where he boarded his appointed train, but the conductor would not let him into any of the regular coaches. The man was told quite rudely to go where he belonged, the Jim Crow car. The hero of this funny story allowed he hadn't washed in the morning, and the dust of travel must be responsible for the conductor's grievous social miscalculation. He went to the washroom; he started to clean his hands.

They were black. An even-hued black. Then he looked into the mirror. His face was the same color. He not only looked darker than white; he was quite visibly a Negro. A great oath precedes the final line which is presumed to be the funny part of this little anecdote: "I know what's happened" are the next words of the man. "It's very simple. They woke up the wrong man!"

I left the teller of this tale in the coffee shop, but I found I couldn't leave the tale itself. Like the affidavit I read at the start of the broadcast, it seems to have become a permanent part of my mental luggage. I sketched in my imagination a sequel to the stranger's funny joke. I saw the man of business who'd gone to bed a white man getting into an argument with a conductor. I saw a policeman boarding a train at the next station and taking the man of business out on the platform and beating the eyes out of his head because the man thought he should be treated with the same respect he'd received the day before when he was white. I saw a man at the police station trying to make him take a drink, so the medical authorities could testify that he was drunk. I saw the man of business bleeding in his cell, reaching out with sightless hands through unseen bars, gesturing for help that would not, could not ever come. And I heard his explanation echoing down the stone hallways of the jail: "I know what's happened. It's very simple. They woke up the wrong man."

Now it seems the officer of the law who blinded the young Negro boy in the affidavit has not been named. The boy saw him while he could still see, but of course he had no way of knowing which particular policeman it was. Who brought the justice of Dachau and Oswiecim to Aiken, South Carolina? He was just another white man with a stick, who wanted to teach a Negro boy a lesson—to show a Negro boy where he belonged: in the darkness. Till we know more about him, for just now, we'll call the policeman Officer X. He might be listening to this. I hope so. Officer X, I'm talking to you. Officer X, they woke up the wrong man. That somebody else, that man sleeping there, is you. The you that God brought into the world. All innocent of hate, a paid-up resident member of the brotherhood of man. Yes. Unbelievably enough, that's you, Officer X. You, still asleep. That you could have been anything, it could have gone to the White House when it grew up. It could have gone to heaven when it died. But they woke up the wrong man. They finally came for him in the blank grey of dawn, as in the death house they come for the condemned. But without prayers. They came with instructions. The accumulated ignorance of the feudal south. And with this particular briefing they called Cain, for another day of the devil's work. While Abel slept. Wash your hands, Officer X. Wash them well. Scrub and scour, you won't blot out the blood of a blinded war veteran. Nor yet the color of your skin. Your own skin. You'll never, never, never change it. Wash your hands, Officer X. Wash a lifetime, you'll never wash away that leprous lack of pigment. The guilty pallor of the white man.

We invite you to luxuriate in secrecy; it will be brief. Go on. Suckle your anonymous moment while it lasts. You're going to be uncovered! We will blast out your name! We'll give the world your given name, Officer X. Yes, and your so-called Christian name. It's going to rise out of the filthy deep like the dead thing it is. We're going to make it public with the public scandal you dictated but failed to sign.

We pause now for a word from the philosophers. A short reminder regarding the matter of payment and cost. Nothing is paid back. That does not happen. Not on earth. A favor cannot be paid back; neither can a wrong. We say a criminal pays for his crime, when we lock him up, a murderer pays for his murder when the state murders him, but really the state is hiding an unsightly object. Society is merely sweeping its dirt under the carpet. We may sometimes manage to cure the thing called "crime," but the man called a criminal is never punished; he can be inconvenienced or tormented or done away with, but he can never pay for what he has done. If the ledger is ever balanced, it is not by him, but by some other man having nothing to do with him. It is balanced by deeds of virtue. By unrelated good works. The evil-doer's agony doesn't show up in the books. Only that fiction known to us as money can be paid back. The true debt, the debt of a friend to a friend or a foe to a foe outlives the principles involved. So much for payment.

Price. That's something else. There's a price for everything. There's nothing that does not have its cost. Joy and inspiration and mere pleasure have a market value precisely computed in terms of their opposites. The cost of youth is age; the cost of age is death. You want love? The cost of love is independence. You want to be independent, do you? Then pay the price, and know what it is to be alone. Your mother paid for you with pain. Nothing, nothing in this living world is free. The free air costs you the life-consuming effort of breath. Freedom itself is priced at the rate of the citizenship it earns and holds. What does it cost to be a Negro? In Aiken, South Carolina, it cost a man his eyes. What does it cost to wear over your skeleton a pinkish tint officially described as "white"? In Aiken, South Carolina, it cost a man his soul.

Officer X may languish in jail. It's unlikely, but it's possible he'll serve as long a term as a Negro would serve in Aiken, South Carolina, for stealing bread. But Officer X will never pay for the two eyes he beat out of the soldier's head. How can you assay the gift of sight? What are they quoting today for one eye? An eye for an eye? A literal reading of this Mosaic law spells out again only the blank waste of vengeance. We've told Officer X that he'll be dragged out of hiding. We've promised him a most unflattering glare of publicity. We're going to keep that promise. We're going to build our own police line-up to line up this reticent policeman, with the killers, the lunatics, the beastmen, all the people of society's zoo. Where he belongs. If he's listening to this, let him listen well. Officer X. After I've found you out,

I'll never lose you. If they try you, I'm going to watch the trial. If they jail you, I'm going to wait for your first day of freedom. You won't be free of me. I want to see who's waiting for you at the prison gates. I want to know who will acknowledge that they know you. I'm interested in your future. I will take careful note of all your destinations. Assume another name and I will be careful that the name you would forget is not forgotten. I will find means to remove from you all refuge, Officer X. You can't get rid of me. We have an appointment, you and I. And only death can cancel it.

Who am I? A masked avenger from the comic books? No sir, merely an inquisitive citizen of America. I admit that nothing on this inhabited earth is capable of your chastisement. I'm simply but quite actively curious to know what will become of you. Your fate cannot affect the boy in the country hospital for the blind, but your welfare is a measure of the welfare of my country. I cannot call it your country. How long will you get along in these United States? Which of the states will still consent to get along with you? Where stands the sun of common fellowship? When will it rise over your dark country? When will it be noon in Georgia? I must know where you go, Officer X, because I must know where the rest of us are going with our American experiment. Into bankruptcy? Or into that serene tomorrow, that plenteous garden that blind soldier hoped for when he had his eyes, and with eyes open, he went to war. We want a world that will lighten his darkness. You're sorry for him? He rejects your pity. You're ashamed? He doesn't care. We want to tell him soon that all America is ashamed of you. If there's room for pity, you can have it, for you are far more blind than he. He had eyes to see and saw with them; they made out, if nothing else, at least part of the shape of human dignity, and this is not a little thing, but you have eyes to see and you have never seen.

He has the memory of light. But you were born in a pit. He cannot grow new eyes to open the world again for his poor bruised head. Never. No. The only word we can share with the martyr to carry him from the county hospital to the county grave is word concerning your eyes, Officer X. Your eyes, remember, were not gouged away. Only the lids are closed. You might raise the lids; you might just try the wild adventure of looking. You might see something; it might be a simple truth. One of those truths held to be self-evident by our founding fathers and most of us. If we should ever find you bravely blinking at the sun, we'll know then that the world is young after all. That chaos is behind us and not ahead. Then there will be shouting of trumpets to rouse the dead at Gettysburg. A thunder of cannon will declare the tidings of peace, and all the bells of liberty will laugh out loud in the streets to celebrate goodwill towards all men. The new blind can hear, and it would be very good if they could hear the news that the old blind can finally see them. Officer X, you'll find that you can wash off what should be washed, and it will be said of you, yes, even you, they awakened the right man.

Now it's time to say goodbye. Please let me call again. Next week, same time. Until then, I am always . . . obediently yours.

August 4, 1946
Hello, this is Orson Welles speaking.

Last week, I read you an affidavit from a Negro soldier named Isaac Woodard. You remember he was taken off a bus in South Carolina by a policeman and beaten until he was blinded in both eyes. I have a formal letter from a Mr. H. Odell Weeks, who, it seems, is the mayor of the city of Aiken in the state of South Carolina. Where, according to the soldier's affidavit, he was blinded. The mayor encloses affidavits of his own, sworn to by the city recorder, by the city chief of police, by a couple of patrol officers. Now, these gentlemen deny all knowledge of the incident.

"It is indeed unfortunate," writes Mr. Weeks, and these are his exact words, quote, that you did not fully verify this story before you broadcasted it. Unquote. The mayor goes on to say that since my broadcast went out to the nation, and since, according to the affidavits, whose accounts are wholly untrue, he the mayor urges that I have the courage and forthrightness to retract the wrong I've done his city. Giving to my own retraction the same emphasis that I've placed on the original broadcast. Well, Mr. Weeks, I hardly know how to make affidavits of your city recorder and city policeman as emphatic as Mr. Woodard's in the hospital for the blind. If it turns out to be true that the city of Aiken is blameless of this hideous scandal, it is my duty to make that innocence as public as possible. I hope to be able to. But: I must warn you that denials are never dramatic. And if I'm to say something exciting about Aiken, it will have to be something better than that a Negro boy was never blinded in its streets.

I look forward to giving the subject of Aiken all the emphasis it deserves. But I am bound to fail without some affirmative material. There are thousands of cities where Negro soldiers have not been blinded. I hope it will be my privilege to announce that your city is one of these. But since the broadcast is going to go out, as you put it, to the nation, let's spice up the retraction with a little good news. I won't ask you what the city of Aiken has done for Negro soldiers or for Negroes or for the blind. I'll only ask you if you're willing to join with me in a manhunt. A man dressed as a policeman blinded a discharged veteran. The blinded boy swears that his tormenter told him he came from the Aiken police. It is surely a more urgent matter for you to apprehend this impostor before he commits further outrages in your city's name than it is to exact from a commentator the cold comfort of apology.

You'll get the apology when the facts are clear. Until then you must understand why it must be deferred. After all, Mr. Weeks, I have not only the affidavits of your policemen; I have also the affidavits of the blinded soldier. Working on the meager clue that there's also an Aiken county, I've sent investigators there and to your city, who should bring out the truth. Unless it is too skillfully hidden. The soldier might easily have made a mistake, but there's a man in a policeman's uniform who made a worse mistake. And all the retractions in the world won't cleanse the name of Aiken. Till we find that man. I assure you Mr. Weeks, I do not doubt the word of your police chief, your patrol officers, or your city recorder. But neither do I doubt the word of the blinded Negro boy. His suffering gives his oath a special validity. And I would take it against the Supreme Court and the President of the United States.

Let us say he misunderstood what was said to him. Or let us say he was lied to. But just saying that isn't enough. Your city's honor is certainly more important than my pride. But honor and pride are piddling trifles beside a pair of eyes. If it is your point that the boy was lied to, it is my point that we must refuse to rest until we've unmasked the liar. If you want me to say that this awful thing did not happen in your city, then there's an American soldier who believes that it did happen in your city. And I cannot forget that. It is to him, Mr. Weeks, that you should address your first and most indignant letters. They will of course need to be transcribed in braille.

And now I see my time is just about up. That's all I have to say to you, for the moment, Mr. Mayor of Aiken. And you, ladies and gentlemen, thank you very much for coming to this part of your dial at this part of a Sunday. Please let me join you next week at this same time and . . . let me hear from you. Your letters are much appreciated. We like reading them on this program. Till next week then, same time, same station. I remain as always, obediently yours.

August 11, 1946
This is Orson Welles.

I've spoken these words before but not on the radio. To be born free is to be born in debt. To live in freedom without fighting slavery is to profiteer. By plane last night, I flew over some parts of our Republic where American citizenship is a luxury beyond the means of the majority. I rode comfortably in my plane above a sovereign state or two where fellow countrymen of ours can't vote without the privilege of cash. I bought my breakfast this morning where Negroes may not come except to serve their white brothers. And there I overheard a member of some master race or other tell all those who listened that something must be done to suppress the Jews.

I have met southerners who expect and fear a Negro insurrection. I see no purpose in withholding this from general discussion. There may be those in that outcast 10 percent of the American people who someday will strike back at their oppressors, but to put down that mob, a mob would rise. I'd like to ask please, who will put down that mob? The scaly dinosaurs of reaction, if indeed they notice what I'm speaking here, will say in their newspapers that I'm a communist. Communists know otherwise. I'm an overpaid movie producer with pleasant reasons to rejoice, and I do, in the wholesome practicability of the profit system. But surely my right to having more than enough is canceled if I don't use that more to help those who have less.

My subject today is the question of moral indebtedness. So I'd like to acknowledge here the debt that goes with ownership. I believe, and this has very much to do with my own notion of freedom, I believe I owe the very profit I make to the people I make it from. If this is radicalism, it comes automatically to most of us in show business, it being generally agreed that any public man owes his position to the public. That's what I mean when I say I'm your obedient servant. It's a debt payable in service and the highest efforts of the debtor. The extension of this moral argument insists no man owns anything outright since he owns it rent free. A wedding never bought a wife. And the devotion of his child is no man's for the mere begetting. We must each day earn what we own. A healthy man owes to the sick all that he can do for them. An educated man owes to the ignorant all that he can do for them. A free man owes to the world's slaves all that he can do for them. And what is to be done is more, much more, than good works, Christmas baskets, bonuses and tips, and bread and circuses. There is only one thing to be done with slaves. Free them.

If we can't die in behalf of progress, we can live for it. Progress, we Americans take to mean, is a fuller realization of democracy. The measure of progress, as we understand it, is the measure of equality enjoyed by all men. We can do something about that. The way our fighting brothers and sisters looked at it, some of them dead as I speak these words, the way they looked at it: we're lucky. And they're right, we're lucky. We're lucky to be alive. But only if our lives make life itself worth dying for. We must be worthy of our luck, or we are damned. Our lives were spared, but this is merely the silliest of accidents. Unless we put the gift of life to the hard employments of justice. If we waste that gift, we won't have anywhere to hide from the indignation of history.

I want to say this. The morality of the auction block is out of date. There is no room in the American century for Jim Crow. The times urge new militancy upon the democratic attitude. Tomorrow's democracy discriminates against discrimination. Its charter won't include the freedom to end freedom. What is described as a feeling against some races can't be further respected. Feeling is a ninnyish, mincing way of saying something ugly. But the word is good enough for race hate when we add that it's a feeling of guilt. Race hate isn't human nature; race hate is the abandonment of human nature. But this is true: we hate whom we hurt. And we mistrust whom we betray. There are minority problems because minority races are often wronged. Race hate distilled from the suspicions of ignorance takes its welcome from the impotent and the godless. There are alibis for the phenomenon, excuses, economic and social, but the brutal fact is simply this: where the racist lies are acceptable, there is corruption. Where there is hate, there is shame. The human soul receives race hate only in the sickness of guilt.

The Indian, the Red Indian, is on our American conscience. The Negro is on our conscience; the Chinese and the Mexican American are on our conscience. The Jew is on the conscience of Europe. But our neglect gives us communion in that guilt. So that there dances even here the lunatic specter of anti-Semitism. This is deplored, but it must be fought. And the fight must be won. The race haters must be stopped. The lynchings must be stopped. No matter who's going to be governor of Georgia, the murders in Monroe must be avenged. Gene Talmadge might call it foreign meddling, but the governor-elect who, you remember, campaigned on the Bilbo platform of race hate needs to be told: that all the states in the Union and all the people in them are concerned. Immediately, personally concerned when a mob forms in the sovereign privacy of Georgia. The mob said it was taking care of things in its own way, then we're going to have to take care of the mob our own way.

Those who take the law into their own hands are going to learn about some laws that'll tie their hands. We'll write those laws, and we'll enforce them. To do him justice, old Gene went and issued himself a statement. After the killings in Monroe were public knowledge, he said the killings were regrettable. But old Gene's made it plenty clear, he doesn't figure any foreigner has the right to poke around asking embarrassing questions. I am sending old Gene a copy of the dawn sermon of the tolling bell, but I don't suppose he'll get the point. The point is, of course, that no man, even Gene Talmadge, is an island entire of itself. Point, of course, is that even Georgia is a piece of the continent. The American continent. And if a clod be washed away by the sea, or if a colored man and his wife are murdered on a dusty country road, America is the less.

And then there's the soldier in the hospital. The blind soldier. The soldier said he was blinded, and the mayor and the chief of police in the place where the soldier says it happened are most indignant with me for repeating what he said and swore to. The *Times* the other day was full of their official protests. Sent under seal all the way up to New York City via the inviolable borders of Aiken County, in South Carolina. My investigators are still hard at work on the case. If the soldier was wrong about the place, I'm going to do something about it. But he isn't wrong about his eyes. He lost them. I'm going to do something about that. All the affidavits from all the policemen in the world won't protest his eyes back in his head. Somebody, somebody who called himself an officer of the law, beat that boy with a stick until he lost his sight. Now, that somebody is nobody. He's vanished, he's never been heard of, he hasn't any name, well . . . he's going to be heard of. The blind soldier has my promise of that. That somebody is going to be named. Editorials and lots of newspapers and lots of people are writing to me to demand to know what business it is of mine. God judge me if it isn't the most pressing business I have.

The blind soldier fought for me in this war. The least I can do now is fight for him. I have eyes. He hasn't. I have a voice on the radio; he hasn't. I was born a white man. And until a colored man is a full citizen, like me, I haven't the leisure to enjoy the freedom that colored man risked his life to maintain for me. I don't own what I have until he owns an equal share of it. Until somebody beats me and blinds me, I am in his debt. And so, I come to this microphone not as a radio dramatist, though it pays better, not as a commentator, although it's safer to be simply that, I come in that boy's name, and in the name of all who in this land of ours have no voice of their own. I come with a call for action. This is a time for it. I call for action against the cause of riots. I know that to some ears, even the word "action" has a revolutionary twang, and it won't surprise me if I'm accused in some quarters of inciting to riot. Well, I'm very interested in riots. I'm very interested in avoiding them. And so I call for action against the cause of riots.

Law is the best action, the most decisive. I call for laws then prohibiting what moral judgment already counts as lawlessness. American law forbids a man the right to take away another's right. It must be law that groups of men can't use the machinery of our republic to limit the rights of other groups. That the vote, for instance, can't be used to take away the vote. It's in the people's power to see to it that what makes lynchings and starts wars is dealt with. Not by well-wishers, but by policemen. And I mean good policemen. Oh, for several generations there may be men who can't be weaned away from the fascist vices of race hate. But we should deny such men the responsibility in public affairs exactly as we deny responsibility to the wretched victims of the drug habit. There are laws against peddling dope; there can be laws against peddling race hate. But every man has a right to his own opinion, as an American boasts, but race hate is not an opinion; it's a phobia. It isn't a viewpoint; race hate is a disease. In a people's world, the incurable racist has no rights. He must be deprived of influence in a people's government. He must be segregated, as he himself would segregate the colored and Semitic peoples. As we now segregate the leprous and the insane.

Anything very big is very simple. If there's a big race question, there's a big answer to it. The big answer is simple. Like the word no. This is my proposition: that the sin of race hate be solemnly declared a crime. What makes this difficult is the conservative fear of raising issues. Well, let's admit that this fear is often no more sinister than an honest dread of going to the dentist, but let's respect the effectiveness of reactionary manipulations of that fear, which is the fear of anarchy and revolution. It is put to wicked use against the same general welfare conservative opinion seeks to protect. Forced to acknowledge Hitler's enmity, conservatives are loathe to admit that even as he surrendered in Europe, he succeeded in America. Let conservatives evaluate the impudent candor of fascism in Argentina today. And be reminded that the heroic survival of our liberty is no proof of its immortality. Our liberty every day has to be safe from marauders whose greed is for all things possessed by the people. Care of these possessions is the hope of life on this planet. They are living things; they grow. These fair possessions of democracy. And nothing but death can stop that growth. Let the yearners for the past, the willfully childish, learn now the facts of life.

The first of which is the fact of that growth. In our hemisphere, the growing has begun, but only just begun. America can write her name across this century, and so she will, if we, the people, brown and black and red, rise now to the great occasion of our brotherhood. It will take courage. It calls for the doing of great deeds, which means the dreaming of great dreams. Giving the world back to its inhabitants is too big a job for the merely practical. The architects of freedom are always capable of hope. The lawmakers of true democracy are true believers. They believe quite simply in the people, in all of them. Only the devout deserve the trust of government, for only the devout can face the unimaginable vistas of man's destiny. God grant them steadfast hope and the rest of us enduring patience. For we must not expect from any leadership a shiny ready-made millennium in our time. No one of us will live to see a blameless peace. We must strive and pray and die for what will be here when we're gone. Our children's children are the ancestors of a free people. We send our greetings ahead of us to them.

To history yet unmade, our greetings. To the generations, sleeping in our loins. Be of good heart. The fight is worth it.

That just about means that my time is up. When my time's up, it's time for me to say goodbye, and to invite you please to join me, the same time, the same station next week. Until then. Thank you for your attention. I remain as always, obediently yours.

August 18, 1946
This is Orson Welles speaking.

A motion picture in which I play a part was scheduled for a couple days running last week in Aiken, South Carolina. But the film was banned. Well, I'm used to being banned. I've been banned by whole governments. The Nazis in Germany have banned me, and the fascists of Italy and Spain have banned me. Here at home, the merest mention of my name is forbidden by Mr. Hearst to all his subject newspapers. But: to be outlawed by an American city is a new experience.

The movie in question is neither controversial nor obscene. But I'm in it, and for the taste of Aiken, that makes any movie too offensive to be endured. Not only was the actual celluloid driven out of the city limits, as with a fiery sword, but in defense of civic sensitivities and to protect the impressionable of Aiken's youth from the shock of my name and likeness, a detachment of police officers working under the direction of the city council itself solemnly tore down such posters as the local theater manager had been rash enough to put up by way of advertisement. And burnt same, together with all printed matter having reference to me, in a formal bonfire in the public streets.

I'm also informed I've been somewhat less officially "hanged" in effigy. And while I have an apology to offer Aiken, it's been suggested that I would be ill-advised to deliver it in person. Since I brought to your attention the case of Isaac Woodard, the case has grown to an issue of the most heated popular concern. It deserves all the national interest it's getting. Isaac Woodard is the veteran whose eyes were beaten out of his head by a policeman, in the streets of a place in South Carolina, that Isaac Woodard thought was Aiken. He said so in an affidavit, and when I read his affidavit on this program, the mayor of Aiken, the chief of police, and others, subsequently preoccupied with the public burning of my name and picture, sent affidavits of their own protesting innocence.

My problem was the choice of affidavits. The boy had been blinded. That was the one clear, brutal fact. And I stuck to that with a promise to Aiken's officialdom that I would apologize for publishing the veteran's testimony when and if my investigators could show a decent doubt. The records were amazingly brief. The policeman who delivered Woodard to the hospital was not named. This is most unusual. The place where the attack occurred was not mentioned in the report. This is almost unheard of.

But my investigators, the investigators of the National Association for the Advancement of Colored People, and the investigators of the FBI have together narrowed down the search to the town of Batesburg, some nineteen miles from Aiken. And this morning comes word that the search has been narrowed still further. I have before me wires and press releases to the effect that a policeman of Batesburg, a man by the name of Shaw or Shore or Shull; it is given three different ways here. The flash is just before us, Chief L. L. Shaw. Pronounce it however you want it. Or want to. Has admitted . . . that he was the police officer who blinded Isaac Woodard. Thirty miles from Aiken. In South Carolina. This is in Batesburg.

I give you a few more of the facts. He has corroborated an army statement, has police chief Shull or Shaw, that ex-serviceman Isaac Woodard was struck on the head with a blackjack. Chief Shull or Shaw says he was called to the bus one night last February to arrest Woodard who, and I'm reading from a Press Association, he said was drunk. Shaw claimed to have hit Woodard across the head when Woodard tried to take away his blackjack. He added that the blow may have landed in the veteran's eyes. Shull or Shaw, the police chief, described the eyes as swollen the next day when Woodard was fined and then driven to a veterans' hospital, at a doctor's suggestion. Now, you remember from the affidavit, and from further reports of our investigators, that Woodard said he'd been offered liquor after he was attacked by the police, which he refused. And investigators at the National Association for the Advancement of Colored Peoples have discovered three other occupants of that bus. All of whom claim, in affidavits, that Woodard was not drunk, nor was he drinking. Woodard, you remember, appealed for medical aid. And also, according to the UP, Shaw or Shore or Shull brands these stories as lies. He has volunteered no information for this, that was unearthed by the investigation. Well, the good citizens of Aiken must be surely so glad to hear this, that my apology tendered herewith and as promised, most abjectly, will come as merely an incidental comfort.

Batesburg, unlike Aiken, has turned out to be to blame. We're getting close to the truth. We have the admission of a man that he was the officer, the officer whom I call X. I would like to remind Officer X, otherwise known as Shull or Shaw, of another promise, a promise I made to the blinded Isaac Woodard. If Chief Shull or Shaw is listening to me now and it's more than possible that he is, it gives me pleasure to repeat that promise. Officer X. We know your name now. Now that we've found you out, we'll never lose you.

If they try you for your crime, I am going to watch the trial, Chief Shull. If they jail you, I'm going to wait for your first day of freedom. You won't be free of me. I want to see who's waiting for you at the prison gates. I want to know who will acknowledge that they know you. I'm interested in your future; I will take note of all your destinations. Assume another name, and I will be careful that the name you would forget is not forgotten. Officer Shull or Shaw, police chief of the city of Batesburg. I will find means to remove from you all refuge. You can't get rid of me. We have an appointment. You and I. Only death can cancel it.

August 25, 1946
This is Orson Welles speaking.

The place was Batesburg. Isaac Woodard thought it happened in Aiken. He was wrong. I've repeatedly explained Woodard's mistake and repeatedly apologized. But I broadcast his affidavit, and now the city of Aiken having banned my movies, burned the posters in the streets, and hanged me in effigy, is threatening, believe it or not, to sue me for the sum of two million dollars.

Well, if I had all that money, honestly, I wouldn't mind owing it to Aiken for the pride of having finally put the blame where it belonged. The blame belongs, as I say, in Batesburg. Batesburg, South Carolina. It was Monday, February 13, 1946. A minister and several workmen saw the police chief of Batesburg and a highway patrolman pouring buckets of water over the head and body of a soldier who'd been arrested the night before. What the policemen were washing away was blood. And between each bucket, they stopped and asked the soldier, "Can you see yet?" Each time the soldier answered, "No."

The soldier was a Negro. We know now that his name is Isaac Woodard. And that the police chief had beaten him the day before. And blinded him. With a blackjack. When I stumbled on the story several months later and brought it to public attention on this program, the name of the guilty policeman was unknown and it looked as if it always would be. I promised to get that name; I have it now. The minister and the workmen provided our investigators with one clue, and there were other clues, all led to a single man.

All clues led to Mr. M. L. Shull. Chief of police in Batesburg, South Carolina. Now we have him. We won't let him go. I promised to hunt him down. I have. I gave my word I'd see him unmasked. I've unmasked him. I'm going to haunt police Chief Shull. For all the rest of his natural life. Mr. Shull is not going to forget me. And what's more important, I'm not going to let you forget Mr. Shull.

Now, here's a letter. It goes like this:

Well, Mr. Welles. You've just lost yourself an ardent fan. That little speech you made on the radio about that Negro got his eyes poked out did it. You don't know a thing about this case, and I'm quite sure I heard the correct side of the story. Being as I live in the very state in which it happened. And proud of it. But it seems that the Yankees always have to pick on somebody about something, and especially the South. Well, I'm going to put you wise for once. If the North would let the South alone a while, and not try to bully them, everything would soon turn out just right for everybody concerned. We want the Negro to have a fair chance; we don't believe the two races should mix. However, it seems as if the North is trying its darndest to make a mulatto nation of the whole South. Well, it isn't going to work. I believe that we would all die fighting—men and women, side by side—before we would let a calamity like this happen to the glorious homeland of gallant men and their women, who have certain well-founded beliefs and never take anything from anybody. Now to get back to that story. I've been around associating with the policemen, or round about, and I happen to know the Negro who received the eye injury was extremely insolent, very unruly, tried to make a getaway from a police officer. Seems like you all want to give the Negro a better chance than you would a white man. And my dear man, I shall present a startling fact to you: the policeman in question did not cause the eye injury to the Negro; it was due to a fight the Negro had with another Negro. And he is trying to put the blame on the officer so he will draw a pension. Think that over, Mr. Orson Welles. Doubtless you have lost quite a few fans from that little dramatic speech you made so full of emotion and tragic tears for the man. You ought to be ashamed of yourself. Signed, Your former fan.

Well, we've been getting a lot of those anonymous letters since we broke the Isaac Woodard case on this program. But this answer answered them all. Dear former fan, you say the North is bullying the South. That if the Yankees would stop always picking on somebody for something, everything would turn out just right for everybody concerned. I'm afraid you're missing the point. Batesburg isn't another battlefield of the Civil War. The sides contending over the scandal of Isaac Woodard aren't the blue and the gray. They are the right and the wrong. And on your side of the Mason Dixon line, as on mine, most of the people are on the right side of that argument. Course you're proud to live in South Carolina; you ought to be. I think you'll find that most of your neighbors in South Carolina are ashamed of Mr. M. L. Shull, the police chief, who beat out the Negro soldier's eyes with his blackjack. I'm proud to live in America, but I'm ashamed of Chief Shull and his blackjack. I'd be ashamed of him if I was a citizen of Tibet. Isaac

Woodard was not involved in a conspiracy to make a mulatto nation of the South. He was just taking a bus trip to Winnsboro to meet a young woman who belongs to his race and who bears his name. But Isaac Woodard never got to see his wife. He'll never see her. Never. Isaac Woodard is blind. Why? Because the North is bullying the South? My dear former fan, your startling fact about the eye injury, your words, "the eye injury," those are your words, "eye injury," being the work of another Negro is meaningless. In the face of Chief Shull's own confession, he did it himself. Chief Shull doesn't claim he was defending the sanctity of white womanhood. Chief Shull doesn't claim he was keeping Isaac Woodard from marrying his sister. Well, that's enough of that for now. We'll come back to Mr. Shull next week. And the week after that. The week after that.

Welles's commitment to championing tolerance and nonviolence was life-long.

Speaking at an anti-nuclear rally in New York City on June 13, 1983, to support the United Nations Special Session on Disarmament, in front of a crowd estimated to be more than 550,000, Orson focused his liberal vision on the dangers of where the path of hate can lead:

> There is not one of us who doesn't know that this living world of ours has never known a single moment of such deadly jeopardy.
>
> "What can I do?" is what we murmur to ourselves. What can one person do about all that? Complications, translate them into choice and you're down to just two choices: life or death.
>
> You hear that, Mr. Reagan?
>
> But this is a bipartisan celebration and I came here to praise him, not to bury him. It's true, I didn't come to preach to the converted, but to speak a good word or two for the process of conversion.
>
> What we have now in the White House is an authentic ideologue. His political ideas, which are fortunately not too numerous, like the elderly footprints of the movie stars paving the way to the old Hollywood Theatre, would seem to be embedded in concrete. But wait, just listen to the man three days ago in Germany. He said that he noticed something in one of the placards. It was a placard and it read simply this: "I am afraid." The president, who is the very best of TV speakers, paused at this. But you know that there was something beyond his actor's skill that prompted that pause. I heard for just that moment the rarest sound in politics—the resonance of human truth, for Reagan said, "I am afraid, too." Isn't that exactly what we want to hear from him?

For today, for as long as it is true, let us believe that it was more than rhetoric when Reagan told us that his heart was with the marchers; if only just marching would be enough to do the job. Well, just marching has brought him around to this. Just marching has made him agree to the formal terms of the SALT Treaty.

Not only praise, but all our gratitude goes out today to a president who listened.

~

A 2018 NBC News poll revealed that 64 percent of Americans believe that racism continues to plague our society and our politics. Another 30 percent acknowledge racism is a reality in our land but contend "it isn't a major problem." Three percent admit racism once existed in America but not today, while 1 percent contend racism has never been "a major problem."

Disturbingly, 45 percent of Americans contend that race relations are worsening while 41 percent believe not enough attention is being paid to addressing healing the nation's racial divide.

>"John Brown's body lies moldering in the grave
>But his soul goes marching on . . ."

So, too, the significance of *Marching Song*.

Notes

The Gestation of Genius

1. Kenneth Tynan, *Show Magazine*, October 1961, 2.
2. Barbara Leaming, *Orson Welles: A Biography* (New York: Viking, 1985), 5.
3. Roger Hill memo written on one of the many files he kept on Welles during his years at Todd and shared with the author. Todd Tarbox, *Orson Welles and Roger Hill: A Friendship in Three Acts* (Albany, GA: BearManor Media, 2013), 5.
4. Noble Hill, "1928 *Todd Seminary for Boys* catalog," 8.
5. Roger Hill, *One Man's Time and Chance: A Memoir of Eighty Years 1895–1975* (Self-published, 1977), 114.
6. Hill, *One Man's Time and Chance*, 114.
7. Orson Welles, *Todd: A Community Devoted to Boys and Their Interests* (Woodstock, IL: Todd Press, 1931).
8. Orson Welles, "Hitting the High Notes/Inside Dope on the Opera Stars: *Ravinia Stars Beware*," *Highland Park News*, July 6, 1928.
9. Hill, *One Man's Time and Chance*, 112.
10. Orson Welles, *Inklings*, *Highland Park News*, July 4, 1930.
11. Welles, *Inklings*, *Highland Park News*, July 4, 1930.
12. "The Most Outstanding Affair," *Woodstock Sentinel*, June 10, 1931.
13. "Review of *Winter of Discontent*," *Woodstock Sentinel*, June 19, 1931.
14. Hill, *One Man's Time and Chance*, 118.
15. "A new actor, Mr. Orson Welles, made an excellent Karl Alexander," *Irish Times*, October 14, 1931.
16. Micheál Mac Liammóir, *All for Hecuba: An Irish Theatrical Biography* (London: Methuen & Co., 1946).

17. Hugh Curran, "Chicago Boy Makes Hit as Irish Actor/Aged 16," *Chicago Tribune*, November 29, 1931, C16.

18. Hill, *One Man's Time and Chance*, 125.

19. Hill, *One Man's Time and Chance*, 114.

20. Hill, *One Man's Time and Chance*, 117

21. Hill, *One Man's Time and Chance*, 120.

22. Hill, *One Man's Time and Chance*, 123.

23. Hill, *One Man's Time and Chance*, 121.

24. John G. Fee, *Autobiography of John G. Fee* (Chicago: National Christian Association, 1891), 147.

25. John Almanza and Rowley Rogers, *Birth of Berea College: A Story of Providence* (Philadelphia: H.T. Coates & Co., 1903), 69.

26. Almanza and Rogers, *Birth of Berea College*, 69.

Epilogue

1. Michael Mok, "Interview with Orson Welles," *New York Times*, November 24, 1937.

2. Paul Green, edited by Laurence G. Avery, *A Southern Life of Letters, 1916–1981* (Chapel Hill: University of North Carolina Press, 1994), 650.

3. Simon Callow, *Orson Welles: The Road to Xanadu* (New York: Viking, 1996), 552.

4. Sidney Whipple, *New York World-Telegram*, March 25, 1941.

5. "New Plays in Manhattan: *Native Son*," *Time*, April 7, 1941.

6. Brian Dolinar, *The Black Cultural Front: Black Writers and Artists of the Depression Generation* (Jackson: University Press of Mississippi, 2012).

Index

~

About the Authors and Editor

George Orson Welles, internationally recognized actor-director, producer, writer, magician, and political activist, was born in Kenosha, Wisconsin, on May 6, 1915.

Two years after his mother's death in 1925, Welles was enrolled at the Todd Seminary for Boys in Woodstock, Illinois, where he developed a mutual rapport with the school's headmaster, Roger Hill, and his wife, Hortense, who recognized young Orson's boundless creativity.

At Todd, Welles wrote, directed, and acted in dozens of stage productions ranging from musical comedies to Shakespearean tragedies. Departing Todd at the age of sixteen, he landed in Ireland, where within months he was playing leading roles on the Gate Theatre stage in Dublin.

After nine months on the Emerald Isle, Welles returned to Todd as the school's drama coach and, at Hill's suggestion, co-authored *Marching Song* and co-edited and arranged for staging *Everybody's Shakespeare* with his lifelong mentor.

Katharine Cornell, "The First Lady of the Theatre," invited Welles to join her

Orson Welles in 1933. *The Vitaphone Corporation / Warners / Photofest; Photographer: Vandamm*

1933 nation-wide tour playing the role of Mercutio in *Romeo and Juliet*, for which he received considerable acclaim.

His next stop was Broadway. Under the aegis of the Federal Theatre Project, he directed and acted in a number of innovative, socially conscious plays. Later, he co-founded, with John Houseman, the Mercury Theatre and the Mercury Theatre of the Air. The notoriety of his October 30, 1938, radio adaptation of H. G. Wells's novel *The War of the Worlds* brought him to Hollywood, where he signed a $225,000 carte blanche contract with RKO Pictures to write, direct, and act in two films of his choosing—the first being the brilliantly crafted and highly controversial *Citizen Kane*.

Though highly acclaimed at the time and since, *Citizen Kane* and his second RKO film, *The Magnificent Ambersons*, were major box office disappointments, which led to RKO severing its ties with Welles.

For the remaining four decades of his life, Welles was an independent film producer and director with bittersweet results.

In 1975, Welles received the Lifetime Achievement Award of the American Film Institute and a decade later the Directors Guild of America's D. W. Griffith Award.

Welles was married to Virginia Nicolson, 1934–1940; Rita Hayworth, 1943–1947; and Paola Mori, 1965–1985. In 1961, while filming *The Trial*, he met Oja Kodar, who for the next quarter century served as muse.

He died on the evening of October 10, 1985, shortly after calling Roger Hill on the phone, reflecting not on the past but on his hopes and plans for the future.

～

Roger "Skipper" Hill was born in 1895 and attended his father's school, the Todd Seminary for Boys. After graduating from Todd, Skipper enrolled at the University of Illinois, where he met and married his wife, Hortense Ruth Gettys. The couple joined the Todd faculty and made the school their home for the next four decades.

During his thirty-year tenure as Todd's headmaster, Hill fashioned one of the most progressive educational programs in the county. His educational philosophy embraced the concept that youngsters were "created creators."

The Hills were married for sixty-six years and were the parents of three children, Joanne, Bette, and Roger II. My mother, Joanne, was their firstborn.

Roger and Hortense Hill, 1979, at their home in South Miami, Florida.

At Skipper's memorial in November 1990, my father, Hascy Tarbox, who came to Todd at age twelve, captured the essence of his father-in-law:

> His interests were catholic and he attacked them with zeal. You were one of the chosen if you were fortunate enough to have worked with him. For those who did, he bequeathed the greatest gift a man can bestow upon another, the capacity to make you feel important in a world that often doesn't. The gift of conveying that feeling is precious. Skipper had it.

Todd Tarbox was born in Chicago, Illinois, in 1944. He attended the Todd School for Boys in Woodstock until it closed in 1954.

He graduated from the University of the Americas in Mexico, D.F., and received a master's degree from Harvard University.

Life Magazine featured his first-year teaching experience in "We Love You, Mr. Tarbox," an article highlighting his creative approach to heightening the imagination of children.

While attending Harvard, Tarbox and his wife, Shirley, started Tarbox Books to expand his goals as an educator. Describing the launch of the company, *Harvard Magazine* wrote, "Todd Tarbox is a man with a dream: 'I want kids to think of the written word not just as something done in a classroom, but something that can be done in their rooms, something that can be done on a walk in the woods.' His avowed goal, to 'allow children to be co-authors,' has inspired both children and adults to make up their own books."

He is the co-editor with his wife of *Footprints of Young Explorers* and the author of *See the World, Imagine*, and *Orson Welles and Roger Hill: A Friendship in Three Acts*.

Tarbox lives with his wife and Saint Bernard, Schnapps, in Colorado Springs, Colorado.